LIVING IN FLAN

David J Rodger was born in Newcast
1970. He has published seven novel:
the creator of YELLOW DAWN, a successful role
playing game based on the world formed by his
books.

He has written freelance non-fiction for UK magazines
and had short stories published in the UK, US and
Canada. His presence on the Internet got him a place
in a BBC documentary, 'Through The Eyes of the
Young' directed by Chris Terrill.

He spent 8 years working for a government agency,
within the IT Division, developing a virtual
communications service, before moving into
commercial online project management for a UK
media company.

He now lives in Bristol with a Braun coffee-maker,
writing from a house on a hill with a view of the
Earth's curve. He can be found on the web at:

www.davidjrodger.com

ALSO BY DAVID J RODGER

Novels
God Seed
Dante's Fool
Iron Man Project
Edge
Dog Eat Dog
Living in Flames
The Black Lake

Short Stories
Air Dancer
Arnos Vale
Cloudy Head
Corrupt Moon
Cypher
Dilemma
Devil's Spring
Flinch
House of Heavenly Light
Killing Candy
Masters of Chaos
Merchant of Oropas
Oracle
Pain
Sim
The Tainted Moor

Other Creations
Yellow Dawn – The Age of Hastur
Shadows of the Quantinex
Murder At Sharky Point
Songs of Spheres

David J Rodger

LIVING IN FLAMES

Acknowledgements

Thanks go to Kelvin Wright who gave help when I needed it – bridging a gap between two worlds. To Jo, my amazing partner in crime. To my sister for becoming the rock in the stormy seas of bereavement. Floyd, for his ever present support. And to big Pete – the Lone Pine – who made Hayling island so available as a sanctuary and haven. Also, to Michelle Gordon and Fran Pascoe – who were there at the beginning of this but never saw the end. Special gratitude and admiration go to the real Tarjuan. Thanks also to the boys and girls at Boston Tea Party café (Bath). Finally to the masters of moods, the musicians who created the essential atmospheres in my world: Gary Numan, Dead Can Dance, Vangelis, Trentemøller, Asura, Solar Fields, Hybrid, and all the incredible soundscapes and mixes that arrived from Ryan @ A Strangely Isolated Place.

For Nice Guy Tony

- thirteen years late but better late than never -

Four of the figures were reposed further back from the edge of the roof, silhouetted by the alabaster light of a half-moon; they surveyed the city of Bristol in contemplative silence. The fifth figure, their leader, was leant forward with both arms locked straight, supporting himself against the stone balustrade as he scoured the tangle of small lanes below him with an intense gaze.

The fifth figure uttered a solemn statement with a slow, brassy voice, consonants cracking like bones in the lazy swirl of his vowels.

"This is where it all began."

- From the private journal of Cray: my flesh, my blood, my faith, my disease

1

Dex Rašković knew the city; he knew the quiet places where most people didn't walk after dark. Hopefully the drones wouldn't be programmed to come looking down here either.

He strode through the back streets as fast as he could without looking like he had something to hide; head bowed against the persistent rain, with the hood of the hydrogel poncho pulled up.

Something big and bad was going down; police were everywhere, creating snap cordons and road blocks on all the main routes; the shitty little drones swarming through the pedestrian areas, scanning. It was the scans he was worried about.

With a handgun tucked into his pouch and three kilos of unlicensed gene-twister strapped around his waist, getting stopped would not be good.

Dex was still assuming all the police activity had nothing to do with him; just a case of being in the right place at the wrong time. There had been gunfire and lots of it down by the harbour.

The sounds had brought back uncomfortable memories of fighting skirmishes in the Gulf. Operation Metal Hammer. He'd done the whole slog out there: went in when the war started and came out when it ended, if you could call it an ending.

Maybe Bristol was being hit by terrorists – yet more repercussions from the war? Maybe it was a cop sting gone bad? Or some of the demonstrators camped out by the Carthew Tower deciding to up the ante with a few automatic weapons; not likely, in his view, but crazier things had happened.

He crossed a busy main without looking; all the traffic at a standstill, headlights glittering in the rain. Brisk pace, he entered another deserted lane; things seemed to be getting calmer the further he walked, moving away from the danger zone.

His planned destination was the Strontium. A nightclub situated in the heart of a shabby part of the city known as St Nicholas Market. It was the place he'd been calling home for the past three months, ever since he'd bailed out of Switzerland fed up with low wage private security work and bored of a country where people got angry if you had a shower after nine P.M.

The club and the drugs around his waist were part of his retirement plans.

Bristol was just a big turf war between the Manchester, Cardiff and London syndicates.

The club belonged to Jerry White, Manchester's longstanding crime guru. Dex thought 'guru' was a lame word for a man like Jerry White. Psychotic bulldog with a hard-on for maiming people was more appropriate but he guessed 'guru' had eloquence and helped Jerry cross the boundary when selling crime to 'good' people.

His departure from Switzerland had followed the relocation of his good pal Duke, to the Tonga Islands, who had left to run security for the royal family out there. Duke was a lucky bastard but he'd arranged the introduction to Jerry White and the rest was history.

The club gave Dex presence, access to a lot of people and a grubby income. The gig came complete with a bunch of White's dealers who were there to shift the pentathene IV coming out of Jerry White's labs. It should have been a lucrative cash builder but the dealers were a stable of lame horses and White refused to let Dex recruit his own talent.

It meant the income was nowhere near what Dex had planned on and now exposed him to a risk of defaulting on the drugs-for-cash advance White had started him with. Defaulting on Jerry White would be an invitation for getting his face re-arranged with a sledgehammer.

He had a few grand tucked away in an investment portfolio but again, nothing close to an amount that would let him press eject on England and go live The Life somewhere.

Besides, he didn't want to go on the run. The Strontium might not have been his business, but it was his to manage and that gave him a sense of belonging, of ownership, of sanctuary, that he'd never had before. Not even when in the Forces: always on the move, never more than a month in one place; everything temporary; everything disposable, broken, barely working or dead. That all ended in the Gulf with a dishonourable discharge and the blood of a Norwegian reporter on his hands. Could have been worse; his CO could have managed to prove he'd pulled the trigger and he'd have been serving twenty for murder.

So being the kind of man he was, quick to identify opportunities outside the box, Dex had grabbed the chance to make a lot of cash in one strike

The three-kilos of gene-twister strapped around his gut had come from Jerry White's gland-farm up North. Sixty grand's worth. It had been smuggled out by somebody in White's organisation; somebody willing to get butchered for a chunk of easy money. Dex had bought it tonight, down by the harbour just before all the guns started going off. If Jerry White ever found out what Dex had done...

It wasn't a scenario he chose to consider.

The whole deal had been set up by Henry McVee. Dex didn't know McVee and was a long way from trusting him, but so far the operation had played out the way the skinny kid had said it would. McVee seemed to have a needle into White's organisation; knew the people, knew the operation. Dex didn't know how and knew better than to ask questions. The next stage of the plan was to hand the three-kilos over to McVee who had a buyer lined up in Glasgow.

And there was the rub. Dex didn't trust McVee but he had to rely on him for the final bag.

Dex stepped out of the lane through a metal archway into St Nicholas Market. The market was a decrepit, historical structure of old stone; its open-plan interior converted into a labyrinth of small carbo-plastic stalls selling everything from tarot cards and incense to specialist software services, eclectic paper-format magazines, and the myriad sub-strata of dance music. This time of night everything was closed and the market was deserted; but it made a convenient short-cut to the club. The police and their drones didn't seem to have pushed their snouts this far.

He had only met McVee once, about three weeks ago. Short ginger hair, a weird goatee beard bleached blonde, and as skinny as a rifle barrel; but Dex had sensed a bristling aggression that told him McVee wasn't a stranger

3

to violence. McVee was probably a couple years younger than him; Dex had him pegged as around twenty-five. Man wore shades like he thought he was a rock star.

If the Glasgow deal turned true then Dex was in line to pocket one-hundred and eighty grand. Not a bad return on the sixty he'd just spent.

That's if the ginger twiglet can shift it.

One hundred and eighty grand bought a lot of opportunities. Opportunities Dex knew he'd be able to convert into bigger cash returns. His ticket out of here; but perhaps more importantly, with this pride intact.

He heard the muffled thumping of the club's sound system seeping above ground through ventilation ducts.

It gave him a flutter of euphoria. He was almost home.

The euphoria vaporised when his eyes caught sight of the body on the ground.

Dex stopped and ripped back the hydrogel hood from his head; glancing around quickly he checked there was no-one observing. He stepped a bit closer; the hairs on the back of his neck prickling up.

The body was lying where it had fallen between a row of empty packing crates against one wall. A sticky rivulet of blood was pooling beside an outstretched hand.

Fuck.

He had seen plenty of corpses in the Gulf, he had almost gotten blasé about it back then, but this was the middle of the city and it was close to the Strontium. Too close to ignore. The police would come asking questions.

Another glance around him: the bleak empty passageways of the market stretched off in three directions. No sign of any onlookers.

This was his find.

The rain was hammering down on the corrugated plastic roofing three-stories overhead.

He reached up to the DVFrames he wore on his face and pressed a small stud on the upper edge of the right lens. He'd configured the button to launch a 'sweep' application installed on his PA device, tucked away in the pocket of his cotton cargo pants. The Personal Assistant polled the immediate area for visible broadcast tags. Most people broadcast something, even just a nickname or a "Who Am I" tag.

The DVFrames presented the results as digital overlay superimposed within his field-of-vision. A cluster of red dots about twenty metres to his right described the people waiting to get into the Strontium. But there was nothing broadcasting nearer than that, and the body wasn't broadcasting anything. No PA, stolen, or simply not activated.

Time to find out.

Dex squatted down so he could take a closer look.

The hand was striking: the fingers thick and muscular, covered in calluses; the nails cracked and caked with ingrained dirt. The blood was dark red, almost purple in the poor overhead lighting. Dex moved closer, his heart beating a little faster. The drumming of the rain on the corrugated plastic seemed to grow more intense as if providing a soundtrack to the moment.

The smell of the body hit him then, and Dex had to angle his head away and suck in a breath. Sweat and urine and something else that was indescribable yet offensive to his nose. The man was wrapped up in a dirt stained raincoat; his legs were twisted beneath him, wearing jeans that were wet with water and maybe blood, and a pair of filthy worker boots. A homeless person, he suspected. A wide brimmed hat hid his face. Dex frowned, staring at the visible flesh of the man's jaw and neck. It looked wrong somehow. Easing forward he went to reach out, lift the hat and take a closer look but paused as he noticed an object clutched in the man's other hand. Hard to see clearly in the poor light the object looked like a wooden statue, like one of those African tribal knick-knacks you could buy anywhere.

An empty bottle was kicked nearby, the sound of it skittering and clinking against stone echoed around the deserted passages.

Shit!

Dex stood upright and stepped back from the body. He glanced up and down the passage but saw nothing. His attention went back to the long shape clutched by the dead man against his chest. Dex stepped forward, leant over and pulled it from the dead man's grip.

2

Ruby Torres licked the end of her finger, moistening the tip beneath the acrylic extension of her nail, then dug into the yellow cellophane wrap of pentathene, coating it in the fine powder before sliding the whole digit sensuously back into her mouth.

The drug didn't taste bitter but rather created a chemical flavour that was pleasant and hard to describe; to Ruby it was American Cream Soda but she'd heard other people claim it was like root beer or Jing Pong. A few had suggested other more obscure flavours but she suspected these people were either attention seekers or had never had the real thing, or been able to afford it.

Pentathene wasn't just Class A... it was First Class.

Her lips spread into a proud smirk around the thought.

She walked across the varnished wooden floor of the lounge with long articulated strides, the spiked-heels of her shiny patent leather thigh boots pushing her height imposingly above six foot. A sense of impatience shuddered through her as the drug kicked-in.

"Kerry!" she shouted as a prompt to her flatmate who was still getting ready in the next room. Glimpsing in a tall mirror she caught a flashed reflection of herself, the black leather military style greatcoat flapping open to reveal a stunning ensemble of bare flesh and lingerie, complete with stockings and rubber suspenders.

"Kerry!" she shouted again, keeping her dark brown eyes fixed on the mirror studying the way her facial features, as mixed-race as the creamy coffee colour of her skin, contorted as vocal muscles produced the sounds; "Come on! We have to go!"

A response was hollered back, her flatmate's South London accent giving the words a tough edge, "Alright-alright you fucking bitch. I want to look good for this!"

Ruby closed her eyes and stepped away from the mirror as the drug raked her spine with a tingle of pleasure.

"You'll look good," she assured quietly to herself.

A FEW MINUTES later the two of them were sprawled in the back of a fast moving taxi.

Kerry had her long tanned legs pulled up onto the seat between them. Twenty-three, with wild cascades of blonde hair tumbling across her bare shoulders, she had the crudely attractive looks of a glamour model. Not a classic beauty but she could draw in the men, which was one reason why Ruby liked her company. Dressed in translucent blue-gel hot-pants, matching bra top and a see-through rain-wrap, there was very little left to the imagination.

Ruby's attitude to men was KISS: Keep it Sexy and Stupid. She liked men who could fuck and make her laugh; she didn't do emotional complications or intelligent playmates. Not right now.

She chose not to think about the fact her Secret Lover broke these rules, but he was an exception in every sense of the word. And if he killed the man she'd asked him to, then he would also be her saviour: time was in short supply, but time would tell.

Random slices of music and celebrity conversation discordantly churned through the speakers as the driver fiddled with the radio.

Kerry winced at this, flicked her mane of hair to one side and asked, "Why didn't we just fly to the club?"

Ruby swung her head to present a look of dismay; aerodynes were now commonplace in the city but they didn't come cheap, "I may be made of money, dude, but don't take the piss." Kerry rolled her eyes and turned away.

They arrived at the club a few minutes later; a black painted door with a sliver of mirrored glass at eye level. It was called 'Vibrant' but there was no sign anywhere in sight. The club's management chip recognised the pre-paid tickets on Ruby's PA and automatically opened the door: locking bolts snapping open as they approached. The two

7

bouncers inside glanced at them then stepped back, wolfish smiles splitting their lips. 'Ladies' they said in a coarse Bristol accent.

Ruby and Kerry breezed past and climbed down a steep and narrow staircase, descending into lurid purple light. There was a heavy wooden door at the bottom, banded with strips of iron to create a medieval image. Pushing it open, the electrifying atmosphere beyond swept out to greet the two girls on swirling clouds of dry ice that pulsed with the stuttering flashes of strobes.

Stepping through the dry-ice they found themselves in a long chamber with a low vaulted ceiling of ancient stone. There was a bar along one wall. Men and women stood or sat in groups, couples or alone, clad in lingerie or outrageous costumes, dressed for sex: rubber, PVC, leather, studs, spikes, whips and dog collars. The club was much larger but the rest was screened from immediate sight by black satin drapes. Ruby watched Kerry scanning the crowd.

To one side of the bar was a striking cluster of people. Two middle-aged men in leather shorts, worker boots and biker caps were struggling to restrain a younger, more muscular man. With slicked back hair, the younger man sported a pair of gold `Elvis' shades and a leather waistcoat open over a bare torso. An older woman in a ribbed corset, stockings and suspenders was clamped against him, voraciously kissing him, raking his bare chest with garish red nails. A fourth man, effeminate and dressed to parody a sailor, was crouched down giving him a blowjob.

"Oh my God!" Kerry exclaimed as she panned her head.

A man with long scraggy hair was looking nervously around him. He had been fastened by his outstretched arms to a large wooden crucifix. Chains rattled and slid past his head as the crucifix was suddenly hoisted up into the air with a disturbing creaking sound, tilting him forward.

Kerry turned to Ruby, open mouthed. Ruby was digging deep into a pocket of her leather coat, feigning detachment, smirking as she bopped to the music; she knew Kerry had never been to such a place before and was looking forward to seeing how much she could flex the girl's values. Then Ruby looked up, gripping a cashcard between her fingers; Kerry was staring at her with a rigid expression of disbelief.

"Vodders?" Ruby asked cheerfully.

They got in drinks and found a place to sit on a pair of high stools by the bar. Kerry gawped at a naked woman on her hands and knees strapped to a stainless steel table by

8

her wrists and ankles. Shallow rolls of flab hung down from her girdle, cellulite shuddering across the back of her thighs as two figures behind her, entirely enclosed in rubber and PVC complete with tinted goggles and respirator masks, were abusing her with vibrators.

"Oh my God that is so disgusting, what are we doing here?" Kerry complained, mortified.

"Don't lie, you know you really want to have a go yourself. I bet you'll be doing that later."

"You're a joker!" Kerry snapped back at her, "You're fucking sick you are."

Ruby raised her shaped eyebrows, "You're only jealous, come on, admit it, you're jealous 'cos you're not brave enough to do it yourself."

Kerry looked away, refusing to comment, then began slowly scanning the rest of the club. She turned back to face Ruby, brushing a long curtain of hair out of the way, complaining sourly, "I wouldn't mind so much if they were good looking."

Ruby's fingers dangled down above her glass of vodka, absently playing with the rim as her mind took her elsewhere.

"Alright there?" Kerry asked softly following her lack of response.

Ruby glanced at her then dropped her gaze back to the glass, thoughtful. "Just a rush darling.... narcotics are a little strong."

Kerry was not convinced; irritated she pressed on, "You've been acting like a right bitch. You due on or something? What's wrong? What's up? Is it that thing you saw on the news? That business with the Carthew family?"

Ruby's fingers stopped where they rested on the rim. One of her fingers curled back and flicked forward to strike a perfect nail against the glass with a - chink- sound. Ruby was not aware she had been so transparent; Kerry had noticed her interest in the Carthews. That was not good. She raised her gaze and met Kerry's concerned look, "You've lost me."

Kerry sniffed, exasperated, "Look I know I don't know you. You arrived in this city a month ago, you move in, you have money to party with but no job, and you don't like me asking questions but I consider you my best friend now and I'm worried because you're acting strung out."

I'm acting strung out? That's a laugh, I'm not the one snorting a grand of pentathene a day. Ruby's judgemental thought was based on the fact she only dabbed the drug, a couple of finger-licks on a night out.

"And what is it with this Carthew family? Do you know them or something?" Kerry continued.

Ruby wanted to close her eyes and scream, to keep screaming until her throat shredded and nothing but hot air came out. She gave her easiest smile, pushing away the moody look, "I'm fine! It's just a rush. I need a friend and that is why you're here. I pay, you play. Simple. Now be a darling and give Richy a call. I think we will need to restock our supplies before this night is through."

"I already rang Richy," she said sourly; Kerry had seen through the brush-off but begrudgingly accepted it.

Kerry climbed down from the stool and said, "I'm off to take a pee."

Ruby dropped the smile from her face the moment Kerry's back was turned. Kerry must have read her face earlier when the news came on. Ruby picked up her drink and took a deep gulp. The Carthews. God had cursed them. And now they wanted to rebuild the tower. Ruby involuntarily shook her head at her own thoughts.

For now, she played this shallow game of bright smiles and make-up, and ignored the deep buried hurt that came from being in a place that held so many childhood memories, a place where she had been excluded from.

Where was her Secret Lover right now? Was he here in Bristol, setting up the trap that would lure a monster to his death?

A stolen idol as the bait.

It was easy to think of the plan in motion, of a cold-blooded murder that had to happen, but it was not so easy to cope with the silence: why had he not called her yet?

She could relate to his desire for secrecy, but not even an email or a text message? The not knowing was infuriating, and terrifying. The very idea something like Cray even existed... still existed, after all this time; it was like being trapped in a nightmare she could not wake from. Or worse, a nightmare that had seeped out to contaminate her waking life.

What if Cray turned the tables on her Man, her Secret Lover, and killed him instead? There were risks bringing Cray to Bristol; clues that Cray might string together to form a picture she suspected he...it, had been longing to see for decades.

For three centuries if you believe everything your father wrote before he died, some part of her reflected.

10

Don't believe everything you read, another part of her countered angrily.

All the other stuff was true.

Don't even go there.

A tremor of anxiety clawed into her chest and closed around her heart; she smoothed it away and smiled around another pleasure rush from the drug.

3

The dance floor and bar of the Strontium occupied a vaulted section of the old cellars of the historical market; the ground floor was occupied by the main entrance, cloakroom, stores, and a private function suite; above this, on the first floor, was the apartment where Dex lived and ran his small web of criminal operations.

The doormen knew better than to talk to him when he didn't have his happy-chatty face on. He passed by without a word, keeping the blood-stained statue out of sight beneath the hydrogel poncho. Shouldering through a door marked 'private' into a short passageway, he climbed the steep staircase up to a more solid door. The apartment's management chip recognised the broadcast tags on his PA and unlocked the door before he got there.

Dex hauled the door open, made his way inside: several lamps came on automatically.

He went straight through to the pristine black-slate bathroom and dropped the statue into the sink. Blood spattered the white marble basin. Rainwater ran off his poncho in tiny rivulets. He looked at his hand. His fingers were covered in blood.

Jesus.

He exhaled noisily through his lips. His heart was pounding. A gunfight kicking-off at the harbour area and now a body outside his club. It was going to be a busy night for the Bristol cops.

You could have picked a better spot to die pal.

Dex stared at the red smears congealing on his fingers.

Correction, a better spot to get yourself killed.

Dex wondered if the body was connected to his operations: a warning, maybe? He dismissed it. There was a turf war going on but this was too obscure to be a threat directly aimed at him.

Of course, if the body turned out to be one of his hopeless dealers...

Dex sighed heavily, he nudged the cold water lever with his elbow and began to rinse off the blood. The police would ask difficult questions. They'd already suspect he was part of Jerry White's outfit. How much they knew depended on the quality of their snitches, but at the very least they'd know that Jerry White owned the club.

No, this was a unconnected event. Pure random.

He looked down at the statue in the sink. Made from dark wood, about the length of his forearm but thicker; it looked like two figures, maybe a person cradling a small child, but it could have been something else. Whatever it was, it was ugly. He grabbed it up and held it under the cold tap, turning it slowly, repeatedly, until the running water was no longer stained red. He wondered if the dead guy had any of the new virus strains creeping across the globe; he'd heard there was a nasty strain of Staph sweeping through Asia giving people boils worthy of one of the Biblical Plagues of Egypt. Then there was the bio-plague somebody had recently dumped on Palestine; the world was pointing its finger at Israel and Israel was pointing two fingers back.

He placed the statue on the tiled surface beside the sink. Reaching into a cupboard with his clean hand he pulled out a squeeze-bottle of heavy-duty antiseptic. Dex picked up a sponge and soaked it with antiseptic and emptied more into the sink basin. He had been through enough sterilisation 'washes' in the Gulf to know this was going to sting. Dex put both his hands into the sink and began to rub them with the sponge, building up a soapy lather that had a recognisable medical smell to it. Then it began to burn its way into his skin. Dex made cursing sounds and his eyes started watering, but he did not stop and made sure to scrape deep beneath his nails.

He thought about cleaning the statue but figured the antiseptic would do bad things to the wood, which would not do much good to its value. That's if it *was* valuable; but the dead guy had been clutching it to his chest like it meant something.

Dex let the basin run dry before turning on the tap again and rinsing his hands clean. A cold sweat had broken out on his back and a horrible taste was seeping into his mouth.

Grabbing a wad of toilet paper he wiped down the sink, the statue and the surface it had been standing on. He dropped the sodden wad down the bowl and flushed.

Moving back into the main room of the apartment he walked over to a safe set into the floor, near to a low platform holding his bed. He opened it and placed the statue inside. Then he withdrew the gun from the pocket of his poncho and did the same. Finally, he pulled the poncho over his head, flung it onto the floor, unfastened the Velcro belt packed with gene-twister from his waist and dropped it into the safe beside the gun.

Closing the safe he walked over to a collection of spirit bottles, wafting his hands in a futile attempt to reduce the scorched sensation throbbing through them. He poured himself a large measure of whisky, walked over to his desk and sat down.

Out of habit he lifted his hand to his *Hermes* DVFrames and tapped a command stud he'd configured to bring up a summary report of his investment portfolio. The information appeared superimposed within his field of vision. The top line was Cr 14.8K, held by Swiss Orbital who were managing his account. A rise of 0.8% since this morning. Not much of a rise but everything had been going in the right direction for a while now. Maybe he'd see a better result tomorrow. The mornings were his best time to trade. Sometimes he'd follow the sun, trading in different markets as they opened across the globe. Not tonight, however.

He closed down the report, took off the DVFrames and went to rub his eyes but then thought better of it. Instead he closed his eyes and took a sip of his drink, ran through some figures in his mind letting the alcohol melt away his tension.

He was into Jerry White for ten kilos of lab quality Pentathene IV. That meant he owed White 120,000 credits for the drugs, a sum which Dex was due to pay at the end of the grace period. The grace period ended next week. So far the lame dealers Dex had inherited as part of the White establishment had managed to shift less than three kilos.

Every kilo cost Dex 12,000 credits but was worth 50,000 on the street. Taking out the dealers cut and the fluctuations in bulk buys, Dex was raking in around 30,000 credits per kilo.

So despite the terrible performance of the dealers he was only 37,500 credits short of the 120,000 he needed to pay White. Except, he'd just spend 60,000 credits on the three kilos of gene-twister.

The short version was that he needed to find a little under 100,000 credits to keep Jerry White's muscle-monkeys from paying him a visit, and he had seven days to do it.

If he relied on the dealers, they needed to shift another three kilos within the week.

Glasgow and the gene-twister could bring in 180,000 credits within a couple of days, but Dex didn't want to rush into that just yet. Call it a hunch but there was something not quite right about Henry McVee and his scheme.

Gene-twister was the bio-engineered substance designed to modify body functions at the cellular level. Loaded into custom spikes, typical variants were used for increased athletic performance, body mass, hair and skin tone. It was legal to sell and buy if produced through corporate syndicated labs. And expensive. But cheap and illegal if produced through the growing number of 'gland farms' that usually consisted of immigrants enslaved by their smugglers.

He wanted to let McVee sweat a little. He wanted to explore the option of finding another route to market for the gene-twister; one that didn't involve such a bargain basement price as McVee was proposing; one that didn't carry the risk of McVee walking away with the cash.

Which left him relying on the dealers, for now.

The biggest share of the pentathene IV was with Richy, the man most trusted to handle large amounts and supposedly most able to shift them; but the past few weeks had shown Richy to be about as effective as a bundle of wet blankets. Heavy to carry and of absolutely no use.

Apparently Richy was having 'emotional problems' with his girlfriend. Dex didn't know Richy and didn't care about his problems. Maybe Richy was trying it on; maybe the dealers thought he was soft; maybe they really were just useless...

Dex chucked the remainder of the whisky down his throat, closed his lips with a sour face and breathed in fumes as he considered the violence looming ahead. He was going to have to make a point, lay down some heavy guidelines: people were going to get hurt.

4

The small bedroom was at the front of a filthy terraced house, overlooking four lanes of slow crawling traffic waiting to join the motorway junction south of Bristol. Weak sunlight picked out the accumulated dust on the cheap muslin curtains, hanging from a broken broomstick handle that had been nailed above the window. The room was cluttered with discarded clothes and almost filled by the sagging double bed and a beaten-up wardrobe.

A blue hydrogel cube, pockmarked with cigarette burns, was doing its best to continue functioning as an alarm clock radio: the time displayed was '7:28 AM', the station was playing 'The Sound of Silence' by Simon & Garfunkel.

If Henry McVee was to describe his life right now, he'd say it was in limbo, closer to Hell than to Heaven, trying to untangle himself from the emotional razor wire that had wrapped itself around his fucked-up relationship with Nicky, and ultimately, waiting for a big cash dump so he could bail out of England with his best mate, Spad.

It was satisfying to be able to summarise it like that, he supposed; but it did fuck all to ease to the hurt.

Nicky lay at one edge of the bed, curled on her side with her back to Henry, her face covered by the tangled explosion of thick brown hair.

She was nothing like Danielle.

McVee lay on his back, hands folded across his pale and wiry torso, staring into space with a loosely rolled spliff between his lips. The heavy rumble of the traffic outside was loud and incessant. He visualised the hot swell of

16

exhaust fumes building up outside the row of houses, trapped within the natural geological basin that this part of the city was built within. Shit, he hated it here. This city, this house, this bed. He glanced over at Nicky and let his gaze linger on her long enough to feel his guts clench up with mixed emotions. She was shagging somebody else, he was sure of it. Yet he had no intention of taking her with him when he pressed eject on Bristol, and England: so why all the stress?

Respect.

That's what it boiled down to. A lack of fucking respect. He was busting his guts to scratch a living here whilst he waited for the big score to go through. Meanwhile, she was soaking up his money, eating his food, sleeping in his bed, and not giving anything in return.

Nothing.

So get rid of her, throw the bitch out.

Can't do that.

That makes you a pussy then, don't it..

He rolled his head back to centre and took a long drag on the spliff. Fucking bitch. His balls were the size of water melons it had been so long since they'd shagged. She was tearing his heart out.

McVee's mind switched to the day ahead. His plan was all going like creamy smoke through a bong: cool, easy and beautiful. Dex had agreed to bankroll his scheme and had bought the gene-twister. Three kilos. Sixty fucking grand. Dex had spunk, McVee admired that.

Next step was for Richy to go collect it and for McVee to get himself to Glasgow – a buyer already lined up – and walk away with three-hundred thousand.

A pulse of adrenaline shot through him, leaving him staring at the ceiling with glittering eyes and a tight smile.

Three hundred G's

Dex wasn't an idiot and had made a good job of putting controls in place that would hinder McVee if he tried to run with it. Dex wanted his share. McVee reckoned he could still make it to Portugal if he had the desire, but it would leave Spad out of the joy, and right now Dex didn't need to be a victim in his plan. The only victim was going to be Jerry White.

Mother Fucker.

McVee shoved Jerry White out of his mind and span his thoughts back to Dex.

Good looking fucker. There was some dark in his skin like he had a bit of gypo in him. Maybe that was why White had taken Dex into the crew? Maybe White sensed the gypo part and welcomed Dex with the open arms of distant family? White normally wouldn't breathe in the same air as anybody he considered to be a nigger or rag head. White by name, white by nature. Racist cunt.

He figured Dex was a little shorter than him but much bulkier; the kind of hard-packed muscle mass that came from a lifetime spent in tough physical conditions. Made sense, story was Dex had gone into the military straight from a fucked-up foster family. Another point of connection between them: a life path carved by the need to escape from mad bastard families.

The ex-military vibe showed: bloke could definitely handle himself in a fight, McVee reckoned. The thought caused a wry smile to slant his narrow face. McVee also knew how to fight. Bare knuckle bouts since he was old enough to spit, following in the tradition of his grandfather; and a childhood where violence was the norm.

Dex was going to be his knight in shining black silk shirt and corduroy trousers.

Three kilos of twister.

Three hundred grand, minus a slice for Dex.

Maybe.

Enough money to press eject on England for good.

Hello sunshine, beaches, and surfing; ice cold beers and tanned girls in bikinis. The idea turned his mood around and a smile spread across his dry lips.

He looked over at Nicky, feeling a twinge of regret about leaving her behind; she had no fucking idea about his plans to bail out. He reached across to stroke her bare arm; as soon as his fingers touched her skin she flinched away and jabbed a sharp elbow back at him.

Anger flared through him and it took all his self-control not to land a fist against the back of her head. Ungrateful slag.

He heard some of the other occupants of the house starting to move around.

Irritated that his day was already starting so badly, McVee flung himself out of bed and went to the bathroom. He could picture himself standing there, cock in hand as he directed a stream of dark yellow piss into the stained basin. Skinny chest, slight belly, wiry arms that were strong. His skin was more pale than usual, with a rash of what looked like acne scars running across his upper arms and back: closer inspection would have told you they were cigarette burns and hard puckered indentations, the scars left over

18

from a .22 air-rifle that his older brother and his father would shoot at him.

He knew he looked older than his twenty-five years. Close-cropped reddish hair and bleached blonde beatnik goatee beard. His wiry face held the expression of somebody who had lived a hard life and been burned by it, who had survived but not without the strain cutting his features to a streetwise edge.

He got dressed. Pulling on a frayed army-surplus T-shirt, a blue knitted wool cardigan cum coat thing he'd bought from a charity shop, baggy nylon cargo pants – also from a charity shop – and a pair of nasty Kasterand trainers he'd found in the park near Jacobs Wells road. All of his clothes had gotten the good news from a 'HERF gun' to zap any RFC tags woven into the fabric. Radio Frequency Cookies - used by the marketing corporations to see where you shop, drink, eat and map products to consumer trends, but it was possible for law enforcement and private investigators to use them to track people too; McVee had no desire to be found by anyone. And they *would* be looking. Without a doubt.

McVee picked up his mo-com, clipped it to his waistband, hooked a pair of rubberised headphones around his ears, set the mo-com to radio mode, and left the house for the thirty minute walk to work.

As he walked he picked up the latest news stories: yesterday's gunfight at the harbour had apparently been a clash between rival gangs, although there was sub-media speculation it was part of the growing conflict between rival corporations using mercenaries to crash lucrative deals. Death toll for the bio-plague in Palestine had topped half a million with Israel picking up the blame. Several fisherman murdered on a trawler off the coast of Cornwall, speculation about a psycho boosted with cybernetic implants being responsible. The proposed rebuilding of the Carthew Tower was continuing to cause controversy because the of the Lottery fund being involved; a public-funded venture that would greatly benefit the Carthew business.

And then something that made his blood run cold: a murder enquiry was underway after the body of man was found shot outside the 'Strontium' in St Nicholas Market.

McVee threw down a freshly lit spliff and quickened his pace. He worked in St Nicholas Market. And the Strontium was Dex's place.

When he got to the market he forced himself to behave normally. He could not afford to draw attention to himself in any way right now. Jerry White's crew wouldn't bundle him into a van for a rendezvous with a beating; they'd just shoot him dead and take a photo for White's peace of mind.

So he went through his usual morning routine and grabbed a coffee from Vinda's before opening the shop.

Walking through the Glass Arcade he saw the cordon of yellow police tape right next to Vinda's stall.

Great.

There was a badly scuffed police drone sitting inertly by the cordon. McVee couldn't tell if it was on standby or had been beaten shitless.

Vinda's stall had just enough room for the woman who served, and wide enough for the two customers who sat outside on stools; both were sipping from Styrofoam cups, dubiously eyeing a scab-ridden dog that was eagerly licking the ground within the cordon.

He ordered a large Americano-to-go.

"Things alright with you Henry?" The Asian woman asked as she worked the machine.

"Aye, not bad," he answered above the banging of a metal cup being emptied of coffee grounds.

"Do you think he could have picked a better place to drop dead?" She made a conspicuous glance at the cordon.

"I dunno, like. Maybe you should charge extra for the privilege of sitting next to a crime scene?"

She chuckled, "Why don't you buy yourself a PA? It would tell me you're coming and I could get your order ready!"

McVee twisted round slightly and looked at the drone; he forced a smile onto his lips and patted his mo-com, "This is all I need. A phone and a computer. Don't need people knowing where I am unless I want them to."

I don't need people knowing who I am either.

There was a blast of steam as she pulled a big lever down, "You can turn that off on a PA."

"Then there's little point in having it," he said, perhaps a little too sharply.

She didn't seem to notice; she placed the coffee down on the counter and clipped a hydrogel lid on top. He held out his cashcard, she scanned it with the data-strap on her finger and the value appeared on the card's screen, he thumbed the 'authorise' button. "Take care Henry."

"Always," he smiled wearily and turned away.

McVee took a left into All Saints Lane, passing a decrepit row of tall stone buildings with bulging window frames; one doorway was festooned with tiny security cameras: the entrance to the Strontium. He walked past without even a glance. As far as the rest of the world was concerned, Dex and he did not know each other. He took a right turn, passing through a rusted iron gate into the Covered Market: like a stone barn filled with pre-fabricated shop units. The corrugated plastic roofing above let in light stained the colour of piss.

McVee weaved through the jigsaw of passageways separating the various shop-units, then, coming around the corner of a second hand bookstore the sight that greeted him made him groan under his breath.

A familiar man sat slumped in the shuttered doorway to McVee's shop. It was his friend and housemate, Steve Metcalf, or 'Spad' as he liked to be called.

McVee hurried over. Spad was barely conscious but still saw him coming, he made an attempt to rise then collapsed, fingers scraping carbo-plastic shutters, swearing incoherently.

Spad was twenty-four going on fifty. A bear-like body turning to flab, his bony head was shaved to the scalp; his skin had a reddish, leathery look to it from too much sun and alcohol. He looked up sorrowfully as McVee stopped beside him. Then he tried to say something but his jumbled words were cut off as his head reeled sharply to the side, a startled expression on his face, too drunk to keep it upright.

McVee sighed heavily. "What a mess. Spad, how long have you been here?" Wondering how the police had not found him. Spad made a mumbled response and McVee picked out something like 'just got here.

He pulled a ring of keys from his pocket then kept Spad in place with his knee as he unlocked the shutters.

Getting inside he left Spad curled up on the floor beneath a rack of tie-dyed tops, looking as though he was peacefully asleep.

The shop wasn't his. It was a fleapit that sold crap to the cheap end of the grunge-hippy-goth-teknotribe market: psychedelic clothing, postcards, low-quality silver jewellery, badly carved ethnic trinkets. He was running the place after the owner, Jess, had hired him to help out before deciding she was a trapped spirit and needed to travel the Federated Asian States.

It was an easy gig and the money was good enough to live whilst he waited for his big scheme to play out and pay out.

He plucked the mo-com off his belt and dialled Richy. It rang several times then transferred to voice-mail. He dialled again three more times, each time transferring to voice-mail. He didn't stop. Finally Richy answered, groggy, his voice thick with the sound of somebody who had been crying.

Find another time to lose it, mate.

"It's McVee. I need you to pick up the G-T from our mutual friend."

5

Another night, another club, another after party.

Ruby sucked the end of her finger dusted with pentathene and grinned as her new friend, a very handsome and athletically fit stockbroker, eased the sports car into a parking space near the apartment building.

Kerry was in a second car, currently behind them, being driven by the stockbroker's friend. It had been a race; and Ruby's escort had won. Ruby didn't care about the race. Her dance tunes were playing, thumping through a state-of-the-art sound system; the drugs were good; all her problems were in a different universe. Her Secret Lover had not been in touch but that didn't matter right now.

In the wing-mirror, Ruby watched as Kerry clambered out of the second car with half her breasts hanging out of the skin-hugging cat suit; she could barely walk straight and came tottering towards Ruby's ride. Popping open the door, Ruby pushed herself up from the low-slung seat, grabbed Kerry's hand as she arrived and hauled herself out, then quickly walked away with her towards their building.

Kerry leaned inwards and murmured, "Gorgeous dick."

Ruby smirked; trust Kerry to tear open her present early.

The apartment building was an old 1930's structure with brick balconies and windows framed in white metal latticework.

Both girls staggered through the glass-paned doorway, crying with laughter, with the two men following behind.

Ruby glanced round and saw them looking at each other with conspiratorial grins.

Then everything came to a sobering stop.

Standing a few metres in front of them, blocking the way forward, was a short, fat, bald middle-aged man. Glowering at them, he wore a food-stained T-shirt too small to cover his hairy belly, which even protruded beyond his open brown dustcoat. It was the building's caretaker. He was visibly shaking with rage.

"You! You there!" He shouted loudly regardless of the fact he would have been heard if he had whispered.

"Oh shit," Kerry muttered under her breath, rearing upright as if to demonstrate she had not been drinking or was under the influence of drugs.

"Nutter alert," Ruby added loud enough for him to hear.

The caretaker put a hand on his hip and waggled a fat finger at them, "You've been on that trampoline again!"

"CHRIST! Here we go again: what fucking trampoline?" Kerry snapped angrily. She strode toward the door to their apartment at the end of the short hall, shoving past the caretaker in the process. "There *is* no trampoline!"

The caretaker span round, looked down at her legs, tried to look away but seemed to find his gaze glued there. By now Kerry had managed to get most of her breasts back inside the cat suit, which still left little to the imagination. This was not lust this was religious outrage. Jabbing his finger at her with indignation he shouted, "You've got a fucking trampoline in there and don't try to fool me because I know a trampoline when I hear one!"

"Have you heard a fucking trampoline? I'd like to know how when there ISN'T ONE IN THERE!" she shouted back.

It was a stalemate. The two of them glared at each other. Ruby watched, calmly enjoying the spectacle. She twisted her head to look at the stockbroker beside her; he glanced at her and shrugged, visibly uncomfortable about the confrontation. Ruby wondered if either man would help if it really came to it; Kerry was wired on an addictive narcotic that was known to cause bouts of irrational violence. The caretaker was unwittingly playing a very dangerous game. Ruby remained silent, happy to watch: see how the chips fell. If Kerry got herself into trouble that would be her problem. Ruby could always afford to move somewhere else. She was skilled in the art of vanishing.

Kerry's guy stepped forward and gently began to discuss the issue of the alleged 'trampoline' in the apartment. Kerry seemed outraged that her new companion was even willing to negotiate with the caretaker. The calmness lasted about five seconds before descending into a three-way argument. The explanation from Kerry – *it's not a trampoline, it's me shagging* – did nothing to ease the tension.

A soft beep in Ruby's ear advised her of an incoming call, her PA had let it through the security filter and a voice prompt stated the caller was 'Your Special Man'.

It was her Secret Lover. The noise in the hall was now bedlam. She turned to hurry outside but the stockbroker grabbed her arm to say something like, "Don't worry I'll sort it out," totally misreading her body cue.

Ruby pulled free with an aggression that left him startled. By the time she got outside the call had transferred to voicemail.

"Oh no," she moaned. "Leave a message. Call me back. Please, baby, call me back."

A few moments later a deposited message rang her back; Ruby listened, nervous and excited at the same time. Her lover, the man who could do what needed to be done. The message was short and to the point. Her blood started to chill inside her veins, her mouth dropped open and her breath escaped in a quivering gasp.

She played it again:

"It was a trap. Cray didn't show. One man is dead. I lost the idol. I'm so sorry. Cray will probably come here now. To Bristol. I've failed you. I wish I could say otherwise. I love you. Forgive me."

6

Half an onion sat on a wooden chopping board. A large serrated blade sank into it, paused briefly, and then proceeded to dice it with precision and speed.

McVee glanced over and watched for a moment as Spad put the knife down, pulled open the fridge with a chinking of bottles, lowered himself into a crouch, spliff in mouth, squinting as smoke curled into his eyes. Spad rummaged through the collection of out-of-date takeaway cartons for the packet of meat he wanted to use.

The kitchen area occupied one corner and a side wall of the large living room.

McVee sat on the floor with his back against the base of a decrepit settee, browsing music and news channels on a large and expensive hardscreen that looked out-of-place within the filthy room. Nicky was sat opposite. His attention went back to the screen:

"Look at that wanker!" McVee said, scowling at the image of a man rescued from his house after coastal erosion had brought it tumbling down. It was a miracle the man was alive, apparently; but he had also ignored warnings from local safety advisors, so the report stated.

"Change the channel," Nicky suggested, bored. She was sitting on another sofa that had half collapsed, wearing the sexy white hydrogel raincoat and boots he had bought her last week. She had the best legs in the world. Maybe he could seduce her tonight? Like old times. Stop arguing for once and make her laugh.

McVee grunted and twisted round looking for the remote control – you could control the hardscreen by voice commands through any house management chip, but they didn't have one of those.

Spad straightened up and tapped the fridge shut with his knee, having pulled out a packet of meat. His face was even redder than usual from the effort of crouching down, and his eyes were watering from the onions and spliff smoke. He reached over, took a swig of some nameless alcohol, and placed the packet of meat next to the chopped onions. Then he took a double-glance at the packet and picked it up again, reading out the advice print on the bright yellow label.

"Use by August...next year!" Spad sounded incredulous. Ash dropped from the spliff jutting from his mouth. Still reading the label he muttered, "Happy Eater Long Life Meat." Tossing the packet down onto the bench he grumbled, "What fucker bought this nuclear shit? This isn't pork!"

Spad's voice rose to a shrill pitch.

"This is cancer!"

McVee glanced at Nicky with an amused smirk curving his lips but she didn't respond. A sour taste filled his mouth; he picked up a glass and took a large swig of Jack Daniels and coke.

Without warning Nicky stood up and stormed towards the door.

"You off?" McVee inquired sarcastically.

"Yes." Nicky yanked open the door then paused to look back at him. "Don't wait up for me."

McVee couldn't hide his surprise or the slowly dawning suspicion that crept across his features. Sniffing he swung his eyes back to the hardscreen. Nothing more was said. Nicky left.

He glanced up when he heard the outside door slam shut.

Why was she doing this to him? Why had he suddenly become so detestable? What was it about him she now hated? They'd been together less than three months but it already felt like a lifetime. When he'd first met her, at the bar where he worked most nights, he'd really thought she might have been the one.

Somebody to take escape England with.

He closed his eyes and forced out the hurt. Anger swept in to take its place.

A memory of Danielle flashed into his mind and ignited in the heat of his rage. How different would his life be if...

McVee snuffed out the burning memory.

Spad stood over the cooker, liberally pouring olive oil into an immaculate frying pan. His expression was close to serene. Putting the bottle down beside a bong filled with dirty brown water, he turned to the onions on the chopping board only to find his spliff ash had landed on them. Flustering and cursing, he stooped down and blew it off.

McVee stared at his friend for a long moment. "Don't worry mate, a couple more weeks and we'll be out of here, getting pissed and stoned on a beach in Portugal. Enough money to live like kings for a few years."

Spad's movements were slow and carefully controlled as he scraped onions into the frying pan. Spad looked over at him, "Did Richy get the Glasgow deal sorted out?"

"Not yet."

Spad dropped a load of the onion on the floor.

McVee looked away and let the images on the screen soak up his brain.

A male Asian news reporter was standing in the middle of a graveyard. Behind him rose a steep wooded slope from which protruded the remains of a very old stone tower.

The reporter was saying, "....who leaked the documents to the media, is still not known but the Carthew's are a respected, old money family that have managed to prune away the rot that led so many of the once great families of Victorian Britain into decline."

McVee scowled, "Who gives a shit!"

The reporter continued, "The modern day Carthews are a globally scattered clan but the family seat still rests firmly in Bristol. Although the current head of the Carthew Trust, Xici Carthew, spends the majority of her time at the firm's private villa complex in Taormina, in Sicily, she clearly devotes a lot of time and money on maintaining the original Carthew Estate near Sneade Park. And this tower, by extension, is a part of that estate.

"And it is the Carthew Trust and the Lottery Council that are coming under fire for their plan to rebuild the tower that stands ruined behind me.

"Originally built in the sixteenth century, on the remains of a chapel that dates back to the time of the Holy Crusades, the tower was destroyed in 1737 in an unexplained explosion, allegedly by the Carthews themselves."

The reporter paused to regard the tower behind him for a moment then came back to face the camera:

"So why should the Lottery Council spend so many millions in rebuilding it, when so many other worthwhile causes go needy?"

"Aye, why indeed," McVee agreed, then flicked to another channel, "Feed the rich and *fuck* the poor."

7

Dex led the Detective Constable down the stairs from his apartment. The interview had gone well, he thought, in so far as the DC seemed to accept his statement about not seeing the body when he'd walked into the club.

Outside there was a long line of young people waiting to get past the doormen and into his club; the DC, who was in plain clothes, glanced at them and smiled wistfully. "If only I had the time off these days."

"Got a family?" Dex asked.

The DC nodded with a look of satisfaction, then stepped away and zipped up his windbreaker; the weather had been turning steadily colder the past few days; "Thank you for your time Mr Rašković."

Dex was mildly impressed the policeman had pronounced his surname perfectly. "Not a problem. Any clues about who he was?"

The DC shook his head and stepped a little closer, maybe to avoid being overheard, "Total blank. Strange looking bloke. Stank to bloody heaven didn't he."

Dex found himself almost about to agree with him, stopped himself when he remembered his version of the story meant he could not know how badly the dead man had smelled. Did that policeman just set up a clever trap? Dex conjured a questioning look that transformed into comprehension; "Homeless then, yeah? I guess if they washed, people wouldn't give them any money."

The DC fixed a steady gaze on him for a few moments longer than was comfortable; Dex wondered if the copper had seen him about to agree. The DC nodded once, his gaze became less intrusive, "Probably. There's not a lot of help out there for homeless people, these days. Well, goodnight sir."

"Have a good evening." Dex said with false sincerity and watched him leave. A few regulars were trying catch his eye probably hoping for a look of recognition; he ignored them and went back inside.

He took the stairs with a quick lithe stride, closed the door to his apartment behind him and walked over to the collection of spirit bottles.

A moddy-prompt flashed up within his field-of-vision and then began to spill words along the lower edge of the DVFrames lenses:

GENTEC CORPORATION HAIL DISCOVERY OF 'MYTHICAL' ENZYME TO HALT AGEING PROCESS::: RESETTING THE CELLULAR STOPWATCH WITHOUT INCREASING THE RISK OF CANCER.

The moddy was a piece of software that sat in cyberspace; Dex had configured this one to behave as an agent monitoring his diverse investments. Anything that might create a significant change in the value of his portfolio was to be highlighted. Dex had certain bio-tech players 'flagged' for their work in particular genetic fields.

Dex wasn't in the mood to react. He'd take a look at it later; the London and New Tokyo markets would be closed right now. He could explore trade options in Asia later tonight.

Standing there, he knocked back a finger of Oban then rubbed the palm of his hand over his jaw, thinking things through. That statue would have to go. And fast. Getting tagged for drugs was one thing but that statue could tie him to a murder. There was motive, even if it looked like a worthless lump of tourist trash. It might be worth something to somebody. An antique. Could it be something like that?

He dug his hand into his pocket and pulled out his PA. He went over to the floor safe, opened it, took out the carved statue and carried it over to his desk, placing it directly into the beam of a lamp there. He activated the PA's camera and took several photographs from different angles. "Time to find out what you are and more importantly, what you are worth."

Picking up the statue he kept it under the light and took a closer look; it was the first time he had taken it out since washing it last night. Turning it slowly in his hands it looked even more ugly than he remembered; the wood was black and rubbed very smooth, but the actual figures had

31

been created out of savage and angular cuts, giving their features a tormented look. He decided it was a mother with her baby after all.

"What the heck is that?" he muttered, squinting as he brought his face closer; there was something not quite right about the way the mother was kissing the child.

He flipped the statue round and looked at the base; there was a symbol carved there that reminded him of the letter 'X' combined with a 'Y' but only in general shape. He stroked it thoughtfully with his thumb.

"Whatever you are, you're still ugly." He carried it back to the safe, noting the handgun and the Velcro belt of gene-twister still in there. He locked the safe and walked back to his desk.

"Jay-Jay," he spoke aloud, a phrase designed to snag the attention of the chip managing his apartment.

"Yes?" the voice was male, a bit dull sounding; it was a nice bit of software but ripped by a hacker associate and most of the personality code was missing.

"Dial Richy, place it through encryption."

"Dialling Richy with encryption," the voice confirmed immediately followed by a ringing-tone. Using the encryption channel would crank up the cost of the call significantly, but with the police getting twitchy on his doorstep he considered it prudent.

Richy's sleepy voice came through; then Dex realised he wasn't sleepy but upset. He decided not to ask.

"How's business Richy?" Getting straight to the point.

Richy said business was good.

"How good?"

A few grams since yesterday.

"That's not good business Richy," Dex told him, raising his voice; "That's a waste of my time. You're costing me money, pal. For fuck's sake you're supposed to be good at this."

Richy started crying; he was trying to hide it but Dex could hear the muffled whimpers as he explained he was under a lot of pressure with his woman.

What the fuck?

Dex ignored it. "Listen pal, you've got six days to shift another three kilos of what you've got. Understand?"

Richy complained; Richy said six days wasn't enough time. His woman needed time with him to build the bridges back.

Build the bridges back?

"Look pal, this is getting really fucking serious." His voice was almost a shout now. "I'm not messing about with you. Either you shift three kilos or I come to your place and I hurt you. And if your *woman* is there I'll fucking hurt her too, got that?"

Richy stammered. Richy apologised. Richy promised to sell three kilos.

"There you go," Dex soothed, "It's easy when you put your mind to it. Okay?"

Richy said Henry McVee had been asking about the Glasgow job. Dex glanced at the safe.

"Tell him it's on hold. A few days. Maybe more. I don't know right now."

Richy said OK.

"One last thing, fella. Do you still have contacts up in the university? There was that professor guy who scored off you on weekends."

Richy confirmed the professor was still a customer.

"Right. That's great 'cos I need you to get him to look at these images I'm sending through to you." With the PA in his hand Dex selected the photos he'd just taken and fired them across to Richy. "It's some kind of antique, or it might be. Can you get him to dig around and find out what it is, and see if it's worth anything. Only be a bit subtle pal, 'cos I think it might have some heat on it."

Richy said he would do.

Dex closed the call, clapped his hands and rubbed them together.

A soft beep in his ear alerted him to an incoming call, caller id: Nicky Osbourne.

Here comes trouble, he mused with a smug smile.

"Yeah what do you want?" he spoke in a neutral tone so she could interpret it anyway she liked.

"That's no way to talk to a lady," she protested in her coarse Bristol accent.

"You're no lady."

"Har-har. I'm downstairs. Let me in."

Bloody hell, Dex rolled his head around on his neck. Nicky was a great fuck but she was a complication: her boyfriend was Henry McVee.

"Cat got your tongue?" Nicky chased playfully.

Dex smiled despite himself; "What are you wearing?"

"White plastic rain coat."

"And?"

"White plastic knee boots with come-fuck me heels."

"You'd better come in then."

8

The late-night café was in the city centre. Tables and chairs cluttered a first floor gallery and balcony that overlooked the downstairs serving area. It was a small cosy place with soft lighting and playing chilled out tunes; normally it was crammed with office workers on their break, but at this hour there was only a handful of people.

Ruby sat across from Kerry, the tiny wooden table cluttered with the remains of a half-eaten slice of fudge cake and two empty espresso cups. Both of them had cigarettes jutting from their lips as they talked and only removed them to flick ash. Smoking in public places had been illegal for decades but the owner had a habit and turned a blind eye to people doing the same this time of night.

"What's the job like?" Ruby asked, pushing a smile to one side of her mouth.

"Crap, next subject." Kerry sat back, crossing her long legs and tossing her blonde hair with a petulant twist of her head.

Ruby frowned, "Why do it then? Why work when your every whim and desire can be taken care of by me, your spa and partner in crime?"

"Because I can't live the rest of my life relying on somebody who acts like they could disappear at any second. So the job is crap, but I'm gonna do it. Next subject?"

Ruby thoughtfully flicked her nail against the ceramic saucer that was so small it was almost pointless; she had to applaud Kerry's ability to perceive what was happening around her despite being seemingly lost within a haze of drugs, alcohol and shopping. That came across as so judgemental and condescending, Ruby reflected. Hypocritical in the circumstances; Ruby was enjoying the sparkly, somewhat inane lifestyle. She had not planned spending her time in Bristol like this, but meeting Kerry and moving into the apartment with her had been an introduction to living on lip-gloss and laughter. It was certainly a distraction from cold dank horror of her recent life, the years of rigorous study and self-education; the war with her mother; living with the pain of severed family ties and rejection; and the ever-growing knowledge that the world was a frightening, terrifying place beneath the fake veneers of modern civilisation.

Kerry was watching her, lifting an eyebrow inquisitively.

Ruby smiled and stuck the end of her finger into the remains of the fudge cake; "You have a new man in your life. Let him take care of you." Ruby was referring to the friend of the stockbroker.

"Jesus Rubes, the whole point is for me to be an independent woman! *Next* subject?"

Ruby laughed and licked the fudge cake off her finger. After the phone message last night Ruby had told the stockbroker to leave or sleep on the couch. He'd taken the latter option. Ruby had gone to bed alone to work out what to do next; she could not call her Secret Lover back, he had restricted his phone-tag. It had boiled down to mind over fear. The fear was that Cray would get his hands on the idol; that Cray would make his way to Bristol and realise the significance of the Carthew family name, and then the tower that was appearing so frequently on the local media feeds.

The fear was that everything she had learned about Cray since receiving the package from the solicitor, containing the letters and journal from her deceased father, was actually true. Impossible yet actual fact. A monstrous *infestation* beneath the daily lives of the millions of people who lived and worked in London. Cray, and his small army, burrowing, stealing and feeding beneath the City.

Yet to succumb to the fear was to acknowledge defeat; and that simply wasn't an option in her mind.

So, she buried the fear, compartmentalised it, locked the door on it and turned her back.

Right now she could laugh free from the brain-numbing grasp of anxiety, and pretend to be happy whilst she waited for the next phase to happen.

"He must be something special dude," Ruby said slyly, "He was still in your bed this morning. That never happens."

Kerry said nothing. Ruby pressed on:

"And you were making him a cup of tea and buttering his toast when I walked into the kitchen."

Kerry glared at her in visible discomfort, "Next subject."

"We owe Richy money for narcotics."

"Ugh! Talk about something cheerful why don't you. And just a second ago you were talking about my every whim and desire." Kerry lifted her nose slightly.

"Excluding narcotics. Don't be a sponge."

"I know I know! Jesus you're a bitch. I fucking hate you sometimes."

"Of course you do." Ruby replied affectionately.

KERRY LEFT THE café to go back to the office where she was working the night shift. Ruby waited a few minutes then walked out: a man had arranged to meet her tonight.

She made her way along the boundary of the floating harbour, passing the imposing gothic structure of St Mary's church, eight centuries of history staining its ancient stone façade; then crossed into an area of closed office buildings. She was in no mood for the meeting, but the man was somebody she could not say no to.

She came to a stop at a tract of barren concrete bordered by thick black iron railings that overlooked a wide channel, the channel was flooded near to bursting point – water that was dirty even in the darkness and street lighting, sliding past just a few metres below her.

It was a discrete and out of the way spot for such a rendezvous.

She didn't have to wait long, and turned at the sound of the car approaching followed by a sweep of headlights. The car was American, glossy black paint speckled with a recent rain shower, tinted windows. It drove across the concrete slowly and pulled up alongside her. She opened the passenger door and climbed into leatherette luxury. Subtle smell of Old Spice aftershave. The courtesy light remained on for a few moments after she slammed the door closed.

"Hello," she greeted the driver in a flat tone.

The driver was a tough looking guy in his sixties, short grey hair and a perfect tan. He was dressed in a crisp grey suit and dark lamb's wool coat. He looked at her for a long while before speaking. Ruby stared out through the windshield, feigning indifference.

"How are you?" Tough Guy asked her, tender.

Ruby turned her head to face him, "Fine. I'm fine. What are you doing here?"

Tough Guy gave a quick shake of his head, exasperated, his voice sounding awkward, "Jezelle..."

"Please don't call me that." Angry.

"What the hell are you *doing* here?" he retorted; his frustration brimming over.

Ruby returned her gaze to the windshield. "Doing what my real dad couldn't."

"Bloody hell."

"You don't understand," she condemned his exasperation, "You don't know anything."

He said nothing. A silence stretched out between them.

"How's business?" she asked, finally.

"It would be better with you around."

"I'm busy."

"So I see." His words were sarcastic.

Another long silence.

This time it was Tough Guy who broke it, "A lot of police action around here recently, I heard."

"Nothing to do with me."

He smiled, genuinely, "I would have been gutted to think it had been. Look, Jez-", he stopped himself from saying her real name, then grimaced; "Ruby. It really would be good to have you back in the fold. You're a valuable asset."

"Is that all I am to you?" Her words were edged with hostility.

"Why is it always so bloody difficult *talking* to you?"

Ruby didn't answer.

He stuck out his jaw a little and eased off some tension by fiddling with the cuffs of his expensive coat. "There's always a place for you in the organisation, when you want to come back."

Ruby looked over at him and thought: *you have no idea who I am or what I'm doing here.*

The man had seen her grow up from a teenager, he'd rescued her from a life of hospitals and institutions, he'd shaped her, in a way, but now she felt as if he had somehow overlooked the true essence of her character. He didn't understand that she worked for him only to learn the skills she needed to take *away* from the job. He worked in the grey zone of information. Stolen or otherwise, he traded it, and she was part of that business.

He turned his head and held her gaze for a moment then glanced away; she could tell he wanted to discuss something he wasn't comfortable about. Then he said it, "Did you know your mother's place was burgled?"

Ruby forced her features to remain composed. "No."

"You didn't have anything to do with it?" He looked at her.

"No," Ruby lied.

"She thinks that maybe you did."

Ruby looked away, narrowed her eyes and pursed her lips.

Tough Guy shifted the way he was sitting, "Your mother, she's worried about you."

"Right," Ruby replied, dismissive.

"She's been talking to your sister."

Ruby flopped her head back against the car seat, "Great. What's *that* going to achieve? I didn't think they were talking? And she's my *half*-sister."

"Time can heal wounds like that."

"Blood is thicker than water," she retorted.

"Something like that."

"You don't know what kind of blood runs in these veins," she muttered.

"What's that?" he asked his tone suggesting he simply hadn't heard her.

"Nothing. Anyway, my darling half-sister has done fuck all to help since the lawyers got involved. Remember that?"

"You don't need to remind me, Jez… Ruby, I share your dislike of those parasites."

Ruby sniffed, inhaled sharply, pushed herself forward and made motions she was ready to leave. "Was there another reason why you wanted to see me today?"

"I was in the area. Wanted to make sure you were okay. You're spending a lot of money."

"Passing visit?"

"No. Here for a few days. I'd like to take you to dinner."

Ruby nodded slowly. She popped open the door and climbed out. "I'll call you if I get hungry," she told him, then swung the door closed and walked away, biting her lip, fighting back tears.

9

It was morning. Dex was working through the weekly accounts for the club when the buzzer rang for his apartment. His eyes flicked from the holographic display to the tangled sheets of his bed. Nicky had left less than four hours ago and for a moment he wondered if it might be McVee standing downstairs. Or was it the police?

"Jay-Jay," he spoke to the apartment chip; "Who's at the door?"

The computer transferred a security camera image onto a separate holographic window, floating above his desk. Dex didn't recognise the man standing there. Tall and tanned, with glossy dark hair scraped back in a sort of retro 1930's look; he looked slightly older than Dex and had a very serious face.

"Jay-Jay, give me voice with the door."

An audio-confirmation symbol appeared within the holographic window. Dex leaned back in his seat and rubbed his chin with two fingers, "Yeah, who is it?"

The man spoke with a strong South American accent, "Mr Rašković?"

"Who's asking?"

"My name is Ricardo Tarjuan. I believe you may have something that belongs to me."

"That's interesting, because I don't think I know you." Dex replied. He watched Mr Tarjuan twist his body and angle his neck, scanning the windows and then the cameras above the main door to the club. He leaned in close to the speaker plate:

"Very true.   Yet the body of a man was found near to your club."

Dex breathed out slowly, instantly wary. "Listen pal, I don't know who you are and I don't-"

A perfect interruption, "Mr Rašković, I am a collector of fine and rare art. I am willing to pay a great deal of money, a great deal, to retrieve what has been stolen from me."

Dex pondered his words for a long moment. He absently rubbed his fingers against the hard scar tissue at the base of his skull where the military had taken out the neural interface socket; par for the course with a dishonourable discharge. Richy had been on the phone earlier to tell him an expert was coming over after lunch to examine the statue; an associate of the university Professor. Now this stranger was downstairs. Coincidence? And hinting the statue had been stolen.   Dex sat forward in his chair. "Stay there. I'll come meet you downstairs."

He went over to the floor safe, opened it and took out the Vortek, slipped it in the belt at the rear of his pants and tugged the tails of his shirt over it.

ICE CUBES TUMBLED into a tall glass followed by a jet of carbonated water from the nozzle of the soda gun.

Dex stood behind the bar, facing the empty club, and his visitor who had taken a stool. The man calling himself Tarjuan appeared very relaxed. Dex took the opportunity to observe him more thoroughly. The man's hands were tanned, long fingered but not delicate. They were hands used to hard work. Tarjuan was wearing a crisp white shirt of buffed cotton beneath a casual black suit. One wrist was bandaged. Sinews were clearly visible in the man's neck and Dex imagined he was very strong.   There was a platinum ear-clip attached to his right lobe, Dex saw the 'RoGong' brand name stencilled into the metal. His features matched his accent, South American, very dark eyes, a proud nose, downward curved lips.   It was a face for business.

They had exchanged pleasantries about the club, and the eclectic blend of modern and old in Bristol's architecture. Now there was silence. The lull before the storm? Dex had already done a 'sweep' with his PA. Tarjuan was not broadcasting any personal tags.

Dex slid the glass a fraction toward him.

Tarjuan picked it up and sipped. "Gracias."

Dex stepped back and folded his arms, "You got in here because you mentioned the word money. What's been stolen and what's it worth?"

Tarjuan sipped the iced-soda water again then put down the glass. Dex noticed all his movements were very precise, graceful. "A rare African idol."

Dex frowned to show this did not ring any bells.

Tarjuan regarded him casually for a moment, "You have not seen it?"

"No. What does it have to do with the body found outside? The police came to see me about that but I told them I saw nothing."

"The police. Yes. They say the idol was missing when the body was found. Perhaps somebody ran off with it not realising how valuable it was?"

"Maybe," Dex's gaze went to the bandage protruding from Tarjuan's cuff, "Or maybe the guy who shot him has it?" Dex brought his gaze back to Tarjuan's and held it there.

Tarjuan smiled, an almost imperceptible stretch of the lips. "No. He does not have it."

Dex pondered his situation. Tarjuan was intimating he was the killer of the man outside the Strontium. There was nobody else in the building. Tarjuan was an unknown, and probably very capable of looking after himself and dealing in violence. Who was Tarjuan connected to, or was he a solo operator? Dex wanted to bring his hands down to his side but felt his movements would be too conspicuous. Also, Tarjuan had just revealed something about himself, information that could be used against him. Either he trusted Dex, or he didn't think Dex could harm him.

Tarjuan was gazing at him impassively, apparently giving Dex time to think. After a few more moments, Tarjuan looked down and picked up his glass. "The idol is very rare. Worth a great deal to only a handful of people. If it was sold, I would find out, and I would find out who sold it to them." He sipped his drink.

Dex sensed a threat veiled behind those words.

"Then I'm not sure what I can do for you," Dex stated.

"I would appreciate it if you would call me, if you find anything."

"There's a reward?" Dex asked.

"I can negotiate one."

Dex nodded, "Okay. Give me your phone tag, I'll ask around for you."

Tarjuan lifted his hand and briefly executed a Balinese chop, followed by a couple of mid-air finger taps. Dex realised, with a little bit of shock and awe, that Tarjuan was wearing extremely subtle implants. Contact lenses that replicated the effect of his – what now seemed to him to be clunky – DVFrames, powered by the new breed of molecular generators. He had read about them being available on the consumer market but they were still prohibitively expensive. What about the hand gestures though? Tarjuan was not wearing a data-strap.

As if Tarjuan had read his confusion he wiggled his fingers and explained, "Nano fibres."

"You're kidding me, how much did that cost?"

"Your PA has my tag. I hope I hear from you."

Dex stepped forward, kept his arms folded. "You've still not told me how much the idol is worth."

"In Argentina, where I am from, my family ranch horses," Tarjuan said conversationally, "Once, there was a horse, a big grey horse that always used to throw a rider, because I think, it was very crazy."

Dex narrowed his eyes and listened.

"However, because it was so big and strong, people would come to the ranch and say 'Rico, why do you not ride that grey horse?' and I would say, 'Because I do not want to be thrown.' But, people kept coming and always they say the same thing. So, the horse is beating me, you see? Even though I am not riding it, even though it is not breaking my bones, it is still beating me. Very bad for Rico."

Dex cut in, "Yeah I know this story: Rico the rancher jumps on that horse and rides the fucker until it gives in."

Tarjuan answered in a level voice, "No. I shot it. Business for me, is the same, yes? Right? People are asking me, 'Rico, why do you not have the idol?' I am being beaten, you see?"

Dex nodded.

"Thank you for the soda. Hasta luego. I will let myself out."

THREE HOURS LATER Dex walked into his apartment followed by the expert Richy had arranged to visit. Robert Venson was forty-two, short, overweight, with a ruddy face and thick tangles of brown hair.

"I'm not interested in selling it. I just want an evaluation. Is it worth anything?" Dex restated his proposition, quietly hoping for a straight answer this time.

"Hard to be precise from the images I saw," Venson stepped past him and made a quick sweep of the apartment with his eyes. "If it is as old as I believe, then it would be of great value to.... certain collectors, but on the general market the highest remuneration you could expect to receive, would be novelty money." Venson's neck stiffened as his gaze fell on the desk where Dex had placed the statue. "My-my." Uttered in a soft tone of astonishment.

Dex fell in behind as Venson walked over to the desk and crouched down, hands on thighs to study the object with professional curiosity. "Rather gruesome, don't you think?" Venson said, as he picked the statue up and began turning it carefully in his hands.

"It's a woman holding a child, right?" Dex gave his observation.

Venson sniffed smugly, apparently knowing something he didn't. Flipping the statue round to point the base toward Dex, he gestured to the symbol carved there. "I sent a copy of the images you took to a colleague of mine, an expert in art such as this." Dex groaned inwardly; felt like saying I thought *you* were the expert. No wonder Rico Tarjuan was sniffing around his door. "If this symbol is authentic, then it makes the object significant. You say you *found* this in Bristol?"

Dex picked up Venson's stress on the word 'found'. He decided he didn't like Venson much. He replied, deadpan, "Yeah."

"That would make sense. Bristol had strong connections to the slave trade. It's quite likely this was brought back by a crewman in his privilege chest, perhaps in the hope of trading it for something better. Hardly surprising he couldn't get rid of it, if that was the case."

"Why's that?" Dex asked.

Venson displayed a macabre smile passed the statue into Dexs' hands, "The mother you see there, she's not *holding* the child; she is eating it."

"Is it dead?" Dex stared at the thing in his hands with fresh disgust.

"The child would be alive. There were quite a few pieces like this, all made by the same chap, who used this symbol as a signature. Eating their young had something to do with their religion, I believe."

Dex found himself unable to take his eyes from the statue. His attention focussed on the mother's mouth, which he had mistakenly believed to be kissing the head of the child. Now he could see the detail his brain had failed to register, the lips of the mother were actually pushed up by the fact her teeth were buried into the child's flesh.

"Your name is interesting. Rašković. East European isn't it?"

Venson's question snapped him out of it, "Yes."

Venson pouted his lips, "Thought so. You've got the look."

Dex raised his eyebrows. "The look?"

"Were your parents Croats or Serbs?"

"Croat, so I'm told."

"Oh, I'm sorry." Venson seemed to understand the implicit tragedy in what Dex had said. "You're an orphan. Were your parents caught up in the troubles?"

Dex gritted his teeth, not enjoying the unexpected intrusion into his private world and yet desperate and hungry for any insight into the events that shaped his early life, events he would have too young to have perceived at the time. He gave a blunt response, "Vukovar."

Venson's brow crinkled with comprehension and then smoothed out with confusion; he looked at Dex as if re-assessing his appearance. "Are you old enough-"

"It was twelve years later. After the capture and arrest of Major Šljivančanin in Budapest."

The Major had been the perpetrator of the Vukovar massacre. For some Serbs, Šljivančanin was a national hero. Dex knew you had to have Baltic blood to understand why. His capture sent out shockwaves through the former Yugoslavia and caused an upswell in Serbian-led violence.

One night, several men in tracksuits walked into the entrance of a bar in Vinkovci and lobbed in four hand grenades. His parents had fled to Vinkovci during the Civil War after a midnight dash on foot through over-ripe cornfields, escaping the horrors of the hospital compound in neighbouring Vukovar. They had escaped Major Šljivančanin's brutal round-up and execution of two-hundred Croats from the same hospital compound. So there was a disturbing irony that Šljivančanin was the cause of the attack. Dex had been there, barely three months old. His father had died instantly from the shock of having his left arm blown off. His mother took shrapnel through her right eye and temple but lived long enough to carry baby Dex from the flames that took over the bar.

"It was a terrible time," Venson said with a tone that closed the conversation down. He made ready to leave and stepped away from the desk. Gesturing at the statue he said, "It's a fine piece, and in impeccable condition. Did you have it restored?"

"No."

"I could try and find you a buyer if you are interested in selling."

Dex smiled thinly, his mind coalescing around thoughts to do with Ricardo Tarjuan: "No, thanks, I've taken a shine to the ugly thing."

10

The spirit bottle rotated end to end as it ascended through the air. Several faces at the bar lifted upwards to follow it. The bottle reached its zenith and seemed to hang there for an impossibly long moment, then rushed back to earth accompanied by a growing cheer of anticipation – barely audible above the loud music – and dropped into the hand waiting to catch it.

Spad's hand.

There was a jubilant roar from the crowd of men and women watching, and most of all from McVee who never ceased to be amazed by Spad's ability as a barman.

Saturn Seven was the current place to be and be seen; full of young clubbers wired on narcotics and the boozy hordes that were cruising to fight or fuck. McVee smiled around the spliff jutting from his lips, his eyes half-closed from alcohol and nostalgia as he remembered his own days on the club scene.

McVee's gaze dropped out of focus and his mood tumbled; he felt old, excluded from these people now. They were all Nicky's age. He wondered where she was tonight. He wondered who she was with.

Turning back to face the bar he shrugged off the depressive shroud, and instinctively started clapping as Spad completed another display of bottle-based acrobatics. McVee grinned, clenching the spliff between his exposed teeth, and kept clapping. He loved his friend. Spad was the only decent person in this city and the closest thing to family for him. All the other barmen were dancing and laughing as they served customers, and because they were having fun it radiated into the crowd; Spad held the spotlight though, with his big hairless head, cheeky smile and crazy antics.

Spad flung two bottles up over his shoulders and caught them both behind his back, then he span round, and with the bottles still behind his back, poured a perfect combined shot into a glass full of colours and crushed ice.

McVee applauded again, puffing on the spliff at the same time so that a breeze of greasy smoke accompanied his words, "Fucking brilliant, eh? That boy is like Zippo the fucking clown when he tries to be careful but he can move like holy John fucking Travolta when it comes to serving drinks."

The customer Spad had just served picked up his drink and walked away without responding. McVee sneered after him and considered throwing something at the back of her head but calmed his hair-trigger temper with a familiar trick of mental control.

Turning away from the solid wall of customers waiting to be served, McVee called over to Spad: "What happened to that girl you took out last week?"

Spad squinted, it took a few moments to retrieve the memory. "I took her to the flicks. Bloody disaster."

"What was her name?"

"Polly."

"What happened?" McVee asked with an enquiring smirk splitting his lips.

One of the barmen shouted over to Spad to help out with the growing crowd. Spad lifted his hand to acknowledge it but didn't move. "I bought tickets for Casablanca, right, cos I'd never seen it on the big screen and thought taking her would be smooth, you know."

"Cultured and cool," McVee said breathing out smoke.

"Only I didn't tell her it was Casablanca, just that we were going to see a movie, thinking she would be really impressed."

McVee laughed, more smoke, "Casablanca?"

"She bloody hated it." Spad glumly shook his big hairless head. "As if it's not in colour, it's not even worth giving your attention to, you know?"

"Did you call her a silly bitch?" McVee said in a tone that intimated he hoped so.

"Well, to be honest, you know, the silly bitch bit comes a bit later on, cos at the end of the day...."

"You're out for a shag!" McVee bellowed with male bravado, but inwardly he felt sad for his friend who was desperate to just meet somebody who would love him.

Spad was grinning, "Desperately. You know. She might have had a crap name, and have no culture, you know; if she doesn't like Casablanca of all things. I mean, it's Bogart! But she had a lovely body on her."

"So you shagged her?"

"Yeah-yeah." Spad guffawed then glanced over and spotted the same barman who'd shouted for help now giving him the Evil Eye. Spad span round and reared up towards him. "What? What's your fucking problem, eh?"

McVee settled back and observed the shouting match flare up. Nothing like a good fight between men. Nothing like a bit of blood to bring back battered memories of the old days. McVee smiled around the sour taste in his mouth that was from more than just the spliff smoke he was breathing out. This blunt trauma bullshit was the stuff of his childhood: growing up with a father who thought a good way to toughen up his skinny son was to have his thug-cronies give him a good kicking every few days.

His features stiffened at the recollection. He was free of that world now. His father would never find him here. Nobody, not even Spad, knew who he really was.

11

Ruby was curled up within the hanging-basket chair in the lounge, changing the colours and designs of the polymer resin on her toenails with an electronic stylus and chuckling at Kerry's predicament.

"It's not funny!" Kerry protested, neurotically stubbing out a dead cigarette.

Ruby raised a prophetic eyebrow, "It's love dude. He's taking you to Bali and you said yes. And you said yes straight away."

Kerry pulled a look of disgust, "No fucking way."

"Yes way!" Ruby chuckled, her bare shoulders juddering up and down.

"Shut up Rube, this isn't funny! Fuck, I can't believe this is happening! What am I gonna do, Rube, what am I gonna do?"

Tears of laughter began to gather on the rims of Ruby's eyes: "I think it's fucking funny. Serves you right." Then in a strong Jamaican accent she pronounced one of her Grandma's proverbs, "Wanty-wanty no getty and getty getty no wanty."

"What the fuck does that mean?"

"I'll tell you when you're older," Ruby teased, smiling.

"Bitch!" Kerry brushed strands of long blonde hair from her face as if a nest of spiders was attacking her. She began looking through several discarded packets of cigarettes. "Oh-my-God oh-my-God."

Ruby wondered if Kerry had always been so highly strung, or had the falsetto-voice drama-queen personality developed with her descent into the drug scene? Ruby eased her humour then said, "I don't know how you can complain. He's intelligent. He's groomed. And he's rich. You can get all the narcotics you can cram up your nose."

"There is more to life than narcotics!" Kerry said earnestly.

Ruby doubted Kerry was being sincere and went back to painting her nails, tapping each cuticle with the electronic stylus.

Jumping up from the sofa Kerry grabbed her cardkey and handbag and headed for the door.

"Where are you going?" Ruby asked.

"To get some fags," Kerry called back, already through the lounge door and into the passageway.

"Can you get me some?" Ruby called after her, making it sound bossy.

"Yes," Kerry replied, irritated.

"Getting Vodka?" Ruby shouted out loudly.

"Yes!"

"Kerry?" Ruby shouted even louder this time.

"Yes?"

Ruby paused with a grin on her face, knowing Kerry would probably be standing by the front door, holding it open just twitching to get going. Ruby let the pause drag on. Then in a caustic tone she shouted, "Love you.'"

She heard Kerry laughing and the apartment door clunk shut. The smile on Ruby's face melted away, replaced by a whole load of tension. She breathed hard, closed her eyes, rolled her head forward and rubbed the back of her neck. The novelty of living life with Kerry was beginning to wear thin.

The game of mind over fear was draining her. It had been two days since she'd received the message from her Secret Lover, and had heard nothing since.

What am I doing here?

She put down the nail-stylus and sat forward. Tough Guy wanted her back and it was a tempting offer. Working for him again held an appealing sense of security compared to the uncertainty of her current predicament.

You made this situation, she chided herself.

You made this bed now fucking sleep in it.

Don't back away now you scared bitch.

But the statement her Secret Lover had made about losing the idol. That caused an alarm that was growing in intensity with each and every hour. Where was the idol?

What would happen if Cray got a hold of it?

Words from the journal and letters her dead father had handed over to her began to spill out from the shuttered recesses of her mind, like deformed creatures of a nightmare becoming real.

What have you done, Jezelle?

It was true to say she didn't know what would happen. She didn't know how much about Cray was really true.

She'd arranged for the idol to be shipped down from storage in orbit; delivered as a gift to her mother, Carmel, in Jamaica, the first step in a plan that was to end in the death of the man called Cray. Three weeks ago her Secret Lover had broken into her mother's place, as planned, and stolen it; bait for the trap.

What had gone wrong?

Who had died?

Why was her Secret Lover not calling her?

Her Secret Lover. A silly and puerile name for a man like Ricardo Tarjuan.

The timing of his arrival into her life had been less than a week after she'd discovered the whereabouts of Cray's lair in London. The timing could not have been any more perfect, almost as a herald of divine intervention, a sign she was working towards the destruction of something that was genuinely Evil. That was how she had looked at it.

Now she was wondering: had she been played? Was she the victim of her own grift?

Ricardo was a killer and a thief, but he was also one of a handful of people on the planet, and off-world, qualified to restore ancient artefacts to a particular level. His part-time passion, he called it. When she'd told Ricardo her plan, he'd *wanted* the idol, to hold it and care for it, and do his restoration thing.

Had that desire transformed into betrayal?

Ricardo said he loved her.

The oldest lie in the book.

Her plan to kill Cray was based on speculation as old as history. She'd never met the man. Neither had her father but he'd believed Cray existed, believed Cray was a monster. The journal was evidence, of something at least.

So you're sitting here, living a false life, strung out and going nuts, not sure what to do next, all because of a mouldy journal that could just be packed with...

There's more than just a journal, she countered her internal dialogue. It was true. There were letters, news accounts, all corroborating the impossible story scrawled out in the journal.

Ruby closed her eyes and pressed her fingers against the ridges of her eye sockets.

How had she allowed herself to become so confused?

And what happened to KISS?

Keep it sexy and stupid.

She'd met Ricardo in Marseilles, less than two months ago, in a bar run by Corsican gangsters. She'd been there on work for Tough Guy. Sebastian Bonifacio Stacoli and his men were going to help her hurt somebody who was withholding information on Tough Guy's organisation.

Ricardo had been there, relaxing in the company of men he liked and trusted. He was intelligent, cultured, enigmatic and funny, and visibly held the respect and admiration of the gangsters.

Ruby smiled briefly, sinking into nostalgia as she recalled the moment they'd started talking.

Wine and weed led to a night of passion. She'd left him in the morning. He'd found her that afternoon: he still hadn't told her how he'd managed that feat.

Then they had begun to spend time together.

And she'd realised he could help her deal with Cray; she'd begun to look at him professionally, rather than passionately. She'd closed down her feelings and laid out the plan to kill Cray.

Ricardo had had refused to accept her shutting him out of her heart. In the back of her mind, she suspected he'd agreed to the plan in the hope of winning her back.

Now she wasn't so sure.

Maybe he had simply used her to get the idol for himself?

There was nothing she could do but sit and wait, or give up, pack up and go back to work for Tough Guy. But she didn't want to do that yet.

Everything was up in the air it seemed, and all she could do was sit and wait for the pieces to fall.

12

The Strontium was packed out with the regular Friday night crowd. The music was an energetic throb of ambient bass and overlapping vocals with an Arabic flavour; the latest and very best sounds coming down from the 'bedroom pod' producers in orbit; technicians and astronauts with a creative habit. The air was damp with sweat and heavy to breathe. The laser rigs and holo-projectors picked out the dense tangle of figures cavorting and posing on the dance floor.

Dex sat at his usual perch at the bar. He liked to spend the weekends there, in the club, mingling, pumping hands, sharing grins and casual bullshit. Most of it was meaningless but it pleased him; made him feel a little bit special. It made him feel like he was doing okay.

Tonight was different, however.

His mood was insular, reflective and uneasy.

The conversation with Venson earlier that day had stirred up old recollections and distant sentiments about family, about blood and identity.

Much of who he was now had been forged in the violence and trauma of the resurgent violence in the Balkans. Ever since he'd been old enough to understand the stories of what had happened during the Civil War he'd found himself identifying with the warrior class of men who had stood up to Oppression and ultimately been crushed into the dirt as a result of it.

The stories of undaunted bravery in the face of overwhelming aggression had fuelled his desire to escape the alcoholic thuggery of his foster family, and five feckless foster-brothers.

He joined the military when he was sixteen. Nine months of basic training then three years with a unit in Poole. He completed a communications course and was assigned to Special Forces signals for the SBS, which was where he got his first taste of the black market. He slotted into the support matrix that fuelled and fed the joint operations between SBS, SEALS and the Dutch 1ACG, sliding up and down the boundaries between the Euro-federation, Russia, China and the Middle-East. Working out of camps of large CP tents, with vehicles reversed into them, bristling with aerials and sat-dishes; and with figures prowling from every agency, deal making and deal breaking.

Even back then Dex had the right personality to blend into the mix.

Driving around with Special Forces plates so the police couldn't stop him, he'd worked with the Russian mafia off-loading weaponry stolen from stores and viral splinters from the cyber warfare units; he'd shifted heroin controlled by the spooks onto the Albanians, raising cash for shadow ops where deniability was paramount.

Then he was made a corporal by his CO and put in charge of other marines doing signals. Then he moved to handling landing craft and vehicle units. Took a proficiency course in PARC and rode through selection top of his class.

He became a PARC pilot just as Operation Metal Hammer kicked-off in the Gulf. That's when he became best buddies with Vincent Brent and his pal Duke.

The Powered Assault Recon Chassis were suits of armoured exoskeleton, varying in size and armament depending on the operational criteria. They hosted state of the art hardware, fitted with sensory arrays and control systems which were fed through to the enclosed pilot via cybernetic linkage. His nervous system was literally 'plugged' into the machine. PARCs were hardened against electromagnetic pulse and microwave attacks and could withstand nuclear blast shock up to one megaton per three Millers Compound Ratio.

Dex grimaced as the recollections took him down a familiar path of memory. His first missions had been as part of a covert team sent in to destroy particular infrastructure, none of which had military significance, but which allowed certain corporations to pick up the lucrative contracts to rebuild them. 'Smash for cash' was the term his unit used for the missions.

That was what the Norwegian journalist had been investigating when Dex found him.

Dex blinked as the chunky electronic beats and sweaty atmosphere crashed back into his awareness; he realised he'd been sitting like a statue staring at his drink.

The barman caught his eye and mouthed the words: you okay?

Shit.

He didn't need to be thinking about that dead journalist right now.

Dex nodded at the barman without giving anything away, then knocked back his drink, stood up and pushed himself away.

With a brisk stride he shoved through a leather-upholstered door. It was another route to his apartment. Passing through a couple of short corridors he reached the staircase.

The apartment's management chip unlocked the door as he reached the top of the stairs.

He strode through and called out "Lights".

Nothing happened.

Dex stopped abruptly; the door swung closed behind him and he was left in near total darkness; the dirty sodium glow of the streetlamps outside painted the windows in sharp silhouette.

"Lights," he called out again.

Something small landed on the floor beside him with a heavy thump.

The hairs on his arms and the back of his neck prickled up; he began turning back toward the door, one hand reaching up to press the 'sweep' button on his DVFrames.

Without warning the room was filled by numerous rapid-fire flashes of painfully bright light; it was like a psychotic strobe light. His hands were already in front of his face, his eyes tightly shut but somehow that light still jabbed through his eyelids, pricking the nerve clusters around his retina with a highly complex sequence.

Dizzy, was the thought spinning through his mind as his brain registered the distant notion he was falling.

Dex hit the floor with his eyes open, his mouth slack and drooling.

WHEN HE WAS fifteen he used to buy butane gas canisters meant for refilling cigarette lighters. He took them home hidden in the bag for his school sports-kit and went up to his bedroom, where he could lock the door. Inhaling the fumes took him to an insane high where everything became wonderful, and yet terribly intense at the same time. He didn't know why he started. He only did it a few times. Clutching to consciousness, riding the dizzying high, he used to push his face into the dazzling beam of a reading light with his eyes tightly shut. He would get so close he could feel the heat of the lamp against his skin. Then he would blink. Rapidly. It made his eyes water but he couldn't feel the pain. Combined with the butane the effect was utterly brain-distorting. When he stopped blinking he would stand up and watch the world invaded by streaks and blobs of light.

Opening his eyes now, Dex found those same visual effects racing across his retina.

For a few seconds he was swamped by confusion and the sickening notion his life had just been one big butane-trip. Then consciousness snapped fully back into place. Only one lamp in the apartment was on. He was sitting in near darkness, in a chair beside the floor safe. He couldn't move. Tilting his head he saw why; he had been tied into the chair with what he recognised as parachute chord.

Looking up he saw Ricardo Tarjuan standing a few metres away, quietly watching him. Tarjuan was dressed in dark clothing, criss-crossed with utility webbing and a climbing harness; there was a ski mask bunched between the gloved fingers of his left hand. In his right hand there was a gun.

Dex saw the gun, a compact model from Israeli Military Industries, there was a stubby silencer attached, and felt crushed by a wave of sad resignation. It was all going to come to an end here, in this room. He looked down at his bonds again and knew he was held fast.

"What do you want?" he asked, tilting his face toward Tarjuan.

Tarjuan stepped forward and Dex noted the curves of defined muscles pressed up against the thin fabric of his jumper. "I want the idol. Give me the code to open the safe. I take the idol and I leave you alive."

Dex knew he was in no position to argue. Tarjuan knew the idol was in the safe. He had nothing to barter with. "How do I know you won't just pop a bullet through my brain after you've got it."

"I don't make a habit of killing people."

56

"Try telling that to the guy they found dead outside my club," Dex retorted bitterly.

Tarjuan nodded, "Touché, Senior Rašković. But I'm afraid you will have to trust me."

Dex could already guess the lines of the conversation but his pride was bruised, so he made some resistance anyway, "And if I don't? What if I don't give you the combination? It's a loud bang to blow it open, or a long wait whilst you try and crack the combo or burn through it, but you're travelling light by the looks of it and I don't see any oxy tanks."

Tarjuan smiled, and Dex was unhappily aware there was not a flicker of nerves or irritation in the skin around that smile. "It is a nice safe," Tarjuan said. "American. A Hayman. U-L-group II combination lock, two spring loaded relocking devices, solid hand welded door and body, full-length dead bar to prevent entry by removing hinges, drill resistant carburized lock mount hardplate, half inch solid steel door. B-rate steel body. It will only take me...thirty minutes to get inside, maybe less; but let's say thirty minutes. I don't think anybody will come looking for you in that time. I think we will be quite undisturbed. Is thirty minutes worth your life?"

Tarjuan pointed the gun at him.

Dex tensed his muscles against his bonds, the features of his face contorted as he looked into the simple circular aperture of the silencer. His memory had plenty of bodies with bullet wounds to help feed his imagination. It took a few moments to compose himself again.

"Thirty minutes? Bollocks."

Tarjuan gently gestured with the gun at some point to Dex's right. Dex turned his head to see a black satchel resting to one side of the door.

Dex realised that if he had not come upstairs Tarjuan would have probably got into the safe without him.

"Don't believe everything a sales-rep tells you. Especially the ones in the security trade. Give me the code."

Dex thought frantically, desperate to find another option but all he got was a blank wall.

"The code."

"Okay," Dex conceded, muttering the word with a heavy breath.

Dex told him the code.

Tarjuan walked briskly over to the safe and dropped down into a squatting position. He swiftly twisted the combination dial, pausing for the briefest moment before the final entry. He grabbed the handle and swung open the spring-assisted door. Dex kept his gaze on the gun in Tarjuan's hand.

Tarjuan reached inside and lifted out the Vortek handgun. He showed it to Dex with the flicker of a smile, "Very nice."

He popped out the magazine, slipped it into a pocket, and then returned the unloaded gun to the safe. He lifted out the idol, stood up and walked towards the door.

"How did you know?" Dex asked, silently relieved Tarjuan did not appear to be interested in the gene-twister.

Tarjuan said nothing. He picked up the black satchel, put the gun and ski-mask inside, then pulled out a sheet of soft white fabric that looked like terry towelling, and carefully wrapped it around the idol.

"So what's it worth?" Dex persisted.

Tarjuan placed the wrapped idol carefully in the satchel, pressed down on the sealstrip, then slipped the satchel over his shoulders and yanked several straps to ensure it was tight against his body.

Dex wanted to curse him but played the smart silent game: live to get revenge another day.

Tarjuan walked across the room and opened a window behind the desk; he reached one arm outside and pulled into the room a length of climbing cable that had been left hanging there. As he did this he said, "Two years ago I left a man tied up, thinking his colleagues would eventually come to investigate. He died where I left him. They found him lying in his own piss and shit. I need to know if I can untie you before I go, yes? You're not going to give me trouble are you?"

Dex stared at him, suppressing the pulse of excitement, concealing the notion rapidly forming inside his brain as he realised he would not be left immobile.

Tarjuan came over and stood beside him. "You're ex-military." It was a statement.

Dex broke off eye contact, "Yes. And you?"

Tarjuan stepped behind him and loosened his bonds. Dex flexed his arms and shoulders and felt some of the chord slipping from his body. Tarjuan made him pause with a hard tap to the top of his skull.

Dex watched, barely able to restrain himself, as Tarjuan backed across the room to the open window, and clipped the climbing cable to his harness. In one continuous movement, Tarjuan reached up, gripped the cable outside

58

and with the aid of his feet pushed himself out through the aperture. Tarjuan hauled himself upwards and vanished above the window frame.

Dex wriggled and thrashed his arms and legs, tearing his limbs free from the para chord. The chord tumbled to the floor in loops. He jumped to his feet, ran across to the main door, flung it open and barrelled through, hurled himself down the stairs with his arms out to either side.

At the bottom of the stairs he crashed through the door out into All Saints Lane; his doormen span round and hurried over to him. Dex moved to the far side of the lane and looked up, trying to see the roof above his apartment.

"I've just been robbed. The cunt's up there on the roof. He's got to come down somewhere."

The doormen hovered uneasily.

Then a sound: corrugated plastic roofing crashing against the concrete ground. Dex knew where that would be. He tugged the arm of his biggest doorman, "You come with me." And to the other two, "Watch the club."

Dex sprinted up All Saint's Lane, his doorman close behind him, past the crowd of young clubbers lining up to get in.

Turning into the Glass Arcade he found several groups of people staring up at the roof, three-stories above, and at the shards of shattered corrugated plastic lying on the floor below. He guessed it must have collapsed from Tarjuan's weight running across it. Which meant Tarjuan was now above the adjoining block of buildings. Dex jogged forward with the loyal doorman close behind. A thought struck him, thinking about Tarjuan with his contact lens DVFrames and fancy surgery; he dug out his PA from his pants and switched it off.

He left the arcade and came out onto a main road crowded with taxis and late-night revellers.

Dex tapped the doorman and pointed down the road, "If you see a South American looking guy dressed in black jeans and jumper take him down hard." Dex didn't mention Tarjuan had a gun. The doorman trotted off, his shaved head twisting left and right on a thick stump of a neck.

Dex glanced around him, tracking the flow of people, looking for any sign of a person hurrying through the crowd, causing a disturbance.

Pink shirt. Flamingo pink. Moving swiftly away from him. Black hair scraped back across the skull. Dex felt the features of his face expand as if in slow motion. He stepped to one side, trying to get a better line of sight through the shifting milieu of drunken men and women. Was it him? The pink shirt was like a beacon. He'd be insane to wear something like that. Then Dex spotted the black satchel clenched by his side.

Son of a bitch!

Dex was running before he even had time to finish the thought. Tarjuan must have had a repel-line ready and waiting to get down with.

Dex closed in using quick short strides; side-stepping through the clusters and throngs of revellers.

Less than five metres from Tarjuan's back Dex was dragged to a halt as a meaty paw clasped around his arm. Dex was whirled round in a vice-like grip and found himself staring at a mound of man who was swaying even as he held onto Dex's arm; "Hey where are you going in such a hurry!" The words tumbled out slurred and overlapping.

Tarjuan heard and looked round. Then Dex saw Tarjuan sprinting away, pushing through the crowds like a bullet. The drunk who had hold of him was trying to pull him in close. Dex span toward him and slammed the heel of his hand into the man-mound's nose, sending him sprawling backwards and letting go to clutch his face.

Dex ran out onto the road and then sprinted at full tilt with the quick moving flow of traffic alongside him.

He saw Tarjuan up ahead climbing into a small blue Fuji-Chrysler. The car pulled out just as he got within an arm's reach of it.

"FUCK."

Punching the air in rage he slowed his pace and watched, defeated, as the Fuji-Chrysler accelerated away. His eyes went to the registration plate. He repeated the string of digits aloud.

Striding away he turned his PA back on then dialled a phone tag from the address book. The call routed via his SONY ear-clip.

The connection went straight through to voicemail, a synthetic male chip voice, "This is Viral Five. Leave a name and a tag we can call."

"This is Dex. Call me back pronto."

He cut the connection.

He didn't go back to the club. He kept walking, his mind racing, blood pumping, anger boiling.

After a few minutes a soft beep in his ear alerted him to an incoming call, caller-ID withheld.

Dex answered, "Yeah?"

It was Viral.

THREE IN THE morning and the city was still packed with people milling around in drunken groups.

Dex walked briskly amongst them, his hands shoved into the front pouch of his hydrogel poncho.

Amongst a row of parked vehicles the Land Rover was just another glossy paint job, although some may have noted the completely opaque windows or the serious whip-antenna rising up from the back. Dex rapped his knuckles against the bodywork three times then slid the side-hatch open.

The cramped interior was filled with racks of computer equipment. It could have been a mobile media production suite; blank, unmarked hardware sat alongside a few devices with familiar names, all strung together with neatly tied bundles of cabling.

Dangling within a chair that was half-web, half swing, was a plain-looking Chinese girl. Her tiny body was dressed in a dark red T-shirt and loose fitting jogging bottoms. This was Mai-Ling, twenty-one years old and a professional hacker.

Knowing her dislike for idle chatter, he slid the hatch shut behind him and pulled out his PA. She took it without a word and slotted it into a cradle jutting out between two box-like devices. Everything that seemed important was within reach of where she dangled; her tiny feet were folded up within a strap below her, her knees loosely tucked together. Two cables snaked from separate devices to end in interface ports surgically drilled into the base of her skull.

There was nowhere for Dex to sit; he crouched down onto his haunches beside the hatch. Touching the floor with his hands he noted how swept-clean it felt.

Mai-Ling was squinting at the small hardscreen below the PA/cradle. Dex noticed there were no holographic projectors; no touch matrix displays, no lightware at all. Just solid hardware. The cabling might have looked old-tech to some but he knew from his experience with the hackers in the SBS cyber-warfare unit, that cables were a great way to keep data packets secure within your local network.

He wondered what in-depth view of his life she would be pulling up on that screen.

"Credit's good, Dexter, business going well?" Her voice was choppy, laced with a trendy London dialect.

Dex chose not to comment on her snooping through his financial records, or the fact she used his full name knowing how much he disliked it. "Not bad. Until tonight. I just got robbed by a monkey who climbed in through my window."

She looked at him without expression.

His legs were cramping up so he dropped down onto his backside, and rested his spine against the hatch. He told her the registration number, then explained: "That's the monkey's car. I need you to find out who he really is and where he is. Can you do that? He was using the name Ricardo Tar-huwan, don't know how you spell that."

"Juan, with a `J'. Spanish?" she asked.

"Argentinean. Likes to shoot horses."

"Eh?"

"Forget it."

Mai-ling pulled a flexible touchboard into her lap, fixed her eyes on the hardscreen and began a series of quick-fire keystrokes. Dex sat silently watching her with an undefined, nauseous tension seeping into his guts. Apparently this job did not merit her touching cyberspace through her neural interface.

A few seconds later she swung the chair to face him. "It's a hire car, paid by cash card."

"Untraceable," Dex stated glumly.

"It would be, but your monkey didn't do much to hide from CCTV. I got his face. Crash ran the biometrics through the cam-d-b's for the area around the rental biz. Snagged a trail. Found him using a credit card in a nice boutique. Expensive taste, your monkey."

"Fucking awesome," Dex said through a grin and gritted teeth. "Can you run the tracking thing where you see everything he's done with that credit card in the last few days?"

"Last few days? Want to be more specific?"

"More days more cost for me?"

"You got it."

"Okay, give me the last three days."

Mai-Ling turned her attention back to the hardscreen, fingers blurring on the touchboard. Dex glanced at several of the other hardscreens within the confined space and caught scrolls of digits and incomprehensible glyphs. He asked: "Where does it tell me how much this is costing?"

Without looking at him Mai-Ling said, "You want to shut the fuck up and let me get on with this?"

Dex grinned, "I thought they'd stopped P-M-T."

"The inhibitors give you a thick discharge, white sticky shit that makes your cunt smell. You want to try some?"

His grin faded. "I'll pass."

The silence extended into seconds.

Mai-Ling sat up straighter, her feet swung down and she crossed her ankles. Reading from the screen she said, "Lots of food. He eats well, your monkey. Paid out of a hotel tonight, round the corner. What time did he hit you?"

"Two hours ago."

"Monkey knew he wasn't coming back, checked out earlier."

"Shit," Dex retorted and rolled his head back and round from side to side. Thinking out loud he said, "What about the car? Does he still have it? Has he booked a flight out of England?"

"No on all counts, but.... he's got a reservation for the next two nights at the JAL Royal, London, room four-oh-one."

Dex smiled: "Got you!"

13

No lights were on inside the bedroom; rivulets of rainwater ran down the window illuminated by the orange streetlamps directly outside. Traffic passed in a steady stream below, tyres hissing on wet asphalt. The time displayed on the blue hydrogel cube was '03:09 A.M.'

McVee sat within the lumpy embrace of a sagging armchair, glaring at the wall opposite window, consumed in a slow burning rag, watching the shadows cast by the rainwater and orange light and visualising the dark trails as blood.

Dex wasn't handing over the gene-twister.

Fucking cunt.

Richy had called earlier to give him the bad news; said Dex was putting pressure on all the dealers to shift Jerry White's load.

Dex was into White for a lot of money; McVee knew how it worked. Had seen it all before.

The way Dex was behaving told McVee he should be grabbing the Glasgow deal with both hands, getting the cash in before Jerry White came down on him like a drop-forge hammer. The fact Dex was delaying suggested he was either looking for another way of shifting the twister or Dex didn't trust him.

Or both of the above.

Either way he cut it, McVee was left looking at a black shutter rolling down on his vision of a future chilling in Portugal with Spad.

McVee sucked harshly on the end of a joint and followed with a slug of cheap Happy Eater whisky; he breathed out creamy smoke around the rim of the bottle still resting against his lower teeth.

There was fuck all he could do right now. He couldn't touch Dex, he couldn't torch his club, he couldn't do anything that would risk the fucking pigs getting a handle on him.

He was sorely tempted to ring Dex and give him a piece of his mind, put him in the picture with the kind of shit he could bring down on him. But McVee was working from a position of disadvantage and Dex was a smart mother fucker; Dex would turn the tables and just make McVee look like a limp dick.

Fuck!

McVee sat and glared and raged in silence.

He heard a car pull up outside the house. McVee sat forward and peered down. It was a sports car; the headlights remained on, a pair of man's hands clutched the steering wheel. The passenger door popped open and Nicky clambered out; long legs covered in spray on PVC and glistening in the orange streetlight. Slamming the door behind her she rushed towards the house. The car did not pull away; the hands began tapping the steering wheel.

McVee settled back into the armchair and waited. For a moment he imagined going downstairs, dragging the guy from his fancy car and kicking the crap out of him. But again, he couldn't risk the police getting involved.

The door to the bedroom swung open and the light snapped on. McVee held a hand up to his face to protect his eyes. Nicky gasped in shock and said in her coarse Bristolian dialect, "Henry! Jesus! What are you doing sat in the dark?"

McVee slowly lowered his hand and looked at her. The shiny black PVC revealed the excruciatingly wonderful shape of her curved thighs and firm backside.

Ignoring his silence, Nicky strode quickly to the beat-up wardrobe.

"Where did you stay last night?" he questioned her.

A pause whilst she peeled off her top, a stretchy black thing; she straightened up and turned to face him. His gaze roamed across her breasts then locked onto her eyes, he wanted to see if she looked away, to see the *guilt* burning there; she was staring back at him, defiant, the trace of a smirk at the edges of her lips. Now he felt pathetic asking her; how many times did they go through this? "Where do you think I was last night?"

"You left in a hurry, like. Spad made you dinner."

65

"You didn't seem too bothered when I left. What's got into you *this* time?" She stood there, with her hands on her hips, glaring at him now. For a moment he was swamped by confusion. Was he just being paranoid? He looked at her half-naked body. That was his girlfriend, or was supposed to be. Was it him, driving her away through these constant bouts of accusations? No, he told himself, look at the facts. He tried to think through it but his thoughts were mired in alcohol and weed.

A smug victorious look spread across her face, then she turned away from him.

"You don't seem to want me anymore?" he protested.

"Jesus!" she hissed, her shoulders jostled as she rummaged through the wardrobe, "You're so *weak*!"

The remark stung. A wound to his ego that had been carved around a culture of proving himself through being strong. An ugly mood descended on him, his voice became low and menacing: "So *where* were you last night?"

"I went to Strontium for a while," she said whilst tugging a fresh top free of several others that had become tangled on their hangers. "And then I went to Mark's."

Cunt, his thoughts raged at the wealthy man who seemed to have become Nicky's new best friend. "Is that his car downstairs, like?"

"Yes," she replied wearily, shaking her head; then she turned round, pulling on the top, bright pink and made of a fine mesh that revealed more than it hid. "I'm sorry you can't handle me meeting new people."

"I can't handle you fucking them."

She gave a sour laugh, shook her head. "You're so sad."

He glared at her, resisting the urge to pound her face with his fists.

Adjusting her top she said, "I hoped you'd be happy for me. I'm meeting people who can help me get somewhere." McVee dropped back into the armchair, reeling-in his anger; he guessed she was referring to her half-hearted attempts at getting modelling work. "Mark's invited me to come to Sixty Two Degrees of Corruption in Soho, next week. Mark's buying me an outfit from DV8. He says I can keep it if I do the next month's photos for Liquid Silk."

McVee was nodding with a sarcastic expression, "Take it I'm not invited then."

Nicky sneered with disdain, "Look at you Henry. Do you really think-", she flapped her hand as if deciding against cutting into him further, "It doesn't matter. Mark's got some important people joining us; I don't think it would be a good idea for you to come. You obviously don't like Mark, and I don't think you could handle me having fun there."

His mind filled with sordid images of what 'having fun' meant. He looked away from her, feeling incapable of arguing, or expressing what it was he felt. Rejection and jealously were hard to couch in winning words. He tried to offset his torment by picturing himself paddling out into a stormy green crystal ocean on a surfboard. But the image only half-formed before the memory of Richy's phone call tore it all down. He was stuck here, scraping the bottom of the barrel, slaving away to merely survive, being bled dry by this demonic bitch. And he couldn't see any way out. If he kicked her out he knew he would only be ten times more miserable wondering where she was and wishing she was there; at least here he had a chance to have her again, however remote, there was a chance.

She was standing by the door, already on her way back out. She waited for him to focus on her face, then said, "You're just jealous because I'm the one being taken to London. I'm the one getting the new clothes, stuff you couldn't even afford!"

McVee stared at her, speechless. What about the clothes he had bought her; did nothing he do count?

Scowling at him, she said, "Don't waste your time waiting up for me. I hate it when you do that. I've got my own life. I intend to live it." She flicked the light switch, plunging the room back into shadows.

14

The soft beep in his ear woke him just as the call connected.

"Dexter," Mai-Ling's voice.

Pulling himself upright in the bed he peered around the room of his apartment, disorientated, a little confused; his heart was thumping, his face and body soaked in sweat. It was still dark outside. "Yeah?"

"You can talk freely, got this line buried in thick ice," she said in her trendy London dialect.

"What the fuck," Dex said, his brain emerging from sleep. It was Viral5. He tried to peer at a time display but his vision was all blurred and messed up. He needed to wake-up more. "You hacked my phone?"

The call had connected without him actually answering it.

"I'll get straight to the point. Got a biz prop but first I need to ask how much you have invested in Henry McVee?"

Dex's thoughts stumbled ahead, pulling away from the lingering memory of a nightmare dream he'd started to recall: running across rain slicked rooftops under the icy glare of a billion stars, whilst something vast and utterly monstrous rose up behind him.

He tried to capture the angles of her preamble. Viral could only know the name Henry McVee from the address book of his PA.

He's a small job man. Not much risk, why?" Dex pressed, almost fully awake now.

"So losing him would not hurt your operations?"

Dex focussed on the time display again; it read '06:01 AM'. "Hurt my ops? Not really. Why?"

"His name's not Henry McVee. His name's Micky White."

The relevance of that name slid into his brain like a butcher's knife. He suddenly felt cold; and a shudder went up his spine.

Micky White.

Jerry White's son. Jerry White, the owner of the Strontium, the man behind the gland farms and the pentathene he was busy trying to shift; the mad-dog of the northern criminal scene.

Fuck.

Micky White was the son Jerry White had disowned for supposedly being a 'snitch', the son whose head Jerry White had put a murder contract on. His head felt like it was suddenly spinning: what the hell was McVee/Micky doing here? Did McVee know *he* worked for Jerry? Did McVee have an angle going? What would happen if Jerry White found out Micky had been primed to take three kilos of gene-twister to Glasgow.

Fucking hell, Jerry White's twister. No wonder McVee had a good source in the gland farm, he's part of the bloody family.

"That's very interesting," Dex said and heard the tremor in his voice, his throat was so dry he couldn't swallow.

"Interesting is for spectators. I'm a player, Dexter. Micky White has a bounty on him. It's a lot of money."

Dex thought about it. He turned his head and looked at the streetlight squeezing through gaps around the window blind. He said, "Do you know what will happen to McVee if his father finds him here?"

"It's a lot of money," she replied coldly. "I could do this without you, Dexter, but we have a business relationship. I only found out through you so you deserve a slice."

"Do you know what will happen to me if Jerry discovers I've been looking after his son?"

"I know who Jerry White is. You've not been looking after his son. Micky White tricked you and probably has a plan to hurt his father's business. You've found out the truth and now's your chance to do something about it. Jerry will reward you."

Does Viral work for Jerry? Dex heard himself think. Was this some kind of sick loyalty test? Dex decided that was too subtle a tactic for somebody like Jerry White.

"I feel like you've got me over a barrel."

"Don't be such a dick. If Micky White has a plan to hurt his father, how seriously bad do you think it would look on you if he executed it?"

He couldn't argue with her logic. It would look bad.

"Have you got an idea how to play this?" Dex asked.

"You call Jerry. You tell him what you know. You give me a fifty percent kickback of the bounty."

Dex pondered his options.   He had very little choice; Mai-Ling had him boxed into a corner. "Fifty percent and a favour to me."

"Favours are hard to quantify on an invoice."

"Call it a freebee," he suggested.

"I call that sucking dick – and I don't suck dick, Dexter; you know that."

"You know-" he started, exasperation flooding into his voice.

"What do you want?" she asked succinctly.

"JAL Royal, room 401, can you pop a lock for me when I need you to?"

"That's an expensive favour."

"Define expensive?"

"The other fifty percent," she told him.

"I call that a fucking rip-off. No way."

"Then no play."

His exasperation returned, "All you've got to-"

She laughed, sharp and loud, "You think you know anything about getting a door open in a hotel. This isn't the movies. Door. Important point of security in any fortress. Do you know what kind of people rely on hotels? Security is heavy. Heavy security is risk. Risk is expensive."

"Forget it then."

"Going gung-ho?" she inquired.

"What?"

"Room 401."

"I've got a plan," he stated.

"Ah yes, the military man." Her tone said she was less than confident in his chances.

"What the fuck?"

"So you'll talk to Jerry?" She brought her discussion back on track.

"Give me a couple of days."

"Now would be better," she insisted.

"I need a couple of days, Viral. Understand?"

"You don't have a couple days. Ricardo Tarjuan is likely to leave the JAL Royal this afternoon. I can't keep tabs on him forever, not unless you're happy to pay for it and looking at your credit levels – I don't think you'll want to know the cost."

"What the fuck would you suggest?"

"Get dressed. Get in your car and drive to London now. Do whatever it is you need to do. I can watch your entry. I can open the door. I can warn you if there's shit to warn you about."

Dex pulled a face. He rubbed his fingers through his short black hair. "You don't mess about do you?"

"Life is busy."

"Get much sleep?" He quipped.

"I can sleep when I'm dead."

HE WAS IN London. The BMW crawled across the rain-slicked asphalt of the hotel visitors' car park. The sky was a bruised blue, wisps of dirty cloud, a muted glimmer of sunlight. Dex swung the BMW into a space then switched off the engine. He peered up through the windshield and drizzle at the conical tower of the JAL Royal hotel, it looked like a Gothic church spire rendered from tinted glass and polished metal. Behind the tower, the sleek lightweight form of an orbital shuttle powered across the sky in a steady ascent; Heathrow's HOP Terminal was only a few miles West.

Ahead of him was the hotel entrance, the softly lit reception visible through curved planes of glass, a welcoming sanctuary within the growing mid-morning gloom. Not so welcoming for him, perhaps. Dex pulled out the Vortek handgun and checked again that the safety was on.

Removing the DVFrames – he'd left them on through habit – he placed them inside the glove compartment. Leaning forward, he tucked the Vortek into the waist of his trousers against his back, then popped open the car door, stepped out, swung the door shut and jogged across to the hotel entrance.

A concierge stepped out to greet him and usher him inside beneath a large white umbrella.

Dex nodded his thanks and hurried through. Peripheral vision picked up a couple of heads turning his way from behind reception. He ignored them and moved directly to a bank of elevators, feigning a weary preoccupied expression that he had cultivated to keep security patrols in the Gulf from picking him out of a crowd. The Vortek felt small and discreet against his back; he was not concerned about give-away bulges, or that he looked out of place. He was just another guest on his way to his room.

The doors rolled open to reveal an empty car, he stepped inside and selected the 4th floor.

When the doors closed the brushed bronze surface presented his own reflection: stiff black hair speckled with rain; hard eyes, dark and intense; a strong nose that fitted the square architecture of his brow, cheeks and jaw; broad lips set in a determined line, his olive skin was shiny with a thin film of rainwater and sweat.

He wondered if Viral5 was watching him preening through the camera blister in the ceiling.

Better be, he considered, if he was paying her the whole slice of whatever Jerry White handed over as a reward. An acidic pellet of dread dropped into his guts and fizzed: he wasn't looking forward to that conversation. McVee was going to end up dead.

Patting the left side pocket of a short leather jacket, he reaffirmed where he had placed the carbo-plastic restraints. Tarjuan was going to regret his decision to rob him.

The elevator door opened onto a small landing; Dex followed a sign that directed him down a curving corridor, bordered by an equally curving expanse of tinted glass.

Turning a corner he came upon a group of people filling the passageway, standing around an open doorway. They were carrying open bottles of champagne, chatting and laughing. Dex slowed to a halt as his eyes scanned room numbers. Room 401 was directly opposite where they had gathered. One of the people glanced his way but took no notice of him.

Pretending to have just realised he was travelling in the wrong direction, Dex flapped his hands and turned away.

Damn.

He returned to the elevator, stepped inside and thumbed the button for the 5th floor. He'd wait a few minutes up there and then come down and try again, see if the crowd had fucked off by then.

Gazing back at his reflection he smirked confidently. London was only two and a half hours drive from Bristol. He'd have time to fuck-up Tarjuan Ricardo and be back in time for dinner. Then he'd start looking for a buyer for the gene-twister. Glasgow was a no deal now. He had to hope to fuck that McVee didn't get a chance to blab about the three kilos.

Henry McVee... a-k-a Micky White.

He hadn't seen that one coming.

Dex came out of his thoughts with a frown.

The elevator doors had not opened.

Glancing at the panel he saw there was no longer any indication of what floor he was on. A bubble of worry dislodged itself from his guts and began to rise up through his chest. The elevator did not seem to be moving. Was it stuck? That would be a bloody irony. Surely Viral5 would have spotted that and called him or done something about it.

That's if she's actually paying attention.

He was about to dial Viral5 when the doors rolled apart. The bubble burst at the back of his throat when he saw what was waiting for him, a gasp of disbelief left his lips.

He stood there, at first too stunned to move, then slowly lifted his hands to show they were empty.

15

"Mate, whatever happened about those shootings down by the harbour?" Spad queried as he rolled up a fresh spliff: the question must have crash-impacted into his brain like a meteor hurtling in from some far distant realm of space and thought. He was sitting naked on a straight-backed wooden chair where he'd been silent for the past hour or so.

"What?" McVee blinked into semi-awareness.

"There was a gunfight down by the river, remember? I was wondering what happened."

"Don't know," McVee replied, his voice low and lethargic. Lying on the collapsed sofa in the lounge he held a forearm across his brow, shielding his eyes from the rainy light coming through the window; a half-empty cup of tea balanced on his belly. It was mid-morning and he was late opening the shop. Nicky had not returned since last night. He'd spent the night on the sofa, unable to cope with the symbolism of the empty bed.

"They're still looking for that documentary fella who was there, and that big German nutter who's with him but the news just totally dried up about the shooting." Spad stated, perplexed.

"Aye, it's all bollocks anyways, Spad, never believe nothing you see on the news. Rule number one, like."

Spad nodded absent-mindedly, concentrating on getting an even distribution of weed in the angle of paper currently cupped in the palm of his hand. McVee watched him, his eyes concealed within the shadow of his forearm. There was a gentle smile on Spad's reddish sun blasted and alcohol pickled face. At least Spad was happy: good old fucking simple Spad.

He had not told Spad about Dex putting the kibosh on his drive to Glasgow. Maybe it was just a temporary delay like Richy had said, but his instincts were screaming: Dex is dropping you.

Cunt.

McVee's guts churned over. More delay. More risk of being found out. He knew his father had people looking for him, and knew what those people would do if they found him. McVee rolled his eyes shut. How had his life come to this? Living between two walls of fear and pain; Nicky on one side, and the risk of being found by his father on the other. Portugal would be his salvation. Total freedom. A clean slate.

Just need the money fella. Just need the money.

Opening his eyes he returned to watching Spad.

"What'ya reckon the truth is then behind the Carthew tower story?" Spad mumbled as he lit up the spliff.

"How do you mean?"

"The news lies, right?"

"Eh, that's a bit of a simplistic interpretation of what I said, like. Not all news, fella. But you could have a point." McVee craned his neck forward and sipped his luke-warm tea.

"Maybe the news is exposing the lie?" Spad suggested, with deep contemplation.

"Aye, maybe. They've no doubt bribed the Lottery Council to give them the money to rebuild the tower. Officially it's to restore a historic building and improve the area, but in reality, what?"

Spad shrugged.

McVee returned his arm across his forehead, "End of the day, fella, has no effect on us."

"Carthews were into slavery and drug running," Spad stated confidently.

"Drug running... how d'ya reckon that?"

Spad leant forward, enthusiastic to demonstrate some knowledge, "Yeah mate, opium. Back in China, us Brits were shipping tons of the stuff from India in exchange for tea, 'cos it wasn't illegal until the Chinese Emperor outlawed it."

Where the fuck did that nugget of detail come from?

McVee raised his arm just enough to show him the puzzled look in his eyes, "I thought tea came from India?"

Spad frowned, troubled that his facts might be flawed. Both of them sank into silence. McVee stroked his bleached goatee beard and returned to his thoughts.

He knew Richy had a serious quantity of pentathene IV. He considered the consequences of fucking Richy over and taking it. Getting that kind of quantity to Portugal without support might be difficult but once there, selling it would be a sinch. Grabbing the pentathene was a potential back-up plan, McVee decided. If Glasgow fell through then he'd have no option but to go for it.

It wasn't like he could turn to his family for any help or comfort. His brother had spent most of his life being groomed to take over the syndicate when Jerry stepped down. Although the only scenario he could visualise Jerry stepping down was in the day he died.

His mother was living in a retreat on a small Island off the coast; she had found salvation from chronic alcoholism through God. Fair enough, McVee mused without much feeling; he considered her as good as dead out there. No use to him and absolutely no support. As for his sister, her idea of family loyalty was making sure she always had one hand glued to Jerry White's credit cards.

Nothing like Danielle. She had always dressed smart. Cultured and sexy, that was how he'd seen her. And she had loved him unconditionally. Not because of who his dad was, or because she'd lived on the fortress-estate his dad had created up in Manchester. She'd penetrated the tough shell McVee had welded together around his personality and shown him how to be relaxed with himself. She had shown him his true self.

McVee stared across the room without blinking and without seeing, his mind dragging out old, familiar and painful memories.

Danielle had been the daughter of one of Jerry's 'lieutenants', a vicious bear of a man who handled Jerry's interests smuggling immigrants, supplying the prostitution rackets and gland farms. He had a taste for the spikes the farms produced. The combination of spikes and heavy drinking exaggerated every aspect of his nastiness.

McVee brought a hand up to cover his eyes, hiding the tears forming there. He remembered the night. It was rare to hear sirens on the estate. He had rushed out, along with many others, and found the ambulance outside Danielle's house. Two fuzz-mobiles were already there, and his father talking angrily with several pigs. Jerry White was already weaving his lies. Danielle's father had come to him, blood stained and shaken: he had kicked and punched Danielle to death. For no good reason, other than she had crossed him whilst he was lost in some inner chasm of madness.

Jerry and the rest of the estate tried to cover up the murder by pinning it on a gang that had been attacking the syndicate's interests. McVee had demanded vengeance but Jerry had refused outright, pointing out the value of Danielle's father to the syndicate. That's when things had started falling apart.

The pigs didn't buy the cover-up. One pig, a promotion hungry detective sergeant had stitched him up. Pulling McVee in for questioning about the murder, the pig had then released him *after* making it look like he'd squealed. Jerry White had put a contract on his head: a dead or alive bounty for his 'snitch of a son'.

McVee blinked away the wetness layering his lashes; subtlety rubbed his fingers around his eyes, then pushed himself up into a sitting position, the cup of tea in one hand. Spad was reclined with his eyes closed, smoking the spliff.

"You gonna Bogart that joint, my friend?" McVee called over.

Spad was so lost within his own world he almost leapt out of his skin; the spliff tumbled to the floor in a cascade of ash.

McVee laughed, his shoulders shuddered and a smile cut his face, "You're fucking useless, fella. You're crap but I love ya."

16

Dex stared at the four security guards on the other side of the elevator doors when they opened. Each of them carried what looked like a thick stubby flashlight; he recognised them as stun batons, expensive versions that could discharge a disruptive field effect.

"Do you have any weapons?" one of the guards asked in a calm voice with deliberate slowness; he was a slim, wiry type, with an unyielding stare. Not your average rent-a-guard.

"No," Dex replied; he guessed they would search him but chance might be on his side. Starting to lower his hands he said, "Would you mind telling-"

"Keep your hands by your head, sir." The thin guard reinforced his command with an aggressive jab of the baton towards him.

Dex did as asked; it was no joke getting 'zapped' by one of those things. He had used larger ones during Operation Metal Hammer, in the Gulf, for crowd control: the field radius was able to take out a group of people at a time; but every now and then, some of the people he hit never got back up. Their brains shut down and the body died. It was much less common with these smaller devices but had still been known to happen. Besides, they caused headaches Dex seriously wanted to avoid.

The four guards flowed into the elevator and took control of him and the small area. Roughly they turned him round and made him face the wall with his legs splayed. The elevator doors closed and Dex felt the car begin to descend.

One guard jabbed the business end of a baton against his ribs, ready to fire; another guard grabbed his hands and locked them behind his neck. The thin guard came in close and started picking through his pockets, brushing down his legs, checking his waist. Finding the Vortek he pocketed it without comment and continued searching.

Dex said nothing. He didn't want to prompt them into subduing him.

The guards were dressed in simple grey suits with the JAL Royal logo neatly embroidered on breast pockets. Had Tarjuan hired them? Or did this have nothing to do with Tarjuan? Were they simply working for the hotel? Maybe somebody had noticed his gun?

The elevator came to a stop and the doors glided open. The guards stuck close, worked together and propelled him out into a sub-basement. Then through a fire door marked 'staff only', down a bland concrete corridor, up a staircase, along another corridor – this one had a coat of paint and photos of corporate buildings in glass frames. The photographs were real, printed on paper and not digital images displayed on cheap hardscreens. A moment later they stopped outside a polished wood door marked 'Manager'; one of the men knocked then pushed the door open, the others marched him inside.

Sitting alone behind the manager's desk was Ricardo Tarjuan; wearing a dark blue suit and a cream coloured shirt with crisp collar and cuffs. A shoelace bola in place of a tie; a horse skull cast in metal, it looked like platinum.

"Mr Rašković!" Tarjuan greeted as if delighted to see him.

Dex was guided into a chair on the other side of the desk.

The thin guard placed his Vortek in front of Tarjuan; Tarjuan eyed it for a moment before picking it up.

"We meet again," he said dryly, and appeared to be referring to the gun; there was a playful tone to his voice.

Tarjuan ejected the magazine from inside the handle, pocketed it, and then placed the unloaded weapon back on the desk. Dex noticed the jumble of datacards beside the gun, each transparent slice of hydrogel the size of a credit card and one side filled with a clear image of him. The image was recent. It meant Tarjuan had anticipated him coming after him and briefed hotel security.

Dex glanced at the guards; all four were watching him. He rolled an eyebrow and turned slowly back to Tarjuan; noticing one wall of the room was filled with hardcopy photographs of men and women, a mixture of police mug shots and private bounty sheets.

This was the third time Dex had met Tarjuan. Like him, Tarjuan was charismatic and sure of himself; yet the idea that Dex held something in common with this man now seemed a wild error of judgement. A delusion based on ego and an over-inflated sense of his own abilities. Ricardo Tarjuan was of a rare calibre of criminal; the kind of operator that could prowl the gutters of any inner city street or the marble and gilded halls of the ancestrally rich, with the ease of a shadow.

Whereas Dex was a bastard orphan, the toughened product of a childhood playing truant from school, raised within in an estate, he saw Tarjuan as the culmination of an educated life within a wealthy sun-baked enclave. A privileged criminal.

Tarjuan looked at the guards, "Thank you for your assistance. You may leave now."

The guards left without a word.

When the door closed Dex folded his arms across his chest and fixed a steady gaze on him. "Nice setup. What deal have you got going on here?"

Tarjuan glanced at him, smiled briefly then pointed at the gun, "Were you going to use this?"

"Depends on whether you apologised."

Tarjuan rocked back in the seat and laughed freely. "Apologised. Oh I like that. *Perfecto!* Apologise…" He seemed to be genuinely delighted.

There was a knock, and the door opened. A middle-aged man in a smart black suit walked in carrying cups and a cafetiere on a silver tray; he silently placed the tray on the desk then stepped back.

Sitting forward Tarjuan said with gratitude, "You are too kind, Mr Grayson."

The man smiled thinly, "An interrogation need not be uncivilised, señor Tarjuan. Are these arrangements to your satisfaction? Would you like me to call the British police?"

"That will not be necessary," Tarjuan replied, appreciative.

"Very well." The man nodded, obliging, then turned and left the room.

"And that was?" Dex asked, bemused.

"Mr Grayson."

"Who is?"

"Director of Security." Tarjuan lifted the cafetiere and sniffed; the scent pleased him; he gave the cafetiere a swirl with his hand and looked across at Dex, "Your pride is feeling damaged. You've come here to prove yourself. I think you already have. Not many people could have done what you did. I applaud you."

"Skip the Zen master speech. What do you want?"

Tarjuan poured two cups then responded: "Straight to the point."

"You must want something otherwise I'd be outside with broken limbs."

"Nothing so crude," Tarjuan softly implored; he put down the cafetiere. "Black for you, yes?"

Dex nodded, leant forward and picked up a cup. It was good coffee. He watched Tarjuan watching him.

Tarjuan looked away to spoon in some brown sugar and stir, probably for longer than was necessary but Dex could sense the South American was calculating what he was about to say: "I'm involved in a job here. I could use your help."

A smile tugged the corners of Dex's lips. This wasn't what he'd expected. This was a potential bonus. He paused to take another slow sip, getting his mind into a negotiating stance. "What's the job?"

Tarjuan fixed a level gaze on him, "For you, twenty thousand credits. Cash. And you help me kill a man."

There was a long pause. Dex had already decided he'd do it, subject to the answers to certain questions he was about to ask. Strangely, it wasn't just the money or his reliably cold-indifference to the idea of murder: Dex was aware that a part of him was excited by the prospect of working with an operator like Tarjuan.

Tarjuan remained silent, his eye-contact became less intense; he supped coffee and waited.

"Okay. Who's the target?" Dex asked, keeping his tone neutral; he wasn't agreeing to anything just yet.

"A bad man," Tarjuan said over the rim of his coffee cup.

"Come on, you'll have to do better than that."

"A self-made monster who has become a problem for my client," Tarjuan replied.

"Where?"

"Here, in London."

"When?"

"Tonight. Is that a problem?" There was no charity in the question.

Dex shook his head: no, there was no problem.

Another pause, Tarjuan was watching him.

Dex puckered his lips thoughtfully, then asked: "Did you kill that man outside my club?"

"Perhaps. The man tried to rob me."

"Really? Just a random crime?" Dex queried, dubious.

"His name was Mortice. He'd come to Bristol to buy something from me. Instead he tried to steal it. The consequences speak for themselves." Tarjuan's tone suggested he was closing down this particular line of conversation. "Your coffee is getting cold."

Dex nodded, reached forward and picked up the expensive designer cup.

"So what happens to the statue now?"

"I restore it. I take care of it, yes. And then it is handled as appropriate to the situation."

That sounded a bit vague to Dex but he didn't press the point. Tarjuan was talking, that was important. "So how did you know I had it? The statue."

"It is an idol by the way."

"Okay, the idol. Can I ask how you knew I had it?"

"One of your employees. A man calling himself Richy. He was asking questions at the university. That flagged him to me. Venson, the man that came to see you: he was working for me."

Tarjuan knocked back the last of his coffee and sat forward. It was decision time. "So. Are you in?"

Dex nodded: he was in.

17

Saturday afternoon. Rain was coming in from the east, according to the weather forecast. Ruby was curled up within the hanging-basket chair in the lounge, absently gazing at the hardscreen mounted on the wall: several media feeds were running, the sound activated on the local news and weather.

Swish computer graphics ran through a timeline, bright green and dark blue patches tracking across London towards Bristol on the weather map.

It was a distraction from the ever-growing turmoil of her thoughts. No word from her Secret Lover. No sign of anything untoward happening around the Carthew Tower. The news had shown live footage of the remains of the tower, poking up above the tree line and surrounded by gravestones that were centuries old. Protesters were still camped outside the walls of the cemetery where the tower was situated; several police officers in street patrol armour and a number of private security contractors ensured the workers were left un-harassed.

The workers were excavating a centuries-old tunnel that had collapsed around the same time as the tower. Their aim was to reach the original basement, then clear and reinforce the foundations in preparation for the main structure to be restored. Speculation was emerging that the tower had been deliberately sabotaged and brought down with gun power, fuelling the raging debate about why the Lottery Council should be using public money to help rebuild it, especially at a time when other local charities were being denied funding.

Ruby knew it *had been* sabotage. She prayed the workers never got to discover the horrific reason behind it. An event that the journal from her dead father spoke of. MacAleavey's journal. An event that was as old as some of the gravestones in the cemetery.

The workers were going into a network of natural and manually expanded tunnels that riddled the subterranean landscape beneath Bristol.

Was MacAleavey's journal honestly a true account? She wondered and shuddered as she recalled the words she'd read.

Was it telling the truth about what was buried down there?

The doorbell rang.

Ruby picked up her PA and tapped an icon to mute the media feeds coming through the hardscreen. The heavy bass chords of zomba-funk rumbled through the walls from Kerry's room; she was still packing for Bali.

Ruby wasn't expecting anyone. If Kerry missed a caller because she had her music too loud, so be it.

The doorbell rang again.

A twinge of apprehension flickered through her. Ruby climbed out of the basket-chair, barefoot and dressed in jogging bottoms and a sports bra; she padded out of the room into the hallway. As she moved, she used her PA to connect to the front door camera.

Part of her had hoped it would be her Secret Lover standing there. Instead the small hardscreen showed a stocky, blonde-haired man who didn't seem much older than twenty-five. He looked groomed and was wearing an expensive coat and leather gloves. She stopped just outside the doorway of the room she'd come from.

Don't know who you are.

Don't want to know who you are.

She was about to rotate and return to the room when the doorbell rang again.

Ruby examined the face of the man as best she could. There was a serious stubbornness to his features. This wasn't a social call.

A quick pause to listen confirmed that Kerry was apparently oblivious to the caller. The music was loud and Ruby could hear her singing along out of tune.

Ruby moved to the apartment's door, yanked it open and move rapidly with long stealthy strides across the parquet floor of the ground floor hall to the main entrance of the building.

The doorbell rang again.

"Jesus!" she hissed.

She unlocked the door and swung it open.

The blonde man jolted with surprise and stepped back.

Ruby blocked the doorway and glared at him.

He took a moment to drag his gaze from her hostile face, past her cleavage, down her exposed midriff, jogging bottoms, to her feet and back up again.

"Miss...Jackson," he began, confidence flowing into his words, "I represent your mother."

Without warning she lunged forward and took the man down in a competent demonstration of Dajudano. The man hit the ground, the back of his head up against the small doorstep. Ruby's knee on his throat.

"You fucking *prick*," she snarled out the words crazily, "Have you been following me?"

The blonde man was choking. Ruby eased the pressure for a moment. He began to explain, "Your mother has hired me -achk!!" Ruby re-applied the pressure to his throat, she bent down to bring her face to his, lips parting to expose her teeth.

"Never show your face here. Never bring that world into my life here. If I see you again, I'll break your fucking neck and you'll spend the rest of your life in a wheelchair. Got that?"

He nodded urgently, his face flushing violently red.

"Tell *mummy dearest* that I don't need her protection."

Ruby jumped up, stepped back as the man sucked in air and began to massage his throat. She slammed the front door shut then strode across the hall back into the apartment.

The zomba-funk was much louder. Kerry's door was open. Ruby froze and listened for movement. Had Kerry witnessed what just happened? The door to the apartment had been wide open.

Kerry shuffled out from the kitchen looking like she'd been dragged through a hedge backwards.

"Good morning," Ruby greeted, forcing a smile onto her face and calming her racing heart.

"Okay, don't say morning!" Kerry complained in a voice that was groggy with a narcotic come-down, hangover and lack of sleep. "I hate packing. Do you hate packing? Can you help me pack?" It was a monologue not actually directed at Ruby. Kerry wandered back into her room and closed the door.

18

Dex mulled the question over in his fuzzy brain for the umpteenth time, still unable to come up with an answer he believed: what would he have done if Tarjuan hadn't got the drop on him?

Each time he went through the scenario it boiled down to two options: shoot Tarjuan with the Vortek or tie him up and hurt him. Either way it was an inelegant solution to a problem that he was actually responsible for; he'd lied to Tarjuan about not having the statue - or idol as the South American referred to it. He'd come to London half-cocked. Out for revenge with a dumb-ass plan. Compared to Ricardo Tarjuan he was an amateur.

Dex gave a psychological shake of his shoulders and tried to throw off the sense he was somehow incompetent. Being with Tarjuan was tarnishing his sense of self-worth.

He got back to the op, started picking out the contents of the backpack Tarjuan had handed him; they were in the back of a rental van parked about a hundred metres from the target. The vehicle license tags had been changed and would be changed back before returning the van after the op.

'You with us Dex?' Tarjuan asked wonderingly, a rolled-up ski mask covering his perfectly groomed hair.

'Yeah,' he responded, snapping back to the moment at hand.

Wearing a pair of clear surgical gloves, Tarjuan picked up a Fabrique Nationale 8-80 from the sports bag by his feet, slid out the wire stock and tried the weapon for size into his shoulder, ducking his head to squint through the open sights.

They'd spent the day... shopping.

The backpack by Dex's feet was different but the contents inside were identical; wearing the ubiquitous surgical gloves he reached inside and took out a pair of tactical-DVFrames. Clear hydrogel they look like safety goggles but they'd been rigged to display targeting information and weapon status. A lot different to the chunky but stylish *Hermes* brand he normally wore, and a heck of a lot less sleek than Tarjuan's contact lens variety.

Slipping the thick elastic strap of the DVFrames over the top of his ski-mask, he made sure it wouldn't interfere with rolling the ski-mask down over his face when he needed too.

The backpacks and everything in them had been prepared in a sterile environment: free of hairs, fingerprints or drips of sweat, anything that might contain DNA and a trace back to the source of the op. Both of them had already switched off their PAs and stuffed them into a space between the spare wheel box and the plywood panel separating the cab from the cargo space.

He picked up the FN 8-80 and carried out normal safety precautions. Pulling back on the cocking piece he checked there were no rounds in the chamber, then he allowed the working parts to go forward under their own force.

The 8-80 was a hybrid weapon, considered by many to be a heavy submachine gun instead of an assault rifle. With the stock folded and a shorter magazine inserted, like the fifteen-round mags they were using, the 8-80 could be easily hidden under a regular jacket.

He picked the two magazines out of the backpack and started to load them, grabbing a handful of the fat 5.56mm rounds, pushing them down one by one into the top slot, then adjusted them to ensure they were properly seated. He preferred caseless weapons: no ejected cartridges, more ammo capacity. However, at least Tarjuan had managed to get subsonic rounds; they would preserve the 8-80's baffles and avoid a normal muzzle report.

There were no windows in the cargo space, just an overhead light. They'd removed the light's bulb before starting and were now working in red light provided by a portable device.

From the photos Tarjuan had taken he knew the target building was a two-story townhouse, part of a whole terrace that had seen better days, probably used by students and the unemployed. There was one entrance at the front, a narrow wooden door flush with the street; no front garden, no gate to worry about. Tarjuan had been unable to get any view of the back but he had also been unable to find any rear access routes for garbage and stuff, so it was likely that any rear entrance opened onto a closed yard: it didn't look like the kind of place for sprawling gardens and flowerbeds. Behind the terrace was an old church attached to a small graveyard.

Tarjuan had done a good job and Dex was confident the intel would be reliable. He had a slight concern the op was being rushed but Tarjuan had been able to answer most of his questions:

Was there any technical security? Yes, but Tarjuan had tools to disable it.

Were Cray and his men static, locked down and lying low or were they fluid, moving around, coming and going? Tarjuan described the target as a portal, barely used, with access to a set of underground tunnels Cray had turned into a personal fortress.

Dex paused loading the magazines and stole a glance at Tarjuan, who was too busy loading his own to notice. Underground tunnels...what was that about? Who the hell was Cray and why was he sneaking around beneath London like some kind of Bond villain? Despite the decent intel and some of the answers his instincts were crawling around his guts giving him the jitters.

There was no point talking about it, the op had been planned, he just had to get on and do it.

Several more minutes passed as they completed prep. Whatever Tarjuan's silent history, he'd had military training.

Tarjuan leant forward with an extended arm and a handful of small bean-shaped objects in his open palm. Dex recognised them as tracking beads. He could drop them at intervals like invisible flares; they would be configured to broadcast on a randomly changing series of digital channels, appearing as flashing beacons or waypoints within any visual augmentation device.

Dex tapped the tactical-DVFrames above his eyes, "Are they set to this?"

"Yes," Tarjuan responded.

Dex took the beads from Tarjuan's hand and pocketed them. Each bead could be activated by pinching them firmly for a couple of seconds. In view of the fact they were about to enter a network of tunnels, Dex suspected the beads were going to prove their weight in gold helping them avoid becoming lost.

"What are you doing in my pocket?"

It was Ricardo's voice.

Dex glanced over to see him holding a thin rectangle of hydrogel between his fingers. It looked like a business card. In fact, as Tarjuan flipped it round, it began to look very familiar.

Tarjuan caught his eye. "Your associate. Richy."

Dex muttered under his breath.

"Remind me to throw this away when we get outside the van," Tarjuan told him.

Dex nodded, staring at the business card balefully as Tarjuan slipped it back into a pocket.

Dex checked the straps on his backpack, made sure nothing was going to flap about or make a noise if he needed to move quickly.

Tarjuan reached over again, this time handing him two small ovoid objects each the size of an egg. They were heavy and covered in small glassy studs; Dex clocked the military markings and guessed they were grenades of some kind.

"Are these what you used on me back in Bristol?"

Tarjuan nodded and found his eyes, as if to check for any animosity that might be brewing in them. "Stutter flash grenade. Condensed light. It is brighter than the sun. Modulates at a frequency that disrupts the nervous system."

"Worked on me pretty fast," Dex commented, examining the markings. He didn't hold any animosity; he was just being curious. "What's the trigger mechanism?"

"To arm it hold down the two studs at the top there. Then twist the upper half round until it clicks. That's it armed. Let go of the studs and it goes off in five seconds."

Dex clanked both of them together and held them in one hand. "Do you have to throw it or can you let them go off in your hand?"

"You'll get a nasty burn if you hold them without thick gloves."

"And to avoid getting zapped yourself?"

Tarjuan tapped a latex gloved finger against his upper cheek bone. "Light filter on the contacts. For you, just look away and cover your eyes with your hands."

Dex put out his lower lip and nodded appreciatively. He slid the grenades into two separate side pockets of the black jacket Tarjuan had acquired for him, then pressed down the sealstrips and tugged the fabric to make sure the pockets were properly closed.

"Ready?" Tarjuan asked, his South American accent coming out strong.

Dex nodded.

Tarjuan switched off the red light. Dex opened the rear door, climbed out as if he was a regular bloke getting out of a work van, slammed it shut again after Tarjuan got out. It was a quiet street with a lot of parked vehicles and few pedestrians, connecting with a main London thoroughfare twenty metres further up. They would look not look out of place.

They both had the 8-80's concealed beneath the flap of warm cotton jackets; the rolled-up ski masks and his tactical-DVFrames would pass them off as workmen. All of the people on foot looked like locals, underfed and frayed around the edges; there was a light rain and people seemed only interested in getting to where they were going. Nobody gave Dex or Tarjuan a second glance.

They were fifty metres from target and walking briskly; he could see the row of houses that were a match to the intel images. The church tower beyond was painted in shadows and the dirty wash of sodium street lights. A lot of the houses were boarded up. This wasn't a place with a close community or for families. The cold damp air carried the bleak, dank atmosphere into his lungs. Dex gritted his teeth and focussed on the op-sec, observing for stags or any sign they'd been noticed.

He checked time in the top right corner of the tactical-DVFrames, barrel temperature and ammo count were presented in the bottom left, a small smiley-face icon showed that the 8-80 was pointing nowhere near where he was looking. As soon as he brought the weapon up, a digital crosshair would appear within his field of vision giving him lethal accuracy.

The moment to worry had been and gone. There was only so much planning that could be done; after that it was in the hands of his training and a solid dose of luck.

The target was in darkness, no lights on. The street lighting revealed grimy windows covered by heavy drapes. They didn't pause or hesitate but moved straight towards the front door like they belonged. Taking on a target from the front was always a fucking nightmare.

Tarjuan stepped up to the front door, pretended to ring the cluster of doorbells, then focussed on the door itself and started doing his stuff. Keeping close, Dex lifted his gaze to the windows as if wondering why nobody was answering the doorbell, casually he glanced at the target windows.

"Ok," he whispered so that only Tarjuan could hear him, "All windows are closed, curtains closed, lights off. If there's life in this place then it's at the back."

Tarjuan responded a second later, "Scan complete, no technical alarms. Doing lock."

Glancing down he saw Tarjuan working the lock with a tiny pick and wrench tool, he prayed there were no deadbolts along the top or bottom.

A dog kicked off somewhere in the near distance. Nothing to do with them. The sound of heavy traffic filtered down from the main road, highlighting the solitude and quiet of the street itself. There was no access to other main roads through here, it wasn't part of any driver rat run; anybody using the ATG, allowing their vehicle to be controlled by London's vast traffic computer network, would be kept away from streets like this one.

His heart rate was climbing, he swallowed a few times, and moved his tongue around trying to get some moisture back into his mouth.

Tarjuan's voice, a whisper, "I'm in."

Then Tarjuan pushed the door open and vanished inside. Dex followed him in, rolling down the ski-mask as soon as he was beyond the threshold and then brought his weapon up. Thin green-neon crosshairs appeared within his vision. Tarjuan was four steps in, next to the wall, ski-mask down, weapon up, covering the hall. The hall was narrow and unlit. A closed doorway was on their immediate left. Ahead was a narrow, battered looking staircase that ascended and vanished into the second floor and darkness. The hall ran straight through the house, again vanishing into darkness. All the heavy drapes on the windows were sealing the place from any indirect light. Dex glanced up at the ceiling and saw the light fitting had been removed. There was a smell crawling up his nostrils, rotten and unpleasant, slightly familiar yet nothing he could place.

The sound of outside seeping into the hall was noticeable; if somebody was in and decided to stick their head round the corner to investigate, it was going to get very messy very quick.

Half turning his body, Dex pushed the front door to, aware of the silence rushing in. The darkness rushed up the hall and swallowed them. Dex lifted a hand to the tactical DVFrames, pressed a stud that had been configured to apply a low-light filter. The hallway and door reappeared in his vision, rendered in shades of green and black.

Glancing behind him he confirmed Tarjuan was doing his bit and keeping cover. He checked the safety was on, crouched down and placed the 8-80 on the floor, then took time to ease the door back into its frame avoiding any clicks or other noises.

Picking up the 8-80 he stood upright; moving slowly to avoid knocking barrel against the wall he turned back to face the hall then started moving forward, lifting his feet and checking each footfall for creaking floorboards beneath the threadbare carpet. He pushed safety onto the next setting, single shot, and then eased his finger onto the trigger, ready to respond.

Tarjuan glanced over at him and Dex nodded, giving him the sign to proceed to the next stage.

In silence, Tarjuan crouched down and lowered his 8-80 to the floor, then reached into a pocket and extracted a thin, flat device. The hardscreen blinked on, sizzling brightly through the low light filter; Dex averted his gaze and watched their surroundings. He was pretty certain the place was deserted, but this device would help Tarjuan confirm that.

Remaining crouched Tarjuan held the device out in front of him and then began to move in a slow arc towards the rear of the building, then around to cover the closed room beside Dex, and then up and around, covering the upper floor. It took about three minutes to complete.

Dex caught glimpses of the building's structural lines mapping themselves onto the hardscreen but kept his attention on the staircase, the rear of the hall and the closed doors.

Abruptly, Tarjuan switched off the device, pocketed it, picked up the 8-80 and stood up. He gestured for Dex to approach him.

Dex came over, careful with each footfall.

"There's nobody here," Tarjuan whispered, placing his mouth next to Dex's ear. "Doorway beneath the staircase leads to a basement. Our way in, is down there."

The junk-cluttered basement looked as if it hadn't been touched in decades, and yet Dex got the impression this appearance was contrived. Visible in the green and black rendering of the low-light filter, there was a clear path leading from the base of the steps, through the floor-to-ceiling stacks of old furniture and sagging cardboard boxes, to a small open area dominated by a metal hatch in the floor.

Dex stood with the 8-80 held ready to use, his augmented gaze alternating between the stairs they'd come down, and the hatch where Tarjuan was now kneeling, doing his thing with the locking mechanism.

The hatch was secured from the other side. From below.

It meant Tarjuan's intel continued to be spot on.

There was an atmosphere to the house and the basement that stirred up a sense of unease in Dex's mind.

"Hey..." he whispered to catch Tarjuan's attention. Scans had showed there was nobody within ten metres of the hatch in any direction, including below.

"Mister Rašković," Tarjuan responded in a low, querying mutter, not looking away from what he was doing. There was a chunky tool in either hand; both were cluttered with electronic sensors. Dex imagined digital overlays mapping themselves across Tarjuan's vision through the DVContacts.

"You make those things?" It wasn't the question he had been about to ask but he got the vibe that talking wasn't really on the menu.

"Yes." Muttered in a conversation-killer tone.

Dex knew a little about what was down there. He'd been sceptical about the idea of somebody creating a criminal base below the streets of London; Tarjuan had responded with a simple explanation: there were thousands of tunnels below London that the authorities, rail network and utility companies have forgotten about.

Cray, the man they were here to kill, had formed links between some of the tunnels, barricaded others, and alarmed every entry point. There was a concentric set of inner boundaries, all leading to a heavily defendable internal living area. This house represented the nearest portal to that living area.

There were a handful of houses like this scattered through the network, above ground, providing discreet access or emergency bolt-holes.

A soft –*click*- caught Dex's attention. He looked over at Tarjuan to see the South American starting to pack away his tools, still on his knees; his 8-80 was lying on the ground beside the hatch.

Dex watched the hatch.

Tarjuan looked over at him and gestured as if to ask, are you ready?

Dex nodded, moved over to stand above the hatch, covering it with the 8-80 whilst Tarjuan leant forward and slowly prised it open.

The stench that wafted up from the opened shaft made Dex gag. Tarjuan whipped his head away as if he'd been physically struck. Dex rolled his head up and around as if trying to keep it above water, but he forced himself to look back down.

The shaft was a vertical drop. A corroded metal ladder hugged one side of it.

Dex stared. Nothing moved down there.

Tarjuan slung the backpack over his shoulders, grabbed his 8-80, then hauled himself over the edge of hatch and began to descend.

No fear, Dex mused. He watched Tarjuan, the contours of his shadowy figure picked out in fine bright green lines, as he went down one rung at a time. Stopping every few rungs to listen and to scan.

It was a descent of about twenty metres.

At the bottom Tarjuan quickly brought the 8-80 into a fire position and took a moment before looking up the shaft and giving an all-clear sign.

Dex followed, leaving the hatch open above him, glad the shaft was wide enough to accommodate him and the backpack without needing to dick around with lowering the pack before or after him.

A pale amber beacon began to pulse within the digital overlay placed across his vision by the tactical DVFrames. Tarjuan had activated a tracking bead and dropped it by the base of the ladder. Small digits showed distance in metres and an orientation arrow, revealing direction and whether he was above or below the bead's physical location.

Nearing the bottom, Dex emerged through the ceiling of a wide, high, curving shaft lined with concrete. The darkness down here was absolute and the low-light filter would have struggled to show more than basic contours, but Tarjuan had switched on an invisible-spectrum torch fixed to the barrel of the 8-80. It created a cone of bright green digitally rendered visibility surrounded by a wash of lesser clarity.

Dex stepped down onto the solid floor, which was dry and relatively uncluttered. He brought the 8-80 up into a fire position then reached down the barrel and turned on the invisible-spectrum torch fitted there.

Twin cones of bright green rendered illumination swept the walls and both ends of the tunnel.

The stench was so bad down here Dex tried to avoid breathing in through his nose, but he could still taste it in his mouth with every breath.

"Bloody hell," he whispered, "It smells like something died down here."

Tarjuan nodded, his features concealed by the ski-mask, which itself looked freaky in the green digital view: his head was an oval blob of darkness with light green circles where his eyes and mouth would have been. Tarjuan glanced down at the thin, flat scanner in his hand, then gestured towards one end of the tunnel.

Dex watched a few flies buzz through his field of vision.

He couldn't guess what purpose the tunnel used to serve, or why there should be an access shaft leading up to the basement of a house. Had it always been there or had Cray built the shaft to requirement?

What *was* that stench?

Another pale amber beacon burst into life ahead of him, matching where Tarjuan was right now. Another tracking bead had been dropped.

Together they moved down the tunnel, Tarjuan staying up front, the cones of green rendered visibility sweeping left and right with practised ease as the barrels of the 8-80s followed their gaze.

Dex paused to turn around every few steps, pushing away the solid darkness behind them with his own cone of green rendered visibility.

He shuddered and didn't know why. Something about the darkness back there. It was so immense and seemingly infinite. Where did the tunnel lead? Who else was down here? His eyes latched onto the receding outline of the ladder leading up from the floor into the ceiling. That was their way out. A big part of him just wanted to head that way now.

Having travelled only thirty metres or so, Tarjuan reached a point where the tunnel had been sealed with a brick wall; with the alien colours of his digital vision there was no way to tell how old the obstruction was. In the floor of the tunnel was another shaft, this one without a hatch. Dex stepped up to the edge and peered down, directing the invisible beam of the torch into it. Another ladder. A ten metre drop. A dozen or so flies were hovering around rim.

Tarjuan caught his attention, made a hand-gesture that said he was going down. Dex nodded, stepped back and took up a cover position.

A pale amber beacon flared up after a minute; the small digits revealing its distance below him. Dex stepped forward and looked down again, and saw the green-contoured form of Tarjuan giving an all-clear signal.

Dex descended; again, the shaft wide enough for both him and his backpack. The ladder was wooden, solidly constructed and felt new.

Unbelievably the stench was getting worse.

When he reached the bottom he saw why.

"Oh my god," he muttered almost without control.

THEY WERE IN a corridor with walls, floor and ceiling made of wooden planking. It was as if the corridor had been constructed inside a larger, unseen space. The corridor stretched off in both directions; curving gently and vanishing into the absolute darkness at the far reach of the torches and the ability of the DVFrames to render useful visual data. This was a fragmentary perception as all of his attention was focussed on the gory items nailed to the walls in a small area surrounding the base of the ladder they'd just descended.

Severed body parts; limbs missing most of the flesh and muscle, with sinew and tendons connecting clumps of rotting tissue stuck to the bones. Loops of entrails, dangling from metal hooks, glistening in the green digital rendering, and crawling with maggots. Dex gagged again and this time nearly doubled over as his body wanted to retch. He clamped a gloved hand to his mouth and held everything in.

Flies buzzed around his face and bounced off the thin fabric of the ski mask.

Jesus Christ what the hell is this?

Tarjuan was studying the walls, something burned into the wood, a large symbol, appearing black against the bright green planks.

Dex waited to regain control of his senses.

From nearby came the abrupt rumble of something large and moving at speed. The wooden corridor physically vibrated. Then he heard the squeal of metal on metal and Dex recognised the sound of a train passing through London's Underground. That made sense. There was a Tube station less than two hundred metres from the target house above them.

Air blasted through cracks in the walls, wafting the stench down the corridor and sending the flies into a flurry of activity.

He kept his mouth closed and reluctantly breathed in through his nose. He didn't want those flies dropping into his gob.

Tarjuan was watching him.

"Are you alright?" the muttered question was laced with his South American accent.

"Yeah, just a bit freaked out," he replied in a whisper.

He saw Tarjuan wiggle the thin, flat scanner in his hand. "There is nobody near us but I think we are getting close to where they are. Do you need to get your nerves together?"

Dex bristled with irritation; he straightened and adjusted his grip on the 8-80, "I'm fine. Seriously. Let's do this."

Then his eye went back to the marks burned into the wooden planking of the walls. The same symbol had been repeated several times. He realised why it looked so familiar:

"I know this symbol," he gasped. It was the same as had been carved into the base of the statue. Looking back at Tarjuan's figure he hissed: "What's going on here?"

"You're doing a job and you're getting paid for it," Tarjuan responded coolly, his voice barely above a whisper.

The paradigm of command and commander reasserted itself within his brain. This was no place for a discussion. That's how you got dead. There was a connection between the statue and the man they were here to kill, so be it. It wasn't Dex's place to question that.

"Come on then," Dex muttered.

He just wanted to get the hell away from there.

Tarjuan whirled away, weapon up, and began to move at a quick pace down the gently curving corridor; his long-legged stride made fleeting contact with the floor and made minimal sound.

Dex followed, repeating what he did in the upper tunnel, pausing every few paces to turn and sweep the darkness behind them.

The corridor had an undefined purpose. Possibly connecting disparate parts of the tunnel network. Or maybe something else? Dex didn't have enough information to guess.

Tarjuan slowed and then stopped. Dex saw one wall of the corridor had become worked stone, as if they were flush with the side of an old building. There was a solid looking door. Tarjuan began scanning it with the device in his hand.

Dex moved past him a couple of paces and jabbed the 8-80 into the darkness that stretched ahead of them, the cone of green visibility showed nothing but bare floor and walls that were once again made of closely aligned wooden planks.

Sweat was building up beneath the ski-mask and his skin was beginning to itch. He worked his jaw in exaggerated motions in a vain attempt to get the material to move a little and scratch.

A couple of flies circled into his line of sight.

He stepped back and checked on Tarjuan's progress. Tarjuan had the tiny pick and wrench tools back in his gloved hands, working on the physical locks of the door.

Dex went back to observing the angles, keeping the 8-80 up and ready to fire.

This was the outer perimeter, he hypothesised. Every boundary he'd seen so far was locked from the 'other side'. None of these routes were general access or transit routes. It gave him reason to relax a little. It was unlikely that a person or persons were going to come strolling along.

But what if they'd triggered an alarm, something they'd missed?

And what kind of people nailed bits of bodies as a gang totem?

Sick puppies, he thought and grimaced.

A glance towards Tarjuan revealed he'd cracked the lock. Dex moved over to where he was crouched in front of the door, pocketing the tools and picking up the 8-80.

"I'm getting interference," Tarjuan muttered, irritated.

"What do you mean?"

"Something is disrupting my scanner," was the taught response.

"Like what?"

Tarjuan shook his head and Dex couldn't tell if it was frustration with the interference or with him.

A pale amber beacon lit up in his field of vision. Another tracking bead dropped.

Holding the 8-80 with one hand Tarjuan grabbed the door handle with the other and began to ease it open. Dex moved to the wall next the door and pressed himself flat against it.

Tarnished yellow candlelight fluttered into the corridor through the gradually opening aperture. The low-light filter on the DVFrames compensated and thinned out the green and black rendering to allow more of reality to penetrate his vision.

A rat darted out of the opening and scurried away into the darkness of the corridor.

Tarjuan paused, in the wash of soft light Dex saw the South American's eyes widen and begin to dart left, right, up and down.

Dex didn't say anything, just waited.

Tarjuan bobbed back a little and then to one side for a better peek into the room. Something had him spooked. Tarjuan reached into his jacket and extracted a stutter-flash grenade. Arming it, he stooped down, bending at the knees, rolled the grenade into the chamber beyond and then turned his head away. Dex heard the grenade roll and skitter across what sounded like bare concrete. It stopped. Dex looked away and closed his eyes. A spatter of light flickered through his eyelids, reflected off the walls of the corridor. Then it ended. He looked back, saw Tarjuan pushing the door wide open and stepping through with the stock of the 8-80 jammed into his shoulder. A number of flies swirled and buzzed in the open doorway.

Dex followed, the 8-80 in shoulder, barrel following his eyes as he swept the angles. The chamber was clear, but it wasn't empty. His brain registered what he was seeing and locked down his shock reaction. Naked bodies hanging from the ceiling. Tarjuan seemed to be doing the same, his gaze hovering over the macabre centrepiece of the space they'd entered: a cadaver on a large table. Several dozen rats lay on the floor, twitching; their nervous systems temporarily frazzled by the grenade.

The chamber was part of the basement for some kind of industrial building; cold, grey stone walls, a high ceiling, evidence of heavy machinery long since removed. There was one exit, a carbo-plastic doorway set into a blocked up archway, currently closed. Various candles burned in metal holders placed on random surfaces, casting enough dirty light to illuminate the key features but failing to dispel the thick shadows that clung to the corners like smoke. The state of the candles suggested the room was frequently used.

There were about a dozen rotting bodies dangling from the ceiling, shrouded in shadows it was still possible to see their skin was darkened by decomposition; their bare feet hung at about head height. A solid butcher's table occupied a space near a square drain grille set into the floor. The floor around the grilled was smeared in overlapping blood stains, some sticky; some ringed with a dark crust. On the table was a partially dissected corpse, bloated, blackened and glistening wet, well into advanced decomposition. Maggots were dropping from the table onto the floor, wriggling amongst the old blood.

He'd seen plenty of dead bodies during his career as a soldier, many in a worse state than this one, but the scene this corpse occupied presented an entirely new league of grotesque horror. There was clear indication the cadaver was in the process of being eaten. Slowly. Over time. The missing sections hadn't been cut away; they'd been gnawed, chewed and ripped.

Dex wanted to believe this was the work of the rats or of some dogs allowed to run amok amongst the tunnels, but he couldn't get out of his head the image of the statue: the mother biting down into the soft skull of her living child. The same symbol connected that statue and this location.

He stomach clenched and he gagged on an upsurge of bile. Dex held it back. Acid in his throat.

The contents of the walls began to filter through to his startled consciousness. Strange symbols. Daubed in what looked like charcoal. Nothing he recognised but they evoked a curious, deep seated sense of dread.

He no longer wanted to be here. He didn't want to go any further in.

But he was here on an op. There were rules and his conditioning as a military man. He'd been scared before and gotten through it.

Tarjuan seemed to have gotten over his shock and was now by the dangling corpses. The South American reached up a latex-gloved hand and grabbed one of their feet; squeezed it, peered closely, then sniffed it. He turned the foot and studied the inside ankle. Dex alternated between watching this macabre inspection and scanning the rest of the room, the 8-80 always following his line of sight. His heart was hammering his chest. His breathing was barely under control, his body craving more oxygen.

A gasp of surprise from Tarjuan. Dex snapped his attention back on him and saw the South American stepping away from the body he was examining, bringing his weapon up.

Dex watched.

Tarjuan glanced over at him and then back to the body. "It is alive," Tarjuan whispered, a little too loudly as the sound echoed around the large chamber.

Dex heard it. An audible moan. Was it his imagination, the fluttering candlelight and dancing shadows, or did that dangling foot just move?

Tarjuan backed away and came over to him. The South American's eyes were wide and wild.

"There are needle marks in the flesh," Tarjuan stated, "These bodies are being decayed whilst they are alive."

"What the hell for?" Dex retorted but some part of him knew the gruesome answer even as the whispered words tumbled from his mouth.

"There is religion here. I do not like it."

Dex saw Tarjuan's gaze settle on the butcher table. In his mind he heard himself say: come on, let's get out of here. But in reality he remained silent.

Tarjuan was caught up in a swirl of thought, then blinked rapidly and brought his gaze back to Dex. "Whoever is doing this is a genius with chemical and organic compounds."

"Uh-huh," Dex muttered, "It's not going to do them any good once you pop them with this." Gesturing with the 8-80. "Come on, let's do this."

Tarjuan moved briskly towards the carbo-plastic door ahead of them. Dex breathed out heavily, steeled himself and moved forward.

At the door, Tarjuan began waving the thin, flat scanner over the locks and hinges. Dex didn't say anything. All his senses were tuning into what might be beyond the door.

Tarjuan returned the device to a pocket then reached forward and took a firm grip of the handle, the 8-80 held in his other hand, partially resting against his hip.

Dex stepped back to take up a cover-fire position. His eyes zeroed on the green crosshairs hovering over the door.

Tarjuan turned the handle and began to pull.

Dex heard a sound like a cough, and then saw Tarjuan stagger and collapse to the floor, his limbs flailing uselessly as he desperately tried to stand again. In the same moment a not-too-distant alarm bell went off.

"What the hell!" Dex cursed and went over to Tarjuan who was lying on his side, attempting to reach a hand to his shoulder. Crouching down Dex could see why. Several tiny spikes, like darts, were embedded into his neck and left shoulder. The door had been booby-trapped. Old school style. Nothing that would show up on Tarjuan's scanner.

Above the clamour of the alarm Dex heard a sound like half a dozen bodies pounding along a wooden floor, heading their way.

He looked down at Tarjuan. The South American was in a shit state. And he knew it.

"Nerve toxin," Tarjuan coughed out the words, his whole body was going into a rigid spasm, every muscle trembling.

"Christ, what do I do?"

"Nothing," Tarjuan sucked in an urgent breath, "You'll not get out of here carrying me. Get back to hotel. The idol is in my room. In a bag." Tarjuan's eyes went wide beneath the skin-tight ski-mask. He bared his teeth with the effort of the next breath. He was desperate to get the words out. "Canvas. Green bag. Use my PA get into room. Money...too. Go back Bristol. The girl, my client, Ruby. In Bristol. Ruby Torres. You *must* give her the idol. Promise-"

Tarjuan slumped onto his back, exhausted, panting heavily and shuddering uncontrollably. His eyes were doing their best to focus on him whilst sliding around in their sockets: all sorts of nightmare thoughts must have been going through his head.

The welcome party was getting close. There wasn't time to fuck about. He slapped Tarjuan on the shoulder, gave a nod, pushed himself up from the crouch and began a hasty retreat.

Tarjuan's mouth flapped open and closed but barely a sound came out. Dex guessed the word being formed, a final plea for confirmation: promise me. Or maybe a change of heart: don't leave me.

Dex didn't care. He just wanted to get the hell away from there.

Dex backed out from the chamber, through the solid-door and into the wooden corridor. His last glimpse of Tarjuan was of the South American clutching one of the stutter-flash grenades between both hands, fumbling with the arming mechanism.

The DVFrames adjusted to the return to darkness. Once again his vision became rendered in shades of green and black.

As he ran Dex thumbed the safety on the 8-80 from three-round burst to full auto then returned his finger to the trigger housing. If anything got in his way he intended to fill it with metal.

He heard a door crash open from inside the chamber behind him.

He heard a chorus of male voices shouting, low and guttural.

Tarjuan began shrieking as if something had gotten a hold of him and was thrashing him from side to side. The horrific sound injected energy into Dex's legs as he sprinted down the corridor, zeroing in on the amber beacon, and then hauled himself up the first ladder. The stutter-flash grenade never went off.

Dex didn't know if anybody was in pursuit and he didn't want to find out.

Heart pumping; eyes bulging wide; breath ragged; he dashed to the next ladder.

19

"At least I don't have to listen to you whine on anymore," Nicky told him, pausing in her hasty and aggressive bag-packing to pin him with a hostile stare.

McVee glared back at her, speechless with a combination of disbelief and impotent rage. How could she do this? *After everything* –

At the same time aware he was powerless to do what he wanted to do. He wanted to smash her fucking face in with his fists. He wanted to beat her to the floor, grab some cable and hog-tie her, stick a gag in her gob and leave her fastened to the heavy sideboard over there; drag the mattress onto the floor; keep her hostage and fuck her when the fuck he pleased.

Fucking bitch cunt.

But all of that anger was only going to get him noticed. And he *could not* risk that. Not right now. Not at this moment in his life.

"Whine...?" his words trailed off, as she sneered at his incredulous response and went back to dragging clothes out of the battered wardrobe, stuffing them into the large drawstring bag. The bag was technically his, but Nicky had apparently decided her needs outweighed any dispute about ownership.

She was angry he'd turned up. Her plan must have been to sneak into the house, grab her things and vanish whilst he'd been at work. But he'd shut down the shop early and come home to give himself time to think through what he was going to do about Dex, about the gene-twister, and the possible back-up plan of robbing Richy's place for the Pentathene.

He'd caught her going through his stash of things, undoubtedly with a view to helping herself to what she considered worthwhile taking.

Demented fucking bitch. But the idea of her walking out right now...for some stupid reason that really ripped him up inside.

Maybe it was because she was wielding the power here. She was making the decision. Ideally, in his version of this scene, he was the one throwing her out for being such a lying, cheating, slag.

Oh fucking hell, just let her go mate.

McVee nodded at his thoughts, turned away and walked towards the large bay window overlooking the main road below. It was nearly dark outside. The bumper-to-bumper, slow moving flow of traffic filled the street with headlights and splashes of red brake lights reflecting off the rain soaked surfaces.

Portugal's just days away. Let her go. Don't fuck this up.

He listened to the rattle of crappy metal hangers bouncing off the empty interior of the wardrobe as she yanked the final items out.

"I deserve somebody who can actually look after me," she remarked. It seemed she didn't want to just fuck off in silence.

"Yeah, well, he'll get what he wants from you and then tell you to fuck off like I should have done when I met you."

"Whatever. I'll be living in luxury whilst you're slumming it here with that loser, Spad."

He turned from the window and stabbed her with his eyes. Her long, slender figure was dressed in thigh-high black rubber boots, an electric red skin suit beneath a semi-opaque hydrogel poncho that had seams of greenish neon. That was the worst part. Looking at her and knowing he'd never have her again.

She laughed. It was a caustic, high pitch sound descending into a bitter sigh; her face rose and tilted as she let it out. A laugh he had learned to hate. She knew what he was thinking; must have seen his eyes crawling over her body.

"You're pathetic."

McVee gritted his teeth, tensed the muscles either side of his jaw and dug the knuckles of his clenched fists into the soft flesh of his thighs.

He turned back to the window, fixing her fuzzy reflection in the glass within his peripheral vision.

Today was Saturday. He'd make his move Monday. Spend tomorrow putting everything into place. Get Spad ready to make the big departure. Either Dex would give him what he wanted or he'd grab Richy's stash of Pentathene. Either way, come Monday he'd be out of Bristol and on his way to Portugal.

20

Inside the White Room the main lights were on, harshly exposing the grubby reality of the interior whilst doormen were asking people to leave.

It was nearly 3 A.M.

Dex strode in carrying the green canvass bag he'd taken from Tarjuan's hotel room, barely grunting a response to the friendly banter from his staff and late-leaving regulars who knew him. He made a bee-line for the bar.

He needed to cut through the numbness smothering his brain. He needed to get his thoughts in order. He needed to work out what the hell to do next, if anything needed doing at all. Maybe that was that. Maybe it was simply over now.

Every moment since running from the house had been a blur.

He'd got to the van and gunned it. Then he'd changed back into his clothes. All items used on the op, apart from the cotton jacket but including the 8-80, had been left in the van which he'd then set light to in an alley on the edges of Crouch End. A brisk walk and then three separate taxi rides. Back at the hotel a concerned Mr Grayson intercepted his return to Tarjuan's room. Dex had barely been able to speak. Grayson had seen the terror and the shock in his wild eyes and decided he and the hotel wanted nothing to do with it; Grayson had ensured his departure was as swift and effortless as it needed to be.

Inside Tarjuan's hotel room, he'd grabbed what he needed. He'd looked inside the canvass bag long enough to see the statue-idol was in there. Seeing it, and the carved woman biting into the skull of her child had made him shudder and moan out loud. Meaningless words of fear and revulsion had tumbled from his lips. He'd badly wanted to leave the damned and ugly thing there, but Tarjuan's promise stuck to him like an intangible shroud of cold sweaty guilt.

The single thought that had formed at the moment had been simple. Find the client. Find Ruby Torres. Give her the statue-idol and disengage.

Tarjuan's PA had been there. Thirty thousand or so credits, loaded into the cash chip. He'd transferred the money to his PA then turned Tarjuan's off and left it there in the room. Not his problem anymore.

The van would eventually lead back to Tarjuan but Dex hadn't been involved in its rental. Once again, not his problem.

He'd got back to Bristol and could barely recall any part of the drive. It had taken him three hours. The only thought he had in his mind was an image of a large glass of whisky in his hands; everything else was an out of focus montage of grotesque images and sounds and ideas, just beyond the boundary of his consciousness. It was as if his mind had hauled up a sort of barrier between him and the immediate memories of what he'd just been through.

It was an experience he'd had before. Right after shooting the Norwegian journalist. That had been on the cusp of months of sleepless nights and pacing around in darkened rooms doing everything he could to stop himself screaming.

Night demons.

He didn't want to go back there again.

At the bar was an unwelcome sight. He stopped in his tracks and dialled into the scene before his eyes.

Nicky Osbourne, dressed in a scarlet skin-hugging all-in-one. Big black rubber boots. She was drinking, smoking a stim-stick and chatting vivaciously with one of the barmen. The barman should have been clearing or washing glasses. Nicky Osbourne had her cunt-wet claws in the kid.

Dex noted the massive bag dumped by the side of her stool.

What the heck?

Dex gave the place a long slow scan, turning his head. All the staff had noticed him and made like they were busy. All except the barman with his eyeballs glued to Nicky's cat suit.

Bernie. the head doorman wandered over, nodding discreetly towards Nicky and in a low voice told him, "She's been guzzling drinks all night, running up a tab, seems to be acting like she is your woman and got the power of God." Bernie hesitated, a question written all over his brow, then asked, "Isn't she Henry McVee's bird?"

Dex did not meet Bernie's gaze. He felt a dull anger throbbing deep down and dangerous. He patted Bernie's arm in thanks then walked over to the bar.

The young kid with the hard-on glanced over, saw him and nearly jumped to attention.

Dex smiled without warmth.

"Get me a glass and a bottle of whisky. Any one will do."

The kid got to it.

Nicky swivelled round on the stool and tried to hook her impossibly long legs around his where he stood near her. He glanced at her, not giving her his full attention. Nicky's long curly hair hung down either side of her slutty face, her large brown eyes half-lidded in a mixture of alcohol and desire.

Dex stepped away, out of range of her legs and rooted his gaze on the bar.

"Hey baby I thought you'd be pleased to see me?"

Her voice was husky and sing-song, but her words were slurred.

This scene had 'WRONG' stamped all over it.

Anger, frustration, cringing embarrassment and self-loathing disgust crashed together in his already battered brain. They surged up against the locked defences of a mind already in deep shock. He saw himself as if observing from an external point of view. It was surreal and frightening.

He could sense the frown seeping down through Nicky's face. It was the kind of frown that compressed all her features and made her look really bloody ugly.

He said nothing. Stared at the bar.

What the fuck are you doing here?

He wanted to scream.

He wanted to drop down on the floor and cry.

Momentary flashes of recalled imagery began to breach his internal defences. The tunnels. The bodies. Tarjuan falling back on the floor, his eyes bugged wide and glassy.

A glass and a bottle appeared in front of him.

He poured until the glass was half full, still pouring when he moved the bottle away liquid spilled across the bar.

He didn't care. He picked up the glass and realised his hands were shaking.

He guzzled and savoured the hot burning sensation against the back of his throat, sliding down his gullet into his stomach.

"What's up baby? What happened? Are you okay?" she tried to reach over to touch his arm. He flinched away, not looking at her.

"You chose the wrong fucking time to be here." His words had an edge to them that left a silence in their wake. All the staff were no doubt tuning into the scene.

"Don't swear at me. Don't you swear at me."

Dex closed his eyes. There she went again with her weird moral values. Shagging another bloke behind your boyfriend's back was okay, but being foul-mouthed was bad.

He took a slow sip, never shifting his gaze from the bar.

The tension was ramping up.

"I thought you'd be pleased," she began, her voice dropping into a pathetic pitch that suggested she was badly done to. "I've left Henry. I'm yours now." She moved in close again. Her voice dropped into sultry mode, the same tone she used when she told him she was going to suck his cock. "You can have me any time you want now."

He snorted in air through his nose and stood up straight. Put the glass down. Turned to face her. His jaw was jutting out, teeth clenched rigidly against each other.

"Yeah? Well I don't fucking want you. Take your bag and fuck off." He saw the revelation blossom across her face like a slow motion replay. A fragmentary glare, hostility quickly suppressed. She went for another angle:

"Baby, don't do this. You've had some kind of bad news. A bad day, but don't throw away what we have together."

Dex shook his head, nailing her with a stare that was wide with disbelief and dislike.

She brought a sob out, "Don't. Please. I need you. I can't go back to him. I can't stand being there with him. I can't go back to that place."

Dex sucked his lower lip up over his top lip. Nodded a couple of times then dipped his head towards the big bag by her stool. "Take that. Go to the door over there. Get out. Never come back. Never hassle me again."

The real Nicky Osbourne began to emerge from behind the sorry-me visage. Her face turned cold and resentful, edged with a humour that was cruel and vitriolic.

Without another word she slid down from the stool, pulled on a clear hydrogel poncho, grabbed her bag and strode out of the club.

110

Dex picked up the glass and knocked back what was left in there. Then he hooked the neck of the bottle in the same hand as at the empty glass and scooped up the green canvas bag with his free hand. He made his way behind the bar and through the leather-upholstered door avoiding eye contact.

Nicky Osbourne was going to be a bitch of an enemy. And no doubt Henry McVee... otherwise known as Micky White...was going to find out sooner than later that he'd been shagging his girlfriend.

Out of the frying pan and into the fire.

Dex decided he'd get drunk. Find Ruby Torres tomorrow, get rid of the statue-idol. Then he'd dispose of McVee / White, before the scrawny runt became a problem.

21

Sunday afternoon and it was still raining. But somehow, for some reason, Ruby was starting to feel more at ease than she had done in many months.

In her mind, the rain was cleansing, metaphorically. But the idea stuck.

She sat in the hanging-basket chair, clutching a mug of tea that was going cold, staring out of the 1930's style bay window at a grey world being soaked through.

Bristol was being washed of its sins.

And maybe my family too, she thought, but without the stomach clenching grip of emotions that had been accompanying such thoughts lately.

She was wearing the same loose fitting jogging bottoms as yesterday when the dumb blonde guy had made the mistake of calling round; but today she'd swapped the sports bra-top for a long sleeved, rolled-neck cardigan with a thick front zip and Urbow designer markings.

Kerry Lloyd lay sprawled along the length of a sofa, wrapped in a once-white terry towelling robe long since stained with false tan sprays and foundation make-up. She was watching several different shows on the wall-mounted hardscreen, all of them on Bali. Slack-jawed, vacant eyed thanks to a little too much narcotic the night before, her long blonde hair hung down past her face to the varnished floorboards.

In six hours, Kerry would be on her way to London with Gerard – her new man – and then flying to Bali.

Ruby doubted she'd ever see Kerry again. There would be no goodbyes. No notice. Kerry would come back in three weeks to find the final month's rent on the apartment paid for, and no sign of Ruby Torres.

It was over.

Her time here had come to an inconclusive end. But it had ended. Nothing had happened.

She'd call on Tough Guy and inform her status was active again. The work would flood in and in a couple of days she'd find herself anywhere in the world, becoming somebody knew, grafting fragments of reality onto a fabricated identity.

Her Secret Lover was too silent for her sanity, too absent for a comfortable explanation. The idol was gone. Stolen by him or otherwise, she'd lost and somebody else had won.

Take it on the chin, Jezelle. That's what her real father had told her when she'd come home from school, upset by another round of bullying by snobby girls who had learned she was an illegitimate child to a wealthy and married man, a man with an existing family.

Not my family.

Richard Carthew had fallen out of love with his wife and into love with his secretary: Carmel Jackson. From that illicit union had come Jezelle.

AKA Ruby Torres.

Born into a surrogate family riddled with opposing desires, mind-games and bad blood.

Instead of hiding the affair and his illegitimate daughter, Richard Carthew had boldly announced it to those who needed to know. It was a death-blow to a bruised marriage that had been limping along for too many years. Carmel and Jezelle came to live on the Carthew Estate, in Bristol. Richard's wife remained stubbornly in place. As did their two children Xici and Dalton.

Xici, the eldest, went on to become the heiress to the corporate empire after Dalton tried and nearly ruined the company: the result of a dubious relationship with a high-class prostitute and artist called Krysta Stine.

Yet despite their legitimacy, Richard Carthew had almost shunned Xici and Dalton in comparison to the love he'd shown towards Jezelle.

A faint smile crept across Ruby's lips as she recalled a series of encounters and memories with the authoritarian yet adoring man who had been her real father.

He'd entrusted her with secrets that nobody else could know; secrets that nobody else would believe. MacAleavey's journal and a stack of news clippings.

Maybe they were the mad ramblings of a lunatic, supported by evidence that was merely circumstantial and yet concrete to a susceptible mind. Or maybe it *was* true.

About Walter Carthew and William Cannel. About why the Carthew Tower was brought down by Walter Carthew's father during the 18th century. About the Devil monster brought back from Africa by Walter Carthew on the merchant slave ships his family controlled.

The idol was true. MacAleavey had written of it in his journal.

Cray existed. Tough Guy's network had found him, doing just as much as MacAleavey's journal had predicted several hundred years earlier.

So was all the rest true or mere fantasy?

Ruby shook her head. It didn't matter now.

It was over for her here.

"Ugh!"

It was Kerry, making another over-exaggerated disgusted sound.

"What's up dude?" Ruby responded out of instinct.

"There's no fucking narcotic left? How am I supposed to have a good time getting to Bali if I've got nothing to go with?"

Kerry pushed herself partially upright, flapped strands of bleached blonde hair away from her face with more aggression than was required.

"I've tried calling Richy, babes," Ruby told her in a gentle voice, "Richy's hasn't answered all day."

"That's not good enough."

"What do you want me to do, dude, go round to his place?" Ruby suggested, not actually serious.

"Well, yes!"

Kerry had a look on her face that suggested that this was a stupid question.

Ruby sighed and bared her teeth as she forced a smile to appear. "You're off to Bali in six hours. You can wait six hours."

"No I can't!" Kerry snapped, horrified at the suggestion. "Oh my God. I've not even packed yet. I've got so much to do. Oh my God. Oh my God. I don't even know if I'll be going at this rate. What will happen if I miss my flight?"

Ruby eased herself out of the hanging-basket chair. "Take a chill pill babes. I'll get my coat on and I'll get a taxi and I'll go and see Richy. Okay?"

"Don't take long."

Ruby's grin became rigid. She wasn't going to miss this.

114

22

The street consisted of terraced houses dating from the early nineteen hundreds. The houses were a mixture of red brick and grey stone and lay along the ridge of a hill that overlooked the length and breadth of Bristol. Despite the commanding view, the area was cheap and run down.

Dex accelerated the BMW along a short stretch of the road then braked hard and swung the car into a space, a couple hundred metres from Richy's place. He climbed out and set the car alarm.

He was furious. Richy hadn't been answering his phone calls all day.

It didn't help that Dex was suffering the head-throbbing consequences of drinking most of the bottle of whisky 3 A.M. onwards. His guts felt like they had frozen acid sliding around inside. He'd felt worse. His days in the Great Gulf War. Too much downtime before PARC ops, ignoring on-standby policy with a few drinks, or maybe a whiff of something chemical on a battlefield, launched by either side, giving you the feeling like your brain was melting. Back in those days he'd tabbed forty miles overnight through rocky desert terrain, feeling like death warmed up, carrying sixty kilos of gear with hostile patrols scouring the area whilst he zeroed in on the PARC hardware that had been air-dropped in. Compared to all that, today was a pleasant stroll.

It was just getting dark. The rain was still coming down but Dex didn't really feel it.

Determined to keep his sanity on the rails, he was still deflecting conscious attempts to recall and dissect what had happened the previous night.

Ironically, his thoughts over the past few hours had been occupied by the Norwegian journalist. A persistent and lingering feeling of guilt and trashy self-worth. Perhaps there was a one-event lag in the way he handled personal trauma? Dex didn't believe in heaven or hell. He believed in what his senses told him. Humans were hardy biological mechanisms. Thought was a delusion of bio-chemical interactions. And flesh was no match for bullets and bombs. But, whilst he was here and self-aware, he'd certainly do everything he could to enjoy his existence.

And yet...

Was the Norwegian out there, somewhere? Beyond. Looking in on him with... what kind of sentiment?

Bad Ju-Ju.

I guess I'm wondering if I'm cursed, eh?

Dex squinted and wrinkled his nose as the rain began to come down with more intensity, pattering against the hydrogel hood of his poncho.

Richy's place was up ahead, on the right. The upper floor of a house at the end of the terrace; the house had long ago been converted into a low-rent pharmacy with an apartment sat atop. A small gap beyond and then a large, late twentieth century church dominating the corner of the street, its blunt, ugly structure rising above the sagging tiled roof of Richy's pad.

Street lights were already on, throwing a bleak yellowish light onto the drab scene.

No lights were on at Richy's. The pharmacy was closed on Sunday's.

A thought popped into his head. What if Richy had done a runner with the remaining stash of Pentathene? That would be an ironic kick in the bollocks.

His investment portfolio was up but not much, and even with the thirty grand he'd ripped from Tarjuan's PA, he was still seriously short on what he needed to pay off Jerry White before his muscle-monkeys clambered down from Manchester for a visit.

Deadline for payment was Wednesday. There was still time, but with a sort of calm certainty Dex could perceive the whole situation here in Bristol was going to slide into badness.

It shouldn't be this hard to shift a few kilos, for Christ's sake.

Dex shook his head and grimaced. Maybe it was time to grab that job offer in Tonga his pal Duke kept reminding him about? Royal protection squad. Although Dex had always seen it as a shoehorn onto the islands with the ultimate aim of opening a bar for wealthy tourists, if he could get the money together and make the right connections.

He slowed abruptly, nearly came to a stop.

Richy's front door was ajar.

He kept moving to avoid drawing attention to himself.

It could be an innocent oversight, the door left open; but it could further indicate Richy had done a runner.

Or it could mean somebody had gotten to him.

Dex crossed the rain-slicked road, glancing both ways on the pretence of checking for traffic but in reality was scanning parked vehicles for any sign of watchers. He couldn't see anybody. No silhouettes of a figure or figures sat in a car. The rain didn't help.

He got to the door and stopped. Torrents of rainwater were cascading from blocked guttering overhead. He hesitated. He'd come without the Vortek handgun, not feeling it was a necessary tool to hurt or coerce Richy; he could do that with his hands or just the threat of violence.

Some higher realm of senses was tweaking with a dull alarm. This wasn't right.

Straining to listen, he stared at the seam of darkness between the door and the frame.

He began to step away when the sound of somebody approaching made him whirl round, startled.

A woman, late twenties, black skin, Caribbean features, tall, slim and attractive; coloured braids pulled back behind her head; a tiny umbrella held aloft, the underside coated in sodalum, painting her face in muted blue glow. Her clothes were fashionable and clearly expensive.

"Whoa jumpy!" she greeted, a natural grin spilling out from beneath the umbrella.

Her easy attitude and good looks were instantly disarming, Dex found. His tense fight or flight posture dropped away to become relaxed, conversational. "You gave me a fright."

She had large eyes, oval shaped, rimmed in make-up, and Dex recognised a crafty intelligence within them as their stares locked for a prolonged moment.

The moment caused him to frown. There was something about this woman...

Her gaze tracked past him to the door and back again. "Richy not in?"

"You know Richy?" he questioned.

"That's why I'm here, dude," she retorted playfully, lifting one eyebrow. Her gaze went back to the door, "You think he's home?"

"Only one way to find out." Dex turned away, pushed the door open and stepped inside. The woman followed, collapsing the tiny umbrella in a way that prevented it making any noise. The way she advanced behind him revealed a natural sense of caution concealed behind easy moves. He'd seen spec-ops move like that before, when running comms-support for shadow teams moving in on targets embedded in civilian locations. It was beyond a surprise to get that vibe here, from a woman like this, in the hallway of Richy's place.

It made him acutely wary of her and yet his instincts told him she wasn't a threat. He focussed on what was ahead of him:

The narrow hallway stretched all the way to the back of the house; a dog-legged corner a few metres away made room for the staircase leading up to Richy's apartment. A rhombus of misty streetlight sloped through a large window at the far end. Upstairs was in darkness. The pharmacy was on the other side of the hallway wall, occupying the whole ground floor.

"Bloody hell," he muttered.

"What is it?" she asked softly behind him, hovering close.

"Can you smell that?"

"It's not you I take it."

"Ha-ha, not me no." he whispered back at her and smirked in the gloomy light. However, a tension was seeping into him; some subconscious reaction to the scene. This wasn't right. There was something about that smell. A memory he couldn't place.

"I don't think Richy was all that bothered about taking his bins out," she commented.

"Hmm."

They were both standing at the bottom of the staircase.

The woman tried the light switch, it clicked without effect. Dex peered up at the length of flex hanging from the ceiling. The bulb was missing.

"What the heck..."

"Maybe we should leave," the woman suggested. She'd noticed the missing bulb too.

"You can, I need to see what's happened upstairs."

"Then I'll come with you."

118

Dex glanced round to check what her face was saying but could barely make out her features in the surrounding shadows. He couldn't sense her motives for being here but she didn't seem overtly tense; more curious.

Pointing his gaze up the stairs he called out loud, "Hey Richy? You up there?" A brief pause, then he called again but part of his brain clamped down on his vocal chords, so his voice came out with less bravado than he liked, "Richy?"

What is that damned smell?

"Maybe his girlfriend finally did him in?" the woman suggested in a jokey sing-song tone.

"Yeah...maybe," he muttered, unable to shake free from the feeling something terrible had happened here. This was ridiculous. "Bloody hell, let's do this."

He began to trudge up the stairs. Every step creaked with age and decades of damp warping the wood beneath the crappy carpet. The sound doubled as she began to ascend after him.

Near the top, the smell grew stronger and it was as if the darkness had become a solid, impenetrable wall. Frowning, he slowed his pace and reached out a hand in front of him, half expecting to feel resistance. His pulse was throbbing away in his temples.

The woman gasped behind him, "Oh my God somebody is down there."

Then she screamed.

Dex tried to turn round but in the next moment big hands were grabbing at his arms and shoulders. They must have been waiting at the top of the staircase. Lurking in the shadows. Dex lashed out, quick slashes with the edges of his hands, jabs with his elbows. He connected with something fleshy and felt a crunch of cartilage. A grunt of pain and the worst breath ever rolling over him. Blows rained in. Striking him in the face and head. It was as if the bastards could see in the dark. Starbursts flashed up in the darkness of his vision. He was hauled down by massive strength, wrestled to the ground, his legs kicked away. Somebody dropped onto his back, grabbed his face with reeking fingers, and began slamming his head into the floor. His arms were held. Pinned. Distantly aware of the woman shrieking in rage, sounds of her putting up a good fight, men growling, figures surging up the stairs, her gasps and choking gurgle as she took a hit to the neck. Sounded like it. His head was getting a battering. The fear grabbed him then and he screamed.

119

A voice barked out, commanding, and chilling with its low guttural tone: "ENOUGH."

The beating stopped.

BIG HANDS GRABBED him roughly under the arms and began to drag him. His head lolled, senses scrambled. Pain still echoed through his skull. Taste of blood in his mouth. The toes of his i/O trainers slid along carpet and bounced over a door rail.

The hands that had a hold of him were as strong as permacrete. He felt as weak as a fish.

They were now in Richy's lounge. A four metre by three metre rectangle. One of the longer walls was taken up by two sash windows that overlooked the front street. There was only one exit. The door they'd entered by. No lights on but in the wash of street light from outside Dex started picking out details. Two scruffy figures had a hold of him; hooded tops beneath baggy jackets, the hoods slung back. Long greasy hair sticking out in tufts, misshapen heads, something wrong with their jaws. Must have been his brain spinning and bad light to make their faces look so bloody freaky.

They were the source of the stench. Like bad sweat cut with damp clothing and something left to rot in a gutter.

Sounds of the woman being dragged in. She was moaning. Complaining. Frightened.

That didn't make him feel any better.

He was flung backwards onto a sofa. The woman landed next to him. Both of them sat side by side, reeling from shock, subdued by the beating.

Four blocky, ragged, shadow drenched forms now stood around them; stinking the place out.

Dex's gaze tracked to a body slumped on the floor with his back against the wall opposite. Head bowed forward. Legs splayed out in a V-shape. A dark mess running down his front.

It was Richy.

Something wrong with the picture...

And suddenly, with the flood of awful comprehension, he gagged, vomit surging up into his mouth, burning his nose and throat, as he realised what he was seeing, and what it had to mean.

The top of his skull had been ripped open. Pale brain matter and dark gore.

He did his best to contain the spillage. It sprayed through his fingers, ran down his hands and wrists.

The stench clicked into place. The tunnels beneath London.

He reeled at a fragmentary recollection of Tarjuan flipping the business card around in his fingers, inside the back of the van.

They'd found him.

Dex pinned his gaze on the boarded-up fireplace on the other side of the room as if it was a safe-haven for his attention.

The woman next to him said nothing; he could feel her trembling. As he wiped away vomit from his face his thoughts started to slot together. His mind eased out of the shock and into gear. He visualised the layout of Richy's place. They must have had one or two people lurking in the downstairs hall, beneath stairs, out of sight. What were his options now? Leap up and make a dash through the window? The forecourt outside the pharmacy below was old fashioned concrete. He'd probably break something and this wasn't the kind of area where shouts for help were going to rally calls to the police.

If this hit wasn't about drugs then it meant Richy's stash of pentathene was probably intact. Police would be a bad thing right now.

Against his will, his gaze danced back to Richy's mutilated corpse. Memories of the bodies dangling from ceiling hooks and partially eaten on a large wooden table. These people weren't playing by normal rules. He had to get out of here.

Somebody strode into the room. Dex glanced up but caught only a fleeting glimpse of a short and slender figure. Yet despite the diminutive size, there was a presence of immense authority. Dex felt the skin on his scalp contract. Goosebumps riddled his body and brought on a shudder.

Properties about the momentary sight of the figure rapidly slithered through his consciousness. Dex sat motionless, staring at the fireplace again, frozen against the horror of turning his head and seeing what he prayed could not be real. A distended, dog-like jaw, leering below a sideways gaze with eyes that glowed yellow in the shadows. Fucking *glowed*, like lanterns. And flesh, sort of grey, covered in lesions and eaten away by decay.

This had to be the bad light and shadows playing tricks on his mind.

The figure stopped behind him and the woman. A pair of blunt, thickly callused hands came down slowly on the woman's shoulders. She made a whimpering sound.

"I can smell...a Carthew." The figure spoke in a low, deliberate voice that was strangely wet and distorted, like a sickening speech impediment.

The woman stiffened. The figure gently kneaded her shoulders and expressed his grim delight, "Yes. A Carthew."

"What, what do you want?" The woman asked, shakily.

Dex stole a sidelong glance at her. Was she a Carthew? Her clothes spoke of money but everything else about her didn't fit.

"The conventicle." The figure responded to her question.

"The what?" Her tone lacked comprehension.

"The ancient meeting ground of our forebears and the carven Key that unlocks the Gate." He explained her for.

The words seemed to connect with some terrible memory; Dex heard a sob break out within her words, "Oh my God."

The figure stopped caressing; his powerful fingers tightened around the muscles of her shoulders. The woman made a frightened sound.

Dex frantically scanned the room with his eyes. There had to be something he could do. He could leap up and make a run for it. But what if they caught him and did the same to him as to Richy? Fear clutched at his heart and filled his limbs with an awful heaviness.

"Do you know who I am?" The figure asked.

Staring at the floor the woman shook her head, some of her braids tumbling loose. "No."

Dex sensed she was lying. And Dex had his own guess about who the figure was. The target in London. The man Tarjuan wanted to kill.

Cray.

"I am of Anubis, I am brother to his children. Yog-Sothoth, Hermes, Thoth, do these names mean anything to you? Do you see the lines of connection? Arteries of the sub-conscious that guide the flow of...dreams." He exuded a slow guttural laugh. "I am the fornicator of the grave. I despoiled Sulis and she was not unwilling. I am your blood. I am your brother."

The woman made a muffled wail of horror and disbelief; she'd clamped a hand over her mouth and was shaking her head vigorously. Denial.

The figure continued, his voice booming through the quiet apartment: "I have *dreamed*. I have *seen* the shadow fingered Kings of Osiren. I have sniffed at the charnel cloak and licked the bones of dead men's secrets. To me you are sacred, child. We are of the one who brought Jy'kalud through the Spheres. Decades have tumbled through that sink-hole we call Time, whilst I have waited, and longed to know the name of the loins that gave me origin. And then last night, a blessing. A voice that screamed the name. Carthew. Carthew. Carthew. Now tell me, Carthew. Where is the meeting ground? You know, don't you! You have read the books. Tell me. Where does Jy'kalud lie waiting behind the veil of this earthly matter?"

"Cray." Dex blurted out the name: a muttered proclamation.

A momentary blister of silence, a shift in the dynamic of the scene. Dex felt gazes swivel onto him.

"You know my name?" Cray grunted with surprise. Then added, not so surprised: "Ahh, but I know your smell too. The accomplice."

"What happened to Tarjuan?" Dex demanded, suddenly bold. His mention of the South American's name caused the woman to snap her head round and lock an intense stare on him.

Are you Tarjuan's client? Ruby Torres...

So why the hell was Cray calling her a Carthew?

Ruby Torres – fake name.

Cray's voice oozed a response to his question about Tarjuan:

"He gave me the name Carthew. But, then he did not know the right answers to my questions. And neither do you."

"The meeting ground, it's..." he gushed, desperate to portray himself as of use.

"Yes?" Cray was curious.

"I, I, I...." He was utterly lost.

"Pity." Cray pronounced.

Dex twisted round where he sat and looked up at Cray, then gasped out in shock, muttered single syllables of fright then turned away again. He could not believe what he had just seen. Dex shook his head to clear his thoughts. He sensed the woman, Ruby Torres, Carthew, whoever she was, staring at him rigidly. It was as if he was treading onto forbidden ground, at least, forbidden for her. "The Carthew Mansion? Is that what you need to know?"

"No." Cray stopped Dex there. "Mary Carthew followed her husband to the conventicle. The sight of Jy'kalud drove her mad. She was not ordained to see what is sacred. She defied her own God by seeking that which should not be sought."

Dex was thrown off tangent and fell silent.

Cray clasped his hands over the woman's upper arms, and then crouched down from behind; Dex could glimpse the lower portion of his elongated, leering, and rotting face sliding into view.

"Jy'kalud has a legacy," Cray whispered to her. "Did you know that?"

"I don't know anything." She cried, railing.

"But it's *your* history," he mocked, "It's in your blood. Our *Carrrthew* blood."

"I don't want to know."

His moment of cruel humour was cut short. Something had caught his attention downstairs. Cray straightened abruptly then leapt to the doorway like a shadow, hugging the frame and listening intently. The four others shifted uneasily. Dex used the interruption to stare at the woman beside him.

Her eyes did not see him: they were fixed on some indeterminate space between the wall of the room and time past and future. She was lost in some internal world of recollection, dawning comprehension and horror.

A hiss of outrage from Cray's lips, something he had seen from the doorway. Then all hell let loose.

"THERE'S ONE!" A man's voice boomed out from downstairs. A torch beam stabbed through the gloom of the passageway and slashed at the doorway. Cray threw himself away as if shot. The other four forms moved as one, and made a sudden dash *through* the door. Dex couldn't tell if they were desperate to escape or zealous to protect their leader. A bedlam of voices and shouts followed from below.

"Watch out!"

"HOLD IT!"

The sounds revealed a violent struggle; screams of shock and pain in rapid succession. It seemed the four figures were literally fighting their way out.

"AAAA! MY EYES MY EYES!" High pitch and chilling.

Dex registered movement in the room and gasped, surprised, to see Cray still there. Cray took a slow, purposeful step back away from the doorway. The fighting had moved outside; it sounded like the police were losing that one. Inside, three police officers swept into the room in tight formation, decked out in modular segments of body armour, with helmets, goggles and masks, the matt surfaces barely reflecting the streetlight coming through the uncurtained windows. Bullhorn tasers were clutched in their armour-gloved hands. The tasers looked like flare guns. Hand held torch beams criss-crossed the room.

"THREE PERPS, I SEE THREE PERPS!"

Then at Dex and the woman: "STAY WHERE YOU ARE!"

Neither of them moved.

The police voices were amplified and probably transcoded with digitally enhanced aggression via the moulded tactical-mask covering their lower face.

The helmet of one officer angled towards the floor to inspect the body of Richy. A torch beam followed. Dex looked away as brain matter and crimson coloured gore flashed into view.

"WE'VE GOT ONE DOWN!"

From downstairs came shouted voices urgently demanding paramedics and backup. Distant cries of agony or frustrated orders outside on the street.

The three officers in the room were breathing harshly, sweat glistening where their flesh was visible. Apart from that, with the armour and poor light, it was impossible to tell much about them, how old they were, what emotional state they were in, or confidence levels. At least they weren't carrying proper firearms.

A torch beam settled on Dex, a voice, spoken not shouted but audibly tense said, "Nobody move, nobody move, okay."

Another torch beam pinned Cray skulking in the darkest corner of the room. The officer wielding the torch seemed to be a little older, and held more senior rank, grunted in dismay.

"YOU! AWAY FROM THE WALL! I SAID AWAY FROM THE WALL!"

Dex sat motionless beside the woman and observed without looking. He had no desire to see Cray any clearer than he already had.

Cray wasn't budging.

The officer pinning Cray with the hostile beam of light jabbed the Bullhorn taser in his direction, "I WON'T TELL YOU AGAIN. MOVE AWAY FROM THE WALL."

The torches began rapidly growing dimmer.

"What the- ?" One of the other officers muttered.

The third officer stepped away from Richy's corpse, turned and called downstairs, "SOMEBODY GET SOME BLOODY LIGHT ON IN HERE! NOW!"

An amplified voice shouted back, "THE LIGHTS ARE ALL OFF."

A surreal moment of silence occurred. All three officers gave each other prolonged glances, despite their faces being concealed behind goggles, carbo-plastic carapaces and stab resistant mesh; then they began to shake their torches, tapping them against segments of their body armour, as the beams of light dulled to a dirty orange...

...and then winked out.

It occurred to Dex that he should get up and run, but the muscles of his legs were numb with terror. The atmosphere in the room was swiftly transforming. The flesh around his scalp was tingling as if an electric current was kindling the air.

"Did you eat meat tonight, Sergeant?"

The question barked out from the darkness where Cray was now all but invisible.

Looks shuttled back and forth among the three helmeted and masked faces.

"What's that got to do with the price of beef?" the one by the door challenged, misplaced humour trying to offset the growing mood of apprehension.

"Looks like we got ourselves a right nutter, here," another one quipped uneasily.

But the senior officer who Cray had apparently directed his question to was remaining silent, his goggled gaze rooted on the dark corner where Cray was lurking.

Dex felt the woman move closer to him; then she placed her hand around his arm. Her grip was frightened and urgent.

"I said, did you eat meat tonight, Sergeant?" Cray repeated.

"I had steak. What about it?" The senior officer retorted, irritated.

Dex twisted round and stole as glance just as Cray stepped forward into the strangely dimmed pools of street light. The dull light revealed an appalling, marbled discoloration of his skin that was heavily veined. Cray's mouth was something from a nightmare: both his upper and lower palettes had been distended, creating a grotesque, leering smile as his wide lips stretched around the extra bone structure. More abhorrent was the rotting pit where his nose should have been.

Cray was grinning repulsively, "Pity. You didn't notice the...eggs."

"What?" The senior officer gasped.

126

"Larvae. Cheap...meat." Cray pronounced each world clearly and with devastating effect.

The senior officer collapsed to the floor as if rabbit-punched and then immediately began to retch and gag inside of his mask. He dropped the Bullhorn and the torch as his hands flapped at his face, desperate to rip the mask away from the helmet.

"Oh shit! Sarge?"

The other two bounded over to their stricken colleague. The retching transformed into a slopping wet, stomach-emptying wail.

Dex snapped his attention back to Cray to find him watching him with a slanted smile: sunken eyes glowing a sulphurous, dirty yellow. Dex babbled half-formed expletives. Cray swung his luminous gaze onto the woman. The woman's grip tightened vice-like around Dex's arm.

"Your mind is like glass to me," Cray said to her, his tone sneering and triumphant. "I can delve into those secrets that slip like water in the spaces between the spheres."

Dex wanted to lunge up and dash around the sofa; he wanted to smash his knuckled fists into the monster's rotting flesh, to hammer it down, to remove it from existence. But he sat there, motionless, robbed of strength by a fear that was beyond description.

The policemen had removed their colleague's helmet and mask. Swearing, uttering freaked-out noises, they tried to help as the violent vomiting continued, and evolved.

The sounds coming from the policeman's throat warped, rose into a gurgling and flesh ripping scream, then became a growling roar of buzzing as hundreds of flies exploded from the yawning chasm of his mouth.

His colleagues threw themselves back, falling onto the floor, howling in shock and disgust, flapping their hands to bat the swarm away from them.

Cray's eyes burned with refreshed victory as he glared at her. He spoke rapidly and harshly, words distorted by his abnormal jaw and teeth. "I have seen the tower in your mind. The conventicle has been found. Jy'kalud was. Jy'kalud has been. Jy'kalud will be again. You will gather the Key. You will bring it to me there."

Then with a swift pace, Cray surged away, walked into the swelling cloud of flies.

And vanished.

23

"So where did he go?"

Detective Sergeant Coleman pressed the question again. Ruby could see his anger building by the florid colour seeping through the dry, flaky skin of his cheeks, and the side of his neck above the open collar of his crumpled wash-and-wear shirt. It was long past midnight and Coleman was probably cruising on coffee, stim-gum and sleep deprivation.

They were in a featureless interrogation suite within a regional police hub-station. Outskirts of Bristol. Driven there by the police mop-up team, processed under the harsh glare of ceiling mounted strip lights and then frog-marched into here for questioning.

Overheard conversations about causalities on the police side. One officer had his eyes ripped out by a claw-like weapon. The perps had escaped. There was a lot of bad feeling in the station.

She'd clocked the name of the dark-haired, good-looking man she'd been brought in with, during the processing: Dexter Rašković. The duty sergeant had seemed to recognise it. Dexter had been taken to a separate interrogation suite. Smug smiles exchanged between the officers in his wake. Dexter was a target for their type of career disdain. Ruby sensed kindred spirit. She'd be talking to him later, she decided, once the police were done; Dexter knew her Secret Lover. She wanted Dexter to tell her what he knew.

Coleman was part of a cop duo. He and his partner, who'd been introduced as DS Harris, seemed to belong within a larger ongoing investigation. Their accents and attitude said *London.* They had a weary, been through it all before weight on their shoulders, layers of tangible frustration built up with time, yet countered by the visceral hunger of a new lead. What had happened tonight fitted into something else.

Ruby didn't care. As far as she was concerned, and all the police needed to know, she was an innocent victim here. So far her fake ID had held up. It all depended on how deep they dug, and what the suspected.

"Come on Ms Torres," appealed DS Harris, who was leaning against one corner of the cramped room, arms folded across his chest, above a gut that was straining over the belt and smart trousers. Crumpled shirt, no tie, sleeves rolled up; dark blue rings and bags under weary eyes. "Don't play this silent and dumb game with us. What you've said doesn't make sense. Why were you there? What did you really see?"

She wasn't playing silent and dumb.

She was numb. The physical consequences of compartmentalising the corrosive horror of what she had learnt tonight. Cray was very real. And he had put something in her mind.

Or maybe he had merely awoken something that had always been there.

I am your brother.

＊

"People don't just disappear into thin air."

Harris, the short, middle-aged, balding arsehole with the bulging beer gut and bad teeth, stomped back and forth between the walls of the crappy interrogation room. He wasn't buying Dex's version of events. Neither was his partner, Coleman, a younger Detective, physically trim and bristling with a confidence not yet worn down by the relentless slog of wading through the excrement of the human condition.

His face hurt like it had been dragged across gravel. A paramedic had patched him up with spray-on-skin, padded the tender areas with bright white, sterile strip-bandages and micropore tape. There was swelling and the inevitable discolouration of deep tissue bruising.

Tonight, he had witnessed something monstrous, something he wasn't yet able to rationalise, and he was being silent about it because of all the questions such an admission could provoke. Questions that could open up what happened in London. Get him implicated in the disappearance of Tarjuan. A burned out car with illegal weapons. Questions that could complicate his currently detached association with Jerry White: he was already having a hard time justifying his presence in Richy's apartment. He had to keep his nerve and play it cool to stand any chance of walking out of there.

Dex noted Coleman's skin was showing classic signs of stress. High-energy type, probably prone to sporadic bursts of violence and a perpetual frustration that the world didn't move along at his pace or sustain his levels of...*whatever.*

Lifting his hands above the table and splaying his fingers, Dex shrugged and passed a helpless look between both coppers.

"I can't help you if you don't want to listen to the truth. Three of your boys were there. As was that woman. What does the official report say?"

Coleman glared at him like he'd just let off a fart. Harris stopped stomping and moved his lips around his lower face like he was chewing on a problem; he glanced sharply at his partner, who didn't respond, then levelled a prolonged and silent look on Dex. The realisation struck him then, that Coleman and Harris were investigating something much bigger than a violent scrap inside a drug dealer's apartment. Did the police *know* about Cray?

"The official report...," Harris' words trailed off. He snorted, rocked back and nodded his head as he came to a decision. "Don't move. I want to show you something."

Harris left the interrogation room.

✳

The thin slice of hardscreen was the size of a sheet of A4 paper, and showed the gruesome photograph in high-definition, crystal focus, with a vibrant and unwelcome colour palette. Uttering an involuntary sound of disgust, Ruby looked away for a moment then returned her gaze to avoid giving DS Coleman a chance to shout at her, and to show DS Harris that a slab of gore wasn't going to break her.

The image, professionally shot and cropped, showed the mangled and naked body of a woman, lying amongst entrails and shredded clothing in a shockingly large pool of blood. The scene was the narrow landing of a staircase Ruby didn't recognise. She could only tell it was a woman because of the genitalia. Nothing remained of the chest; ribs pulled back or snapped like they were nothing more than twigs; organs and viscera hung out from the savagely opened cavity as if they'd been scooped out and dropped. The interior was a catalogue of reds with yellow fat deposits and streaks of green bile, like some organic rendering of Fauvism. The soft flesh of the woman's face had been completely chewed away down to the bone; bite marks visible in the stringy shreds of muscle tissue still clinging to the jaw and scalp.

Ruby swallowed, or tried to, but her throat felt as if it had been crushed in a vice since the attack at Richy's place. Her stomach shifted; feeling queasy. DS Harris came in close beside her, put a hand on her shoulder.

"Jacki Solomein. Journalist." The detective spoke as if he was showing part of a rare collection. He leaned forward and slid the image off to one side of the hardscreen, immediately replaced by another.

This one showed a muscular man lying across the floor of a bedroom, his body twisted at a spine breaking angle. The top of his skull had been smashed away. A shocking wound. The interior scooped out, pounded and mashed into the carpet. Sickly grey, yellow, white matter that looked like a lumpy mix of porridge and scrambled eggs. Blood was everywhere. A massive handprint on a wall next to the body, crimson, edged in dark rinds of pulped and congealed tissue, dominated the photograph. The handprint occupied a position a metre above the floor, as if the owner had slapped a hand there for support whilst...

Ruby controlled her stomach.

"Peter Todd. Armed robber." DS Harris told her.

The handprint grappled her eyes, held her gaze. It was huge. Something that belonged to a monster.

Who were these people? Why were they victims? Why were the police showing them to her?

*

The copper with the beer belly and bad breath hovered next to him as he dealt out the gory slideshow. Holding the hardscreen like he was wafting a set of family photographs in front of his face. Dex figured Harris was intentionally trying to invade his personal space, wedge levers into his comfort zone. Dex caught the whiff of body odour squeezing out through a layer of spice-scented antiperspirant. The bloke really needed to throw away the shirt and start again.

The photos were gruesome but he'd seen worse: the kind of post-combat mess that got brushed into the junk folder labelled collateral damage.

Until journos got beyond the sterile boundary of media sanctions, got camera-happy...

Got dead.

Flash moment of recollection overrode his state of sitting in the interrogation room. Now, in his mind, he was limping along through desert dust; the hatch of the pilot capsule wrenched open, blackened by the explosive force that had crippled the PARC he was operating. Ambush during a smash for cash op. The long sinewy limbs of the synthetic muscle and carbo-plastic joints straining to maintain bipedal movement whilst compensating for the blast damage. Sweat pouring down his face, gritted teeth, blood spatter on parts of the exoskeleton. His blood. Sounds of heavy contact behind him. Deniable colleagues getting slaughtered. Him on a tight vector for regroup. Sight of a jeep and the dirty black beard of the driver. Something in his hands. Camera. Jeep going into panic reverse. Trying to get distance. To get away. And Dex swinging up the Boris-Tek Auto-Assault rifle. 20mm slugs thundering out of the barrel. Ripping apart the jeep. Massive blood splatter as the driver shredded into burger meat.

A quick inspection of the wrecked vehicle after it ploughed into rocky terrain and crashed.

Dirty black beard on the intact head attached to a shattered torso. No insurgent. No Afghan, Pakistan, Iran or Syrian features. Blue eyes wide in a death stare. Scandinavian features.

A satellite for one of the news corporations caught it all. No footage of *him* though. Dex dodged the official scandal bullet. The damage he caused and internal politics got him later.

"Not a pretty sight is it?" Harris suggested, his voice bringing Dex back into the moment, his eyes shifted focus from internal to external vision. Another mangled body on the hardscreen.

This one showed the body of a man, slumped against the wall of a room in a sitting position, like some grotesque parody of a puppet without strings, surrounded by the signs of a violent struggle. His head was bowed forward, a gaping hole where the top of his skull had been torn open, brain matter spattering his cheeks, lumps of it tumbled onto his lap.

It was Richy.

"Your friend died of massive blood loss and heart failure," Harris told him matter-of-factly. "He'd been alive when this was done to him. They took off the top of his head and then scooped out his brain."

Dex felt his face tighten.

Cray. How did something like Cray come to exist?

Whatever Cray was, Dex wanted no part of it. He'd get the statue-idol back to Ruby Torres, or Carthew, if that was her real name, and then keep as far away as possible.

His only concern now was to try to fix the situation of not having enough money to pay off Jerry White. Maybe Richy's murder could work in his favour? Give him a reason that Jerry and his muscle monkeys would have to accept.

Dex shoved his feelings into deep groove. Sighed and tilted his head at the image before looking up at Harris.

"Yeah. It's ugly. What do you want me to say?"

"Not as ugly as you, you little prick." This outburst from Coleman who'd been leaning back against a wall, arms folded across a big chest. Coleman now stood forward, jabbing a finger in his direction. "Why don't you stop dicking us around and tell us who these psychos are!"

Raising his hands, Dex rolled out another shrug, ending with a nod towards the hardscreen held by Harris, "I can't help you with this. These psychos... I don't know who they are."

Harris span away, dumped the hardscreen on the solitary bolted-down table, took up a hostile stance, hands on hips; fat belly bursting the seam of his stinking shirt. "Look we can turn the heat up here if you want, sonny Jim. Your pal Richy there, he was close with the man who used to run your club. Peter Stable. You know him?"

A slow nod from Dex, "Heard about him. Yeah. He vanished before I started."

"Vanished!" Harris repeated sharply. A cold hard stare. "Your friend Richy was a dealer. Jerry White, he's a big time supplier. You work for Jerry White and there you are in Richy's flat. It's not going to take a jury long to work that one out."

Dex bristled but held his tongue.

Standoff. He traded sullen glares with Harris. Coleman had gone back to leaning against the wall; arms across his chest as he shook his head sadly.

Harris breathed in loudly through his nose. He tapped a stubby finger on the photo image of Richy. "We found nearly four kilos of Pentathene at your boy's place tonight. Must be worth at least a hundred-and-fifty grand on the street. Maybe even two-hundred with the right dealers. That's got to hurt, eh?"

Cold tendrils of fright slid in through the sides of his head. His vision seemed to become surreal and floating for a moment. Then a sickly heat swept through him and he knew his face was flushing red. Harris saw it and smeared a brutal curve onto his lips.

Dex pushed through it: "You said Richy was a dealer. Great detective work. Drugs. Dealer. House." He nodded, condescending.

"Hey listen," Harris began quietly, "I don't know Jerry White. Not my patch. But the briefing I had from Drug Squad didn't paint a pretty picture. If you're involved in this. If you need help. I can get you protected. Just tell us what you know about the people that did this."

Another stubby finger tap on the photo of Richy's corpse.

Harris carried on. Laid out the scenario. Portraying Dex out of his depth. Harris the helpful cop. The caring cop. Coleman remained in the background sneering and absently clenching his fists. Harris was talking to him like he was counselling him on overcoming a phobia; a softly softly tone that was as creepy as it was irritatingly false.

Dex conceded to himself that Harris knew his game, he'd gotten under his skin, he'd made him feel vulnerable. Clever Harris.

Meeting his gaze, Dex couldn't stop a smirk widen his face. Harris sighed, more disappointed than angry, then turned away.

Coleman strode forward, picked up the hardscreen so aggressively Dex thought he was about to whack him with it. Instead, Coleman shoved it towards him and gave the screen a hard drag of a finger, causing the slideshow to zip through a dozen or more gruesome images.

"We've got whole stacks of these. Different people. Same style of death. All connected through forensics." Coleman glared at him. It seemed Coleman wanted to shout but was holding it back. "You want to play smart? Tell us what you know or I guarantee you, because I've been working this case for over a year now, I guarantee you that in a few days you'll be joining the collection."

✳

DS Coleman was a short distance away, leaning across the table, standing with his legs apart, his upper torso bent at the waist, hands propped on either corner with arms supporting his muscular weight, his gaze locked onto Ruby.

"We would probably have been adding you to the collection," he told her with an ironic tone, "but you got rescued, didn't you."

DS Harris was slouched a few paces from his younger, fitter, colleague, hands deep in pockets, pushing his belly out.

Ruby dropped her eyes to the table. She knew where this was going.

"The boys in blue came and got you out," DS Harris said quietly. She could feel his stare crawling over her as if he was inspecting something he didn't like. "One of them's never going to see anything again – not without some surgery and that doesn't come cheap."

Ruby didn't bite.

"A tip off," DS Coleman exclaimed, pushing himself upright and away from the table. "From some private dick who'd been hired to keep an eye on you, Ms Torres. What do you think about that? A private investigator. Very nice."

"Lucky for you, having friends like that." Harris suggested, giving Dex a sidelong glance.

Dex pushed himself up in the chair a little. "She's not my friend. I don't know her. Before tonight I'd never met her."

Private detective or private bodyguard? Dex pondered the question. The latter made sense, if the woman really was a Carthew.

The fat cop rocked back and forth where he stood, hugging his chest, nodding slowly. "A new customer for you, eh? What, was she buying in bulk? Did that warrant a bit of personal attention from the big man? That'll be you, won't it? The Big Man."

Dex tuned out of the mind games. Mainly because he was considering what Harris was offering. Harris had got a hook into his brain. Dex had the fear about Jerry White. About what might happen next. Richy had lost four kilos of pentathene IV but Jerry White might hold Dex accountable. Was Harris offering total amnesty or just the potential of a good word to the drug squad? Dex couldn't ask without showing his hand.

Still one ace up his sleeve, however.

Three kilos of gene-twister.

He decided to keep a cool face on, keep silent until he got out, and then pay Henry McVee a call. A.K.A Micky White. Conclude the Glasgow deal. Ride up to Scotland with him. Get the money before Wednesday's deadline to pay off Micky's father, Jerry White.

And maybe sell out Micky to his dad and curry some extra credit.

Maybe.

"You're not telling me what I need to know, sonny Jim." The friendly, softly-softly tone in Harris' voice was scraping thin.

With a renewed sense of confidence, Dex peeled off a smug grin for the fat cop and found his eyes.

✳

"So talk to me," DS Harris said, economically. "Tell me why Richard Hale get's his head cracked open but you and your friend get to sit on the sofa and watch the party?"

Ruby looked up sharply. "They were going to kill us."

"Sure. You've said that. The report says otherwise. Dexter and yourself were sitting down. You were in conversation. What were you talking about?"

A short breathless sigh from Ruby. "I don't remember."

"No?"

"No."

DS Harris deliberately exchanged looks with his partner. Some silent meaning. DS Coleman shook his head, a sour expression.

Ruby caught it in peripheral vision, her focus glued to the putrid green paint covering the lower section of the wall opposite her. Garish overhead strip lighting. No chance of sleep. She just wanted this to be over. Phase out whilst she went through this bit. Get out of here. Get moving. The police had their collection of corpses. Their theories, their questions and hoped-for answers. But Ruby possessed the truth. How could she even start to explain? They would lock her up again. Antipsychotic drugs. Restraints. Mood stabilisers.

They could try.

Tough Guy got her out. Tough Guy sponsored her. Tough Guy saw the potential and sold it to her mother.

Mother. The term made her face twist with a complex and ugly emotion. True, the private detective did probably save her life but that only meant Ruby was now further indebted to a woman whose only mission seemed to be to control her living actions.

Carmel Jackson. Once the secretary to Richard Carthew and then illicit lover, and then mother to their illegitimate child. Carmel had been repulsed by Richard Carthew's quiet obsession with the family's darker – some would say shameful – distant past. A time when the family ran merchant ships between England, the west coast of Africa and the Americas.

The indelible moral stain of a wealth created through trading in slaves. But Richard Carthew wasn't interested in that. It was the historical ancestor Walter Carthew, the man-monster, the Satanist, the black magician.

Ruby knew her mother as only an estranged daughter can do, but Richard hadn't known the extent to which Carmel would go to try and manipulate people who didn't behave as she thought was right. Carmel was a Christian woman and did not want her husband hunting down centuries-old fragments of what she saw as blasphemous fabrications.

It caused a strain on the relationship. It caused a strain on Richard Carthew.

Richard Carthew died of a heart-attack; young for an old-man.

There were other strains, the pressures of managing an aging business through the cruel evolutions of the modern corporate world; a vicious-tongued ex-wife and an emotionally exhausting relationship with his daughter and son, Xici and Dalton.

But Ruby would never forgive her mother.

The Carthew family folded into the multifarious corporate entity, the Carthew Trust, and morphed into steel blooded creatures at the helm of a vast, global empire that was taking bold steps into the rapidly emerging off-world realm.

Then Dalton Carthew went mad – or had some kind of episode - and stepped down. It was Xici who took control and drove the whole operation forward. By then Ruby, or Jezelle as she was really known, and her mother Carmel, had been socially ostracised, cornered financially and then given a harsh ultimatum: vanish or suffer the consequences. The ultimatum came with enough cash for taking option one to make life very comfortable.

Carmel took the money without question and relocated to Jamaica.

Another point of chagrin.

It left Ruby stranded in a country she didn't relate to in any way, missing the place she'd called home since birth, and even the laboured but real kinship with people she'd called family and friends.

Ruby's failure to settle into the new paradigm infuriated her mother. The final straw had been the package from her deceased father, Richard Carthew, on her eighteenth birthday. The collected components of a mystery that had plagued Richard Carthew's life and now became Ruby's obsession.

Carmel had her hospitalised for her own good.

Her mother couldn't perceive the possibility that Ruby was merely latching onto something that brought her closer to the memory of a father she missed desperately and dearly.

The bitter irony was the fact the mystery was bedded in a terrible truth.

Left undisturbed, unhindered, the worst thing had happened: Cray had found Bristol and the name of his family. Cray knew about the tower. MacAleavey had scrawled urgent warnings about something beneath the tower, in his journal; the journal bought by her father and entrusted to her after his death.

Jy'kalud.

The thing that drove MacAleavey's sister, Mary Carthew, mad with just the sight of it, three hundred years ago.

Mary Carthew sneaking out into the night to follow her husband in the naïve and mistaken belief he was off to meet another woman.

Walter Carthew, the bogey man in the family closet.

Three hundred years.

And here's Cray.

You can't be the same man. It's not possible.

Ruby shuddered.

What was beneath the tower? What had MacAleavey feared so greatly? What had driven MacAleavey's sister - Walter Carthew's wife - to immediate and irrevocable insanity? What had motivated Walter Carthew's father – Ruby's great ancestor - to blow the foundations of the tower into rubble?

Jy'kalud.

The name stirred primal feelings deep with her, like dust choked shadows, black veils of ancient fabric dropping in the sudden breeze of recollection.

"I have to get out of here," she murmured.

"Yeah," DS Harris responded coldly, mistaking her state of distress. "Don't worry, little princess. Your fancy private dick has arranged for a fancy private lawyer to come get you."

***

Outside the police building a new day was starting cold, grey and damp. Alone, Ruby strode across the quiet parking lot with teeth gritted together, jaw clenched, hugging the tall collar of her brown leather Haujobb jacket around her throat. Suffering from an overwhelming state of nervous exhaustion, the chilly air sank deep into her bones. Trying to think was impossible; her mind was numb, her skull packed with ice or so it seemed – everything she was doing right now, from walking to breathing, was taking place through pure instinct.

The basic human machine had taken over.

It was a terrible feeling.

And yet there was *something* alert and conscious within her; a lurking, skulking sentience that did not belong inside of her head.

Am I going mad?

She had started to wonder; might she share the same malady as her half-brother Dalton Carthew?

Her eyes focussed on the sight of a figure waiting for her at the edge of the car park.

She'd half-expected to be met by some black-clad corporate-looking legal type, one of her mum's paid-for minions; or the stocky young blonde man she'd dropped to the ground outside her apartment on Saturday. Was he the one who had kept to following her, and ultimately called in the police?

Instead, she was relieved to see the tanned, shrewd-eyed, craggy face of Tough Guy leaning against the outside of the big American car with tinted windows. Every centimetre of the vehicle's glossy black exterior was speckled with water droplets; Tough Guy hadn't driven there recently. He'd been waiting there some time.

"Hallo rajah," He called out warmly; it was a nickname he'd given her back when she was a teenager. A genuine smile tugged the leathery corners of his old mouth and then he opened up his arms. Ruby stepped into his embrace, pressed herself into the dark lambs wool coat, and held him tightly as his arms closed around her. Cigar tobacco and expensive cologne. Smell of familiarity, security and strength.

"It's good to see you," she almost sobbed the words. "I'm so glad you're here."

"About time they bloody let you out of there."

Ruby held on for a few more moments. She needed to make a decision. Stay in Bristol or leave with Tough Guy.

"Your mum's been busy."

Ruby said nothing.

"Doing my bloody head in," he added.

Holding tight, Ruby closed her eyes and smiled, despite herself, loving the way he said it.

He cleared his throat. "Look, er...there's been a development."

Ruby opened her eyes but didn't move.

"Your half-sister's become involved," he told her.

Blinking rapidly. A montage of images of the beautiful Xici Carthew blended together from memory and corporate promos. The architect of their exclusion from the family mansion in Bristol, and ultimately her removal from England.

He stroked her back. "She's brought in the head of Carthew security. A French bloke. Ex-cop."

"Is that bad for you?" Ruby asked, open-eyed, gaze drifting over the water-speckled glossy paintwork of the car beside them.

"He got you out of here. He wants me to bring you into a virt. Wants to ask you some questions about what happened last night."

"He wants to know what I'm doing in Bristol." It was an accusation; she couldn't hide the anger in her voice.

Tough Guy sighed, struggling a little, "Probably. Yes."

Ruby closed her eyes. She made her decision. She would stay here and see this thing through.

Nobody believed her. She was on her own, again.

Sensing Tough Guy bristle at something, she eased back and saw him staring over her shoulder.

"Who's this? Your boyfriend?"

A glance behind her revealed sight of the smug, dark-haired guy crossing the car park towards them.

"No." She stepped away from Tough Guy to meet him. A wary smile curved her lips. She wanted him to talk about Ricardo; but what did *he* want?

"Trouble?" she heard Tough Guy mutter, loud enough for Dexter to hear.

"Shouldn't be," she replied, looking at Dexter neutrally.

"Hi," Dexter said, glumness seeping through a weary mask of friendliness, a curt nod at Tough Guy, some vague respect like he knew the situation. Then very direct eye contact with her. "Come find me at the Strontium club later today. I have something you want. Don't leave it too late as I'm not going to be around for a while after today."

24

Dex strode away from the car park like a man on a mission. He was on the edge of friggin' nowhere. He hated these parts of Bristol. He needed a taxi. The old hatchet-faced bloke with Ruby Whats-Her-Name didn't look like he was in the mood for offering a ride.

It was freezing and the sky looked like it was going to dump a shit load of rain down at any time soon. Dex hugged his flimsy jacket around his body, absently envying the obvious warmth and protection he'd seen in the long dark lambs wool coat draped over the old boy.

Was he her dad or was he the private protection? Could have been either. The bloke looked liked he could handle himself, despite his age.

Ripping open the hydrogel bag the police had sealed all of his belongings into, Dex extracted his *Hermes* DVFrames and slipped them on. Out of pure habit he tapped the command stud configured for his investment portfolio: the top line, superimposed on his field of vision was Cr 15.5K.

He shut it down without bothering to scan any other details. It was far short of what he needed to pay-off Jerry White and woefully distant from what he'd set as a target for pressing eject on Bristol.

Switching on his PA, he ignored the flurry of message prompts and missed calls, icons fading up into view through the DVFrames, the PA itself vibrating with each delayed alert. Instead, he started searching for the nearest active taxi-tag.

Then his eyes caught site of something up ahead and his pace slowed without him even being aware of it. Two short and burly figures leaning back against an aggressive-looking jeep with dark tinted windows; their thick arms were folded across blocky chests, short-sleeved sports shirts despite the crappy weather, revealing a plethora of army and prison tattoos.

Shit. He knew these two. Jed and Col. Two of Jerry White's lieutenants. He'd met them once before, two months ago, when they'd helped to install him into the Strontium. They were bad news. Pitbulls, with brains and a savage outlook on life. Their idea of fun was hurting people who got on the bad side of Jerry White.

Both of them spotted him and eased themselves upright, arms still folded, casually but purposefully obstructing his path.

"Aye-aye, mate, you look fookin' shite."

This from Col. Strong northern accent. Short hair, badly bleached, so that it was more yellow than blonde, as was the stubby goatee at the end of his jaw; a narrow, rubbery face, probably once good looking before gene-twister added too much fibrous muscle tissue and violence mashed the finer edges of his features. Above the ridiculous goatee, broad lips curved upwards in a monkey-smile.

"Knew you were a farkin' pussy," Jed added quickly, his accent some weird hybrid mix that suggested years embedded in foreign hotspots. His tone was typically sharp and acidic as if every statement was aimed at provoking a fight. "Yer nowt with all that farkin' metal and machinery lonkin' ya along, are ya?"

Dex knew from his previous encounter with them that Jed had taken an instant dislike to the fact he'd been a PARC pilot during his time in Service. Not a real soldier, was Jed's opinion.

Jed was wide at the chest, shoulders, neck, jaw and face. His hair was short and very ginger. Most of the tattoos on his pale arms were mottled with a covering of large freckles. Bright blue eyes, small and round, gleamed with manic tension above a broad grin.

Both of them were comparatively short compared to Dex, but he knew they'd be able to take him down brutally fast and painfully hard if he tried to dick them around, or make a run for it.

Why the hell should I run, though?

Dex gave them both a glum nod and stopped a few paces away.

"You here because of Richy?"

144

Both men traded blunt grins with each other. Col stepped to the jeep and yanked open a rear door.

Jed gestured towards the vehicle, "Get in ya farkin' nob end."

Dex frowned, hesitated. Jed moved over, grabbed him and hauled him towards the jeep. Dex didn't resist. He half-stumbled, half strode with it.

"You're a farkin' liability," Jed told him. "That's why *we're* here. Should be watchin' the footie we should, but nah, wuv gotta com' down 'ere and sort out the mess yer makin'."

Dex climbed in the middle-rear, onto leatherette seats that were surprisingly spotless. He made an irritated sigh loud enough for the other two to hear as Col moved around to the front and got into the driver's seat, and Jed jumped into the rear beside him and slammed the door shut.

"Is Jerry down here?" Dex asked.

Jed guffawed. "Jerry? Na. He doesn't come doon 'ere t' wipe yer farkin' arse. Na. He's brought in Kofi to clean oop this farkin' mess."

"Kofi?" Dex didn't know the name.

"Aye, Kofi, real fookin' nutcase bastard." Col recounted, shoulders heaving up and down with a throaty chuckle. He started the jeep, gunned the engine and pulled away with a slick skid of tyres on wet road surface.

Jed turned his head to look at him. "One o' them enforcers for the Latvian supply thing, ya know, ex-mercenary. Spent years in an Iranian terror trainin' camp during that big war that ya kinda missed."

"Which is funny," Col added, finding Dex's eyes in the rear-mirror, "Cos Kofi fookin' hates them Arab bastards."

"Farkin' ay," Jed cried out, laughing, "Farkin' black Moslem cunt heads divent nah wot hit 'em when Kofi farkin' got busy over there."

Col's eyes flicked from the road back to Dex in the mirror again, "Cos he's a Serb, yeah? And he fookin' hates those Bosnian's and Croats, don' he?"

Sneering nod from Jed, sideways glace at Dex, "Ay. You're one o'them aren't ya? A farkin' Croat?"

"Kofi's gonna fookin' luv meetin' you like." Col added, his words ending in a hacking cough that turned to laughter.

Dex stared straight ahead, past the out of focus view of Col's grinning eyes. Cold acid was leaking into his guts. His face was throbbing and swollen, and through it all he felt the chill of a greasy sweat seeping out. Once again in his life he was no longer in control and he hated it. The edges of Bristol slid past the tinted windows. They were heading towards the city centre. He didn't know what was worse. The idea of meeting Kofi or spending any length of time with these two.

KOFI WAS AT the club. He'd been there some time, apparently, interviewing staff and the doormen according to Col and Jed. Not even eight o'clock in the morning, the place was deserted when Dex got escorted inside, flanked by his two new best friends.

Kofi sat hunched on a stool at the bar, reassembling the components a large calibre handgun with the casual ease of familiarity. Olive tanned skin, leathery and glistening, as if he hadn't washed for a while. Greasy brown hair, chopped almost to stubble on the front and sides, with a straggly mane hanging down towards massive shoulders that stretched the plain black T-shirt to ripping point. His whole body was cast from bulging slabs of rock-solid muscle. Beneath shiny green tracksuit bottoms was the kind of thighs a Ukrainian shot-putter would have been proud of.

Dex mirrored Jed and Col as they came to natural stop a few paces from Kofi who continued slotting the weapon back together; he had only looked up once to glance at Dex as they entered.

The look Dex had got wasn't friendly.

Dex's gaze flickered over the handgun. It was a Boris flechette pistol. Matt black moulded carbon-alloy casing. Some customisation to the loading chamber. He tracked his gaze to the munitions standing tidily arranged along part of the bar top. Saw the yellow and red chevrons on the cylindrical shells. Explosive incendiary. Each shell would deliver twenty or so high-velocity slivers of monomolecular filaments, diamond sharp, capable of shredding soft anti-ballistic armour. The modified load meant they would not only deliver multiple wound points, but together, minute explosive charges, would combine into an almighty hole-punched right through anything soft and organic. The incendiary elements would set toughened armour on fire and cause additional body shock to a wounded victim. It was a one shot kill weapon, and not particularly noisy compared to the kick it could deliver.

At least Col and Jed had shut up. Although their silence only reinforced Dex's growing unease towards the Serb.

The period of quiet observation continued. Dex realised Kofi was making a point, defining the power paradigm. There was a battle-hardened shell to Kofi's demeanour. Dex could easily visualise him in a war-command position. His drilled-in conditioning towards military authority kicked in almost instinctively. Shut up and wait for the CO to speak.

He picked out other details. A thick stump of a neck, mostly hidden from side by the upward curve of his shoulder muscles and the overhanging curtain of hair at the back. Glimpse of combat tattoos curving around the sides and back of his skull, hidden by the hair. A green rubber ear-bead and separate throat-mike, both looking like army surplus. On the glassy bar top, beside the tidy line of ammunition, was an expensive PA branded with the Bryce logo.

Slapping the firing mechanism into place, Kofi began to pick up the cylindrical shells and load them into the weapon's integral magazine that sat inside the chunky hand-grip.

A casual sweep of his head to regard Col and Jed and then those large brown eyes, that were flat and cool like stone, settled on Dex.

"You have the money you owe Jerry, *budala*?"

His accent sounded rural and a far cry from the educated sounds of Belgrade and Zagreb that many Serbs aspired to. Budala. It had been a long time since he'd heard anyone use that insult on him.

"No."

A snort followed by a moment of contemptuous silence whilst Korda loaded another shell into the weapon.

Dex was pissed off and sick of feeling scared by these people. "Listen, the money's not due until Wednesday."

Korda let him finish speaking, bobbing his head up and down as if agreeing with him. Then those cold, soulless brown eyes switched back to him again and Dex felt all last vestiges of hope and self-confidence bleed out of him.

"Kurac-palac-kriminalac," Kofi muttered, accusing Dex of being a wannabe criminal, and then cocked his head slightly to one side. "You don't have the money. You don't have the drugs. The police have the drugs. So how are you going to get the money?"

Dex blew out through his lips. His guts were crunching up into a tight ball. "I...," he sighed, suddenly exhausted, "I can't."

Kofi nodded, satisfied. He looked down at the flechette gun in his hands as he shoved in the last shell; locked the loading slide and yanked back the cocking handle.

Dex tensed.

So did Jed and Col.

"Aye-aye fella, divent gan blastin' that fookin thing round me, right." Col was pointing his finger at the gun as he moved away.

Kofi gave Col a weary stare. Then back to Dex.

"Who killed Rich?"

"I don't know who they are." Dex swallowed to get some moisture back into his mouth.

"Well they knew who Richy was. How's that?"

"I don't know," Dex repeated. Did Jerry White think there was another drug gang muscling in on the territory? Was that why Kofi had been brought in? What about Micky White? Dex could give them that information, but the problem was how to do it without looking like he'd been holding back. And he needed Micky White, aka, Henry McVee breathing and mobile for the next few days, at least until the scrawny punk had gotten Dex to Glasgow and the gene-twister was sold.

Jerry White's gene-twister. Bloody hell, did Kofi know about that?

"Who was the black cunt?"

An eye blink of silence from Dex as he focussed on being seen to be an asset and not a problem. Ruby Torres. Maybe a Carthew. No need to mention that.

"Just a customer, I think." Dex said, glancing at Jed and Col. "Wrong place. Wrong time."

"Huh, yeah?" Kofi sneered. "Story of your life."

Dex bristled but didn't react.

Kofi watched him, then shrugged dismissively. "Why did these people kill Rich?"

"I don't know. Rich...was already dead when I got there."

"You don't know who they are?"

Dex felt a vein jump in his neck. "No."

Kofi continued to watch him.

Jed was hovering a pace away. Dex could sense the ginger git itching to get a punch in. Col had wandered behind the bar, plucked up an empty glass and was now surveying the beers on tap.

148

"You've not been doing anything to bring this aggression against us?" Kofi asked, insinuating he had. "Nothing extra curricular."

"No."

Kofi nodded, making his mind up, coming to a decision. He shifted his weight on the stool as he shifted the focus of his questions. "You know Micky White?"

Dex felt something shift inside his chest. He'd hoped to avoid talking about this. A crossroads had appeared right in front of him. A choice had to be made. He could not hesitate. The words formed in his mind even as he spoke them.

"I've heard of him. Jerry's son. There's a bounty on his head. I've never met him."

Kofi's mouth compressed into a thin line. Dex resisted the desperate urge to keep talking. He'd committed, he had to stay on target. Col was pouring a pint, watching the liquid with vague interest.

Kofi made an angry flicking gesture with the flechette gun held so easily in his massive hand. "Yes you have."

"What? No way." His voice nearly stumbled with anxiety.

"He uses the name Henry McVee."

Dex played revelation and shock. Blank stare. Mouth parted open.

Kofi seemed to be observing him casually now but Dex could sense the predatory instincts working behind the Serb's demeanour. "You didn't know?"

Crossroads again. Stay on target.

"No. Henry? No. Jesus. No I didn't."

"*Jebem li ti mater*," Kofi spat the words, shook his head in disgust. "What did Jerry want in you? *Budala.* You're a waste of space. Micky White is right beside you and you don't see?"

Dex stared. A chill sweat was seeping out under his arms. His face was flushing hot. The swelling and bruising throbbed with a sickening ache.

Kofi came off the stool. Jed backed off a pace. Dex stood his ground. To hell with this Serb. If the flechette came up, he'd make a lunge for it, he decided.

Kofi slid the safety on. "Micky has been here for a while. He's got plan to hurt his father. Being close to you. It helps him. Maybe you want to help him?"

Dex shook his head out of instinctive denial.

Kofi rolled out a shrug and glanced over at Col, who was supping through the foamy head of beer, with something like dismay.

"Good job I come here and fix these problems." Kofi turned his stony gaze back to Dex. "You stay here. I'm going to fix Micky White. Then I come back and you and I have chat. See what kind of problem *you* are."

25

At least the fucking rain was easing up.

Spliff in hand, McVee stood in the window bay of the small, shabby bedroom, gazing down on the busy road below. Hiss of tyres on wet road surface. Bumper to bumper traffic down there but he didn't really see it. His mind was frantically trying to re-arrange the shattered pieces of the plans he'd come up with yesterday.

Richard Hale was dead. Murdered.

He was a nice guy for a drug dealer.

Fucking murdered.

Media was using the words 'violent' and 'savage attack'.

Didn't deserve that.

And no doubt the stash of pentathene IV either stolen by the wankers that did it, or taken by the police.

No plan 'B'.

Today was supposed to have been D-day.

Do or Die day.

Now it was piss-on-your-hands day.

A rim of acidic sunlight was burning through the edges of the tall grey clouds overhead; the yellow glare distracted him momentarily.

He thought about the saying, every cloud has a silver lining. Fucking crap omen if today was anything to go by.

Dex had been ignoring his calls. He'd sent texts. He'd rung and bounced off voicemail a dozen times. Nothing. No response. Either the fucker had been struck by a drone and was lying unconscious in a pool of blood, or he was giving him the fucking 'v' with his fingers.

Most likely the latter.

Whirling away from the window, he stopped and stared into the gloom of the room; faint glow of weak sunlight on far wall.

What the fuck was he going to do? Portugal had been within touching distance and now it may as well be on Mars. Spad was all packed and ready to go, like he was going on fucking holiday or something. The boy hadn't seemed to have grasped the idea they were never going to be coming back.

Yet it seemed like they were never going to leave.

His surging gaze settled on the sagging double-bed. Then moved to the empty wardrobe.

What a shit fucking life.

Maybe Nicky was right. He shook his head angrily, stuffed the spliff between his lips and sucked hard and fast. Flare of red and the edge of oblivion seeping closer with a long deep breath.

He exhaled, turned slowly back to face the world outside. Everything was sliding past without even a glance in his direction. He was fucking invisible. He was a nobody. Not just a man without an identity, but a man without *any*-fucking-*thing*.

Should he go and open the shop? Should he-

"What the fuck..." his words trailed off around a plume of creamy hash-smoke as his gaze locked onto the tall, skinny, sexy-ass figure of Nicky Osbourne, stomping along the pavement this side of the road, towards the house. She was hefting the same big bag over one shoulder; the hydrogel poncho revealing a thick grey wool jumper which stopped above the hot-curves of her backside, black leggings and the same big black rubber boots. Her lioness mane of brown wavy hair was loose and flapping with each angry stride.

A swirl of emotions spiralled through him. First reaction was excitement, immediately followed by anger and suspicion, subsequently trailed by a yearning desire to put his cock inside of her.

She was back, which meant something had gone wrong for her; which meant he had an angle he could use.

Shag her then kick her out.

An insolent smirk curved his lips around the spliff jutting out.

Her long face tilted upwards as she noticed him. He waved. She nodded her head, her features set in grim recognition of the fact he was smiling with glee.

Jogging down the narrow staircase he called out to Spad, who was in the front room on the ground floor, watching day-time shit on the massive hardscreen with the volume pumped up as high as it always was when he was here. All the housemates were out at work.

"Spad mate."

"Yeah?" a bear-like shout came back, slurred from Spad's early morning hit of cheap go-blind vodka and orange squash.

McVee jumped the last few steps, hit the floor of the hallway and kept moving towards the front door. "I've got a visitor. Don't fucking bother me upstairs right?"

"Sure. Yeah. No problem."

His voice was accompanied by the stuttering rapid-fire basslines of a chungo track, blended with what sounded like a history documentary and some world news programme. Spad probably had other feeds running with the sound off. He would mute and un-mute as the visuals grabbed his fancy.

Spad, hopeless fucking legend of male multi-tasking.

Hauling open the front door, he found Nicky standing on the steps leading up from the pavement, her racially-blended features set at a halfway point between desperation and disdain. Typical fucking Nicky. Nothing was ever simple with her. Not even an apology.

He let her in and wordlessly led the way upstairs, without interruption from Spad.

In the cramped bedroom she un-slung the heavy bag and placed it on the floor, near the old wardrobe, as he shuffled over to the window. The spliff had gone out. His mind was in a riot.

"Where did you go?" he asked, surprised by the softness of his voice. His gaze squinted at the fading ridge of sunlight that was losing the battle against the clouds. It was going to rain again.

"Somewhere but it didn't work out."

McVee turned around and saw her standing there, by the bed, narrow shoulders slightly stooped with feeling-sorry-for-herself expression. His eyes crawled up her legs from the moulded calves of the rubber boots, up through slender arcs of her thighs to the joy spot between her legs, just visible below the hem of the dark wool jumper and the poncho.

His manhood stiffened in his pants. He wanted her so bad it was like a mind-crushing hunger for a drug.

"What, that faggot Mark decide you're a fucking psycho and dump you did he?" McVee said it out of spite and a need to show he wasn't going to be a pushover. She couldn't just walk back into his life like this. Not after what she'd done.

She was biting down on her lower lip, the curtain of brown wavy hair framing her face as she looked at him from beneath a furrowed brow. She was debating telling him about something. Something difficult.

"No." She sighed then stood more upright. "It wasn't him."

"Somebody else? Fucking hell Nicky. How many blokes have you had behind my back?" The words tumbled out of him, full of hurt.

She moved away from the bed, came towards him with slow strides. Her arms were open, long fingers extended; the promise of a careful embrace.

He let her close the gap. Smell of her perfume mixed with the tang of sweat, and the coolness radiating off her wet poncho. He let her hands cusp his face. He closed his eyes as her lips found his. Heat flooded from the kiss. Her tongue found his and slid across as it filled and explored his mouth.

His hands grasped her buttocks and for once she didn't smack them away, didn't recoil or reject him. Instead she murmured with pleasure and pushed herself closer.

The kiss built up in intensity. Their hands now sliding and stroking and caressing and squeezing. He was so hard it was almost painful, his cock straining against baggy nylon cargo pants.

A sound from downstairs punctured the dizzy haze of hormones and desire.

He pulled away, aware of Spad: a voice raised in some kind of shout and then abruptly quiet. Something funny on the hardscreen, perhaps?

"Leave him baby," Nicky crooned, lips hanging open, breath panting, gently clawing the back of his head with one hand, pulling him back into the kiss whilst her other hand dug down into his trousers. "He's drunk. He's always drunk."

Her words faded into a mumble as the kiss resumed.

But an alarm bell was ringing inside his skull.

Something about Spad's voice, like a shout, a warning? The way Spad had so quickly fallen silent.

The bedroom door flew open.

Three men strode him. Two he recognised instantly. Col and Jed. His father's favourite thugs. The third man was a stranger. Short, broad, black leather jacket, black T-shirt, shiny green jogging bottoms; he looked like a cross between something the East Euro-federation would groom for their Olympic teams, and a throwback to a distant era of bad rock music. And, fuck, yes, he had a weapon, a big black cannon of a handgun that seemed welded into the fist at the end of his right arm. All three were wearing latex gloves.

Nicky had gasped in shock followed by a stream of panicked words. She dragged her hand from his trousers but stuck close. McVee didn't move, his gaze rooted to the gun, using peripheral vision to track Col and Jed as they split either side and came in to make a grab.

McVee balled his fists.

"Don't be a stupid fuckhead," the Muscle Mullet growled, twisted Euro accent, like Russian or Polish or something, barrel of the gun levelled directly at him.

Jed, with his freckles and ginger hair, planted his hands on Nicky's shoulders and whirled her away with a sick-boy grin.

Col stepped in close behind him, filling the space. McVee knew he'd have a good chance to break Col's nose and jaw in a couple of swift moves. He'd always been quicker than Col. But with Jed, Muscle Mullet and the Hand Cannon, he stood fuck all chance of being anything but dead.

"Hallo sunshine," Col jeered, reaching down and taking a steel grip of one of his wrists. "Fancy seein' you here, eh?"

McVee said nothing. Just drove daggers of hate into Muscle Mullet with his eyes. The other man was as cold as ice, however, and McVee sensed this was not a man who frightened easily, if at all. Col had both his wrists now and looped a strip of hard plastic-stuff around them, tugged it tighter than it needed. McVee felt the plastic bite into his skin and the circulation in his hands back up.

He cursed under his breath but wasn't going to give any of the fuckers the satisfaction of him complaining.

Nicky was talking bollocks. Half pleading, part angry, the rest demented.

Muscle Mullet swivelled his eyes to Jed and gave a sharp jerk of his head, indicating Nicky and then the bed. Jed hurled Nicky brutally away from him, throwing her off balance; her legs connected with the edge of the bed and she tumbled down onto it with a shriek. In a moment that was surreal in its speed and simultaneous slowness, and horrific in the read intention and McVee's inability to do anything to stop it, Muscle Mullet swung the gun at Nicky and pulled the trigger. There was a sound like a brief aerosol hiss followed instantly by a wet, gristle-like sucking and slapping impact. Nicky's chest and shoulder erupted in a spray of blood and mangled tissue. Her body slumped, immediately lifeless, eyes bulging wide and vacant, surrounded by a veil of gore, blood droplets cascading down the transparent hydrogel of the poncho. Spatter marks on the wall behind the bed.

McVee was howling. His whole body strained forward, neck nearly tearing free from his shoulders, mouth yawning open. Pain burst through his hands and wrists as Col held onto him like he was restraining a wild dog.

Even, strangely, as some inner voice within his head shouted *'fuck yeah she got was she deserved'*, his mind was already mapping this killing onto personal history. It was Danielle all over again. Another women he'd loved, murdered by his father's thugs.

Muscle Mullet was laughing, a quiet, shoulder-shaking mirth. "Ah, stop this. She was a whore queen. I do you a favour for nothing, eh? She was fucking your friend. The Croat donkey. Yes? You see? I help you."

The words ripped into his emotions like a storm striking a flimsy structure in a battered landscape. His yelling ceased, he quit struggling and he reared upright, Col still holding on.

Croat?

Muscle Mullet was smiling, seeing he'd scored a direct hit. The lower flanks of his face were actually wider than the low dome of his skull above bony cheekbones that could have been carved.

"What Croat?"

Muscle Mullet continued with an easy shrug of a shoulder, gesturing at the body with the barrel of the gun, "I have to stop her seeing what I did to the man downstairs. She can speak and make us all in trouble. Yes?"

Spad's dead.

The certainty sank into him, chilling the blood in his veins. Yet his mind babbled and words tumbled from his lips: "What Croat? Dex? Are you talking about Dex? Nicky was screwing Dex?"

"Maybe he was screwing her, eh? You see how fate works out? You use Dex to hurt your father, and yet Dex is placed to hurt you. Life, eh?" A dark chuckle. Then

156

movements that said it was time to go. "Come. We go now. We take a ride and we chat about things. About Dex."

26

Dex was sitting at the bar, in the deserted club, supping a whisky diluted with coke when Ruby What's-Her-Name paid a visit. He'd been toying with the idea of grabbing what he could and making a run for it; give his good pal Duke that call, get on a long ride to Tonga and pick up some work. But that's probably what Kofi was expecting, or hoping he'd do.

He walked to the main entrance and let her in, closed the door and strolled back to the bar. She followed him without anything needing to be said.

She'd been back home and changed, it seemed. Now dressed in a long leather jacket that had the kind of cut and durable colour that cost money. Stylish but functional trainers and dark leggings. There was a sleek rubberised bag slung over her back. Something about the get-up suggested she was dressed for doing things. He noticed she was taller than him, but not as tall as Nicky Osbourne, and wider at the shoulders too. Within all her feminine guise, the nails, the hair, the make-up, there was an air of concealment; these things weren't done to enhance her attractiveness, they were worn to hide her aggression.

He was glad to see her. Her presence, and the bruises to her face, was an affirmation that what had happened only last night wasn't a figment of his imagination. It *had* actually happened. In the same way the human mind can compartmentalise the horrors of war, sanitise them with an almost magical mirage of foggy imagery and numbed emotions, it was possible a part of him was merely protecting his sanity – concealing any clear memories.

He'd found it increasingly difficult to accurately piece together the events in London and stitch them onto the lunacy in Richy's flat, so he simply accepted that they were connected.

With Ruby here, he could now hand over the final connection with the stalking terror, and wash his hands of it.

The idol.

For him here were now far more real, secular and grim issues to confront. Kofi, Jed and Col, and whatever Jerry White had in store for him.

"Drink?"

She nodded once in response, watching him with undisguised tension.

He poured her a whisky without asking what she actually wanted, threw in a splash of coke and handed it over. She took the glass with a trembling hand and knocked most of it back in one gulp before setting it down on the bar. Raw nerves, apprehension of the moment or lingering after effects of such monstrous bedlam? He couldn't tell.

"You said you had something for me." She opened, businesslike.

"I'll go get it."

Leaving her in the bar he went out through the leather upholstered door, along the passageway and up the stairs to his apartment. The interlude gave him a chance to formulate what he wanted to ask and say to her. He'd not really thought about it until this moment; but now realised he wanted to know more about what Cray was. What was his connection to Ruby, and to the Carthew family? More importantly, he wanted to know what she'd told the police about Richy, about Richy's drug-dealing, and if she knew what the police suspected of Dex and his operations in Bristol. The police had released him without comment or explanation; leaving him puzzled, wrong-footed and wary.

Dex opened the safe and extracted the wooden idol; long and thin in his hands, he avoided looking at it any longer than was necessary. The thing brought back fragments of memory that were disturbing to recall and made him feel deeply uncomfortable about it.

Then he paused. The Vortek handgun was where he'd dumped it after getting back from London. Along with the Velcro belt packed with three kilos of gene-twister. Decision time. Take the handgun? Leave the gene-twister? Kofi was going to be watching him and had that monster flechette gun; he'd seen those things used on soft targets and didn't rate his chances if he caught a blast from one. Even a grazing shot could shred a limb into a pulpy stump. He hadn't noticed Col or Jed carrying guns, no tell-tale bulges, no posture changes to alleviate discomfort; so, conceivably if he got the drop on Kofi he could dominate and control the situation.

And then what, Mr Rašković?

What *was* the situation?

Did Kofi have anything to use against him other than misplaced ethnic dislike? Or was Kofi merely fishing for dirt? Just being thorough with the verbal intimidation and pat-down to see what filthy secrets might wriggle out? Seeing if there were things that Jerry White would disapprove of?

Like buying and selling gene-twister stolen from White's gland farms by a son who was wanted dead or alive by his own father.

Who you've known about for a couple days now and done nothing with the intel.

Viral5 must have gotten twitchy and sold. Dex couldn't blame her but how much had she revealed about his level of knowledge in the matter?

If things did turn messy it would be better to have the gun than not...

He reached into the safe, tilted the Vortek in his hand to check safety was on, slipped it into the belt at the rear of his black jeans and tugged the tails of his dark blue shirt over it.

His gaze dropped back into the safe. There wasn't a better place to hide the gene-twister, and if Kofi knew about the safe, which was likely, as the club belonged to White, and wanted to poke around inside, then Dex would tell him to stick his Croatian-hating head up his Serbian shit-tube.

Closing the safe, he made sure it was properly locked, then wrapped the idol in a towel and returned downstairs.

Ruby hadn't budged other than to remove her bag and coat, both resting on top of the stool beside her.

The glass was empty.

Dex moved past her and pointed a finger and thumb gun-shape at the glass. His face asked the question: another?

She shook her head, the tension still etched on her features. Her eyes, large and green, slid onto the towel-wrapped object he placed on the bar top between them. He watched her analyse the shape and size of the object and

160

the rapid injection of hope into her features as she sat upright.

It struck him then how much he found her attractive. Not just physically; there was a vibe about her that caught him in the chest.

Her focus was shuttling between him and towel.

He opened his mouth, took a breath, told her:

"It's from Tarjuan." He waited out the emotional gasp that came from her at the mention of the name, then continued: "It's the wooden statue, idol...thing. He said you had to have it. He was pretty insistent about that."

"He had it all this time?" A delighted yet distraught laugh stuttered from her lips; she breathed out and a hundred questions caught on her lips. She stared at him for answers.

He met her gaze.

"It was the last thing he told me. I'm sorry."

The tone he used conveyed the grim meaning to his words. He saw the shadow of sadness roll in and obscure the gleam in her eyes. Tears welled up at the make-up lined rims but didn't spill. She sniffed, nodded, seemed to accept what he was saying; the smile evaporated and her generous lips compressed into a hard line.

It all came out then. Dex started to compartmentalise, to give her a few facts but he *needed* to talk about it now, here, with this woman who was possibly the only other human being he could share the story with and get some real answers. He hoped.

So he told her everything. From finding the statue clutched in the hands of a dead man outside the club, to Tarjuan breaking in to recover it – that brought a brief nostalgic smile to her lips – to his encounter with Tarjuan in London and their disastrous attempt to take down Cray.

The need to talk, openly, frankly, without the risk of being judged was consequently ignited within her.

They shared brief facts and put together a picture that satisfied their basic, immediate queries:

Her real name was Jezelle Jackson. She was the illegitimate daughter of Richard Carthew. Ruby was her preferred name when 'working'. Ruby had the idol shipped down from secure storage in orbit and arranged for Tarjuan to steal it. Ruby had contacts in the realms of highly organised crime – Dex pegged Tough Guy as her conduit but didn't mention this – which she had recently used to investigate the existence and whereabouts of the figure known as Cray. Cray wanted the idol. Ruby wanted Cray dead, and had dangled the idol as the bait in a trap that would see Ricardo Tarjuan deliver a killing blow.

Cray never showed. Instead, he'd sent an acolyte called Mortice with a view to killing the unknown seller and taking the idol, which had some kind of quasi-religious, mystical significance to Cray and his followers.

Tarjuan had fought off Mortice, wounding him, fatally, but he'd also suffered a life-threatening wound. Dex recalled the bandage around Tarjuan's wrist. Both combatants had fled the scene of the trade and attack, Mortice eventually succumbing to his wounds outside of Dex's club. Tarjuan had found grey-market medical help and thought, initially, that he'd lost the idol.

Dex clarified that it was when Richy started asking questions at the Bristol University that Tarjuan was able to discover he had the statue.

The rest was history.

"I get all this," Dex stated, pushing himself up from the stool he drifted around to the other side of the bar. "I get the statue-idol... thing. I get the fact it's really important to Cray."

Ruby shook her head vigorously, "It's more than important. It's *essential* to him. It's a vital part of what he's been longing to find for, well, for..." Her words trailed off with a distant, troubled expression tugging her features. As if she wasn't certain how to frame her thoughts.

Dex sloshed a couple fingers of whisky into his glass, held the bottle towards hers and withdrew it when she gestured 'no' with her hand.

"A very long time," she concluded.

"Yeah. I get that, too." He plonked down the bottle and took a quick sip from the glass, inhaling sharply, gritting his teeth at the burn. "And that he's looking for this con, convec-, what was it?"

"Conventicle."

"Right. Conventicle. Which he said was the tower. Is that the Carthew Tower?"

"Yes." The way her lips curled up, it was as if she was admitting some terrible moral crime.

"So..." he faltered, not sure what he was trying to fathom.

A long drawn out sigh. She closed her eyes and muttered something. Then springing them open she reached over to the stool beside her, plucked up her bag, opened it and extracted a bundle of old-looking papers and a thin book, all wrapped in a floppy sheet of transparent hydrogel. She placed the bundle on the bar top then grabbed the towel wrapped statue and stuffed it into the bottom of the bag, shoving it down as far as it would go.

Dex wondered if she might have been about to get up and leave. Instead, she calmed her movements and began to carefully peel away the sheet of hydrogel from the bundle. It was like watching somebody unpick the death shroud from the face of a loved-one before sending the body on its way.

"My father was an amazing man," she began, her eyes glazed and directed at what her hands were doing. "He had his faults, I suppose. It's like all men with wealth and power do. He was my best friend. We didn't always get on or see eye to eye, but there was a love there that was unbreakable. We had trust. We had a bond."

Ruby lifted the bundle clear of the hydrogel, placing the discarded sheet neatly on top of her jacket on the stool. The assorted papers were hardcopy prints, a few years old judging by their crumpled edges, but a glimpse of their contents revealed they were copies of much older documents. The thin book was ancient, bound in leather and falling to pieces, it looked like somebody's journal.

"My father died when I was a teenager. Before he died, he told me that our family was burdened by a terrible legacy. His blood was my blood, and our blood made us both part of this legacy. He told me I would have to be strong, because one day the Carthew family would be made accountable for the actions of its ancestors. Slavery was only the tip of the iceberg."

Her gaze was now fixed on him, but there was a glassiness to it that revealed her mind was disconnected from what her eyes were really seeing. Dex sensed she was reliving some vital moment of her past. Once again, tears brimmed on the rims of make-up. It didn't seem like it was nostalgia that had her upset; from the quivering tremor in her face it looked to be a complex emotion born out of disconsolation and fear.

He stood silently, listening, and supped his whisky.

She cleared her throat and tapped her badly grazed fingers on the exposed bundle. "When I was eighteen, a package arrived from my father's solicitor containing everything he had found on this legacy. I didn't know until then what an obsession it had been for him. My mother had known but...," her face tightened, she finished quietly. "That's another story. For another time."

Picking up the pace she tapped the bundle again. "The origin of the story comes from the journal of a man called MacAleavey. This is his journal here. MacAleavey was linked to the Carthew family through the East India Company during the seventeen hundreds."

"They shipped tea around the place, didn't they?" Dex hazarded.

"And the rest," Ruby responded with a morose sigh, and gestured that it wasn't relevant. "The journal survived and was purchased by the first member of the Carthew family to really investigate the hushed history of the family. James Carthew. Over a hundred years ago in nineteen-nineteen, a few months after the end of the First World War. James had been in Ypres, and went back there after the war to help co-ordinate the reconstruction, and no doubt profit on the interests of the family business."

Ruby narrowed her eyes and puckered her lips speculatively. "The Carthew name caught the attention of somebody who was also there. A Frenchman who had interests beyond bricks and mortar or extracting recompense from Germany. He knew about the Carthew family's not-so-wholesome past. He approached James with information to sell. My mother, as others had, claimed this was no more than subterfuge and blackmail. The journal was a hoax." Ruby shook her head. "Anyway, the result was James bought the proffered journal and so ignited a study, an obsession as my mother called it, that has been passed down through generations of Carthews."

"So here we are," Dex announced soberly, holding aloft the whisky glass. "Now the opposite side of the story comes creeping out of the shadows, eh? Whilst your family was looking for Cray, right? Cray was looking for your family? His family, even."

"Something like that." Ruby said, sounding defensive.

"Mary Carthew. Who was she?" Dex recalled Cray mentioning the name in Richy's flat.

"She was MacAleavey's sister."

"Shit." Dex responded slowly, seeing the first glimmer of motive for the journal. He knocked back the last dregs of whisky in the glass and pointed at the bundle beneath Ruby's fingers. "So what happened?"

Ruby shifted her posture on the stool so she could look directly at him, and then began to unburden herself of the whole story. Entirely from memory, she told it as it must have been written in the journal. Dex didn't interrupt. He just listened and assimilated, so he could understand the

164

horror that had touched his life, and maybe answer some of the questions he had about the events that had recently occurred.

MACALEAVEY WAS AN opportunist. He was like many of the employees of the East Orient Company during the 18th Century, able to put together a personal fortune making private business deals, forming syndicates and buying small brigs. The Company tolerated this merely because it was confident with its own profits, which were immense.

When the Emperor of China outlawed all trading in opium, MacAleavey and a group of entrepreneurs, including a young Walter Carthew, worked hard to create a an illicit network. They gave massive bribes to port officials in Batavia and Macao, so the officials would overlook the illegal opium when inspecting beneath the hatch covers. They made clandestine contacts with Chinese smugglers and kept the opium moving.

During this time, MacAleavey and Carthew became very close. They became friends. Carthew married MacAleavey's sister, Mary. Then, the history of the Carthew line took a very dark turn.

Walter Carthew did not need to smuggle opium. He *wanted* to. He was an arrogant young man, full of the spirit of adventure that defined the seventeen hundreds. MacAleavey wrote this, but also that Walter Carthew was hooked on primitive religions, in particular the native rituals of the slaves used by the Carthew family for their sugar plantations in Barbados.

Understandably, it bothered MacAleavey because Walther Carthew was married to his sister.

Then Walter Carthew went with the family ships to the Ivory Coast, ostensibly to oversee the transporting of slaves. MacAleavey wrote this, and described a frightening change when Walter Carthew returned to Bristol nearly a whole year later. Rumours sprung up that he and some of the crew who had journeyed with him, had become involved in un-Christian activities. All the men had changed, it transpired.

They seemed to abandon their previous lives, their wives, sweethearts and families, and instead became utterly loyal to Walter Carthew.

At that point, Bristol became alive with sensational gossip. Cemeteries were found desecrated, graves opened, caskets torn apart, and cadavers gone. Some people whispered of necromancy. Others talked of unethical experiments and the illicit trade in cadavers. A few pointed fingers in the direction of Walter Carthew, those that did either quickly retracted their accusations or disappeared. No official investigation ever crossed Carthew's path. All of this, MacAleavey wrote down with increasing alarm and concern for his sister, Mary.

MacAleavey had good cause to be worried. But his fears were realised all too soon and tragically, not before he could extract his sister from the demented relationship.

Mary Carthew believed her husband to be having an affair. It was widely known how much Walter Carthew liked prostitutes. One night, Mary tried following him on one of his frequent nocturnal sojourns. Nobody knows where they went. In the early hours of the next morning, Mary was found stumbling through Bristol's streets, utterly insane, babbling about a living darkness in a pit, her mind gone.

Nobody ever discovered what she saw to cause such irrevocable madness, although the family tower, set upon a wooded slope within Arnos Vale, became the focus for many of the rumours. MacAleavey hounded Carthew with accusations but did not gain a reply. By now Walter Carthew had turned his back on their friendship, and on his own father who had started to become vocal in his concerns about the unwholesome activities of his son.

The journal was filled with theories, and frenzied notes jotted down by MacAleavey after conversations with people who had ideas about what Walter Carthew was up to. Again, the tower and the subterranean caves beneath it came out as the suspected focal point for macabre and unholy rites.

These rumours ended when Walter Carthew's father took a gang of men to the tower and then planted explosives in the cellars as a feverish and horrified reaction to what they allegedly found there. MacAleavey had begged the men to tell him what they had discovered, what might have driven his sister over the brink, but only received vague muttered suggestions: about cannibalism and the worship of a knotted length of carved wood; and whispered terror of some kind of moving shadow, or sentient darkness, that came from the chiselled and sinewy talisman itself.

Days later, the father was found murdered, a knife buried in his side and Walter Carthew, chief suspect in the crime, evaporated from Bristol.

Several years passed. MacAleavey struggled to come to terms with the abrupt silence in the wake of what had occurred. He delved into books of forgotten lore, probed boundaries of knowledge historically forbidden by theologians and scholars of the diabolical. The Gospel of Thomas; the Treatise on the Seventh and the Eighth; the Nag Hammadi Texts; People of the Monolith; and the Voynich Manuscript, but it was in the G'harne Fragments that MacAleavey uncovered the name of the monstrous entity Walter Carthew had worshipped, the entity Carthew had made manifest in the world of men through the spilling of blood and uttering of demonical phrases.

Jy'kalud.

The corruptor of flesh. The diseased One. Associated with a pantheon of cosmic nightmares with such names as Zhothaqquah and its *formless spawn*; Yog-Sothoth, concurrently described by MacAleavey as *Yaji Ash-Shuthath*; and Great Q'thulu, which lies dreaming within a tomb-like temple below the surface of one of Earth's oceans.

MacAleavey began to grasp what Walter Carthew was doing in Bristol and was so terrified he ceased to update his journal with anything but cursory comments; then he relocated to London with nominal plans to emigrate to the new territories in North America.

Yet fate has a wicked sense of irony.

One day, in London, MacAleavey came across a man called William Cannell. He had money and all the comportments of a gentleman, but the manners and appearance of a dog.

Though much changed, MacAleavey instantly recognised William Cannell to be Walter Carthew.

Not long after, William Cannell was killed by an unidentified assailant in the insalubrious wharf district of London.

MacAleavey's journal made no confession to the murder but did suggest he had a hand to play in the death.

"SO WHO THE hell is Cray?" Dex queried, his body pressed up against the edge of the bar as he listened to Ruby's telling of the story. "The son of William Cannell – Walter Carthew?"

Ruby relaxed her posture, folded her arms along the opposite edge of the bar. She shook her head and then

167

stared into the wall of spirit bottles and optics, a haunted look straining her bruised features. "I don't know."

Dex recalled what Cray had said about family and blood, back in Richy's flat, suggesting he *was* related, in some way; but he got the distinct impression from Ruby that she was avoiding that particular subject. He couldn't blame her.

"MacAleavey died on his journey to America," Ruby told him as she pushed herself upright and came back into focus, "French pirates opened fire on the ship he was travelling. Ironically, James Carthew probably bought the journal off a descendant of the pirates who killed MacAleavey."

Dex grunted; mulling through what Ruby had said.

The description of the talisman: a knotted length of carved wood; chiselled, sinewy. Was the talisman the statue-idol-thing?

Dex slung his gaze to the sleek rubberised bag now lying on the bar top. "This talisman MacAleavey wrote about…"

Ruby nodded solemnly, watching him with a caution he thought was unnecessary. "It was found in the attic of the Carthew Mansion, inside an old privilege chest. Probably hidden there by Walter Carthew's father after destroying the tower, and lost to time. It's been a part of the ongoing mystery and obsession of the family since then."

"And the same for Cray." Dex brought the conversation back to the subject he'd started with. "The same obsession, and a part *of* the obsession. He's been out there, beneath London for, Jesus knows how long, some kind of freak mutation, a monster, right? And all this time he's been looking for the statue or idol, this talisman maybe; *and* the location Walter Carthew was using for these weird rituals."

"Yeah," Ruby said quietly, a reflex grimace that showed her teeth.

"So, what happens if Cray gets his claws on that?" Dex gestured at the bag.

"I don't know." Her voice was almost a whisper.

"What did MacAleavey say about it?"

"He didn't."

Dex sighed, pushed himself up straight and walked away from the bar.

"I've got a real situation here," he started, couching his words in a careful tone. "I know you've got this crap going on. But it seems to me that it could all be about a bunch of people fighting over who owns the statue. It's like a religion, isn't it. Thing is, it doesn't involve me. I've got people in the city right now who probably want to break my bones. Maybe even put a bullet in my brain. Do you know what I'm saying?"

"Sure. You're saying you're too damn stupid to see the bigger picture here."

"*Hey-*" He turned to face her, angry, but she crashed through his objection with her words:

"I know the people who've got you dangling on a wire here. I know who they work for. Jerry White. He's violent scum and you're an idiot for having anything to do with him. But that's your problem, not mine." Flash of a cold smile. "They think Cray is a rival gang. They don't know that *you* led Cray here to Bristol and they'd definitely kill you if they did. So Cray *is* your problem, whether you like it or not."

Dex stiffened, slapped by the truth of her insights, and shocked by how much she knew or suspected.

"Yep?" She concluded, dismissive of his stunned reaction. "Look, Cray is here and I know where he is. This situation presents a unique opportunity. Don't you see it?"

"What opportunity? What are you talking about?"

"I'm talking about using the people who are here. I'm talking about killing Cray."

27

"Then this ebony bird beguiling my sad fancy into smiling...."

Some kind of poem. The words rolled off Muscle Mullet's tongue like polished stones, glossy with age, with the ease of practised familiarity.

McVee was slumped in the middle row of the Israeli jeep, beside Jed, dimly aware of the throbbing ache in his wrists where the strip-binders were slicing into his flesh, and the maddening deadness of his hands where the circulation was all but cut off. Col was up front, driving, with Muscle Mullet in the front passenger bucket.

"By the grave and stern decorum of the countenance it wore..."

Muscle Mullet was called Kofi. Kofi looked as chilled-out as a dead fish, staring glassily at the city centre through the tinted windows, the bits of poetry spaced out by long pauses.

Col and Jed were silent. Their usual cocky brashness and sick humour subdued since the killing of Nicky.

McVee hadn't said a word either. He kept seeing the wound erupting in his minds-eye. Again and again. Quiet aerosol hiss, then wet slap and squelch of meat being ripped apart. The life vaporising from Nicky's face in an instant. His howling shriek of misery and rage.

He'd glimpsed Spad as a blur of crimson gore in the doorway to the lounge as Col and Jed had frog-marched him outside.

There's nothing fucking left for me, he thought sluggishly, struggling to compose any consistent line of reason. His brain was numb and remote, as if the inner part of him had been wrapped in thick cotton-wool padding.

"Though thy crest be shorn and shaven, thou, I said, art sure no craven, ghastly grim and ancient Raven wandering from the nightly shore...."

There was no need to kill them. Neither of them were a problem. Why the fuck kill them?

Whichever way the next few minutes or hours played out, it wasn't going to be a good ending for him, McVee decided dimly.

He didn't know what he was going to do. He was just a breathing corpse right now, as far as he was concerned. They were going to take him somewhere and hurt him until he talked. Talked about Dex.

Fucking cunt.

Had Dex really been shagging Nicky?

McVee tried to string small glimpses of knowledge together but couldn't see anything other than his own paranoid suspicions. Nicky had been fucking lots of people.

They're going to torture you and dump your body.

Whatever, Nicky had been a fucked up slag. Dex had done fuck all to help him about Glasgow. An icy sheen of hate began to encase his thoughts. If he was going to suffer at the hands of his dad's thugs, then Dex was going to suffer too. He promised himself that.

"Tell me what thy lordly name is on the Night's Plutonium shore."

28

Ruby could feel the alcohol taking the edge off her fear. Strong urge to have more but that would leave her sluggish and it was vital she was at one-hundred percent for the next stage.

Dexter was sitting on a stool, two away from her, hunched over MacAleavey's journal and the hardcopies of documents related to the family obsession. Most of the research done during the past two generations was now stored on digital files, with copies stashed on her PA. The journal had been treated by a specialist in antiquarian preservation and restoration, a polymer wash that toughened the delicate pages and halted their deterioration through time. Even Ricardo had been impressed. Ruby smiled briefly, the upward curve collapsing under the weight of raw emotions.

She didn't want to think about Ricardo or what might have happened to him in London. No questions for Dexter. Not yet. Maybe later, when this was over.

Surging recollection of Cray's slime-dripping, diseased and mutated face. Yellow eyes glowing in the shadows of the room.

Ruby stamped down on the slithering memories. Caught her breath, heart pounding in her temples.

She consciously turned her thoughts away from the sense of something lurking inside her mind, watching, grinning... *waiting* with anticipation.

Focus on the here and now. Prepare for the conclusion of this nightmare.

The way this moment had come together almost seemed God sent. That was how she wanted to view it. After all, she was enmeshed within the tattered, centuries-old fabric of a battle with an incarnation of Evil, capital 'E'.

Driving away from the police station earlier, Tough Guy had told her all about Richy's associations and the criminal bulldog he had belonged to; almost as courtesy briefing, like this was all a part of one of his jobs.

Jerry White. Mr Gene Twister. An ironic *nom de plume* considering his fascist view on racial purity. A book penned in jail, 'Brothers in Blood', a loyal following from white-supremacists and Aryan-gangs rallying around his chant, 'Your Blood is Your Flag'.

Dangerous and well-connected. Plugged into the same network as Tough Guy, at a much *lower* level.

She'd used the morning with Tough Guy to explore everything he knew about Jerry White's operation in Bristol. And so discovered the belief held by White's lieutenants that a rival gang from London was muscling in on his territory here.

It was savagely perfect. It's was God's will.

Divine retribution.

"Bloody hell." The muttered remark came from Dexter. "I'm glad you told me this and I didn't have to read it for myself. The bloke's handwriting is bad enough but it's almost another language."

"English is a virus," she commented, paraphrasing somebody else she'd once heard using that statement.

Dexter nodded, not really responding, his bandaged brow furrowed as he continued to read.

She considered the fact she was revealing all of this to him. She'd told Ricardo nothing about the true horror of what she believed Cray to be, merely painted a picture of a deranged man with a criminal lifestyle padded in the pursuit of occult thrills.

Was there guilt there?

I am responsible for Ricardo's death.

She tried the statement for fit.

It didn't and she shrugged free of the concept.

She switched mental tracks and her eyes locked onto Dexter, and his trim, well-proportioned figure. Noted the blocky shape of the handgun tucked down the back of his jeans, pressing up against the shirt. She'd seen the way his eyes, although striated with broken blood vessels, had dilated behind the lenses of his DVFrames when he'd been gazing at her, the flare of his nostrils and subtle blushing of his cheeks. Another penis that found her desirable. Yawn.

Ruby admired intelligence and physical strength. Dexter was smart, but too full of himself to be attractive, she decided. Whereas Ricardo's toughened shell had glimmered with a sophistication that was crotch-soakingly seductive, Dexter's persona was one step up from a thug. He was a lad with brains.

Which made him useful, and expendable.

Her thoughts flipped to Kerry. There was a sense of closure in Kerry's absence from their apartment in Clifton, which felt appropriate. Kerry had left a note on the lounge mirror scrawled in Ruby's favourite lipstick:

GONE 2 BALI U BITCH. HOPE U CHOKE ON THE P. SEE U WHEN I GET BACK. LUV U. Kx

No you won't, Ruby declared silently. *I'll be long gone and all of this will be just a bad memory.*

A noise at the door, sound of several people walking into the club. Dex sat bolt upright then pushed away from the stool, the journal instantly forgotten.

In a flash, Ruby was up, scooping the journal and papers together. She grabbed the slim bag she'd brought along and more or less stuffed them inside, pressing them deeply down onto the towel-wrapped object, the idol, at the bottom of the bag.

The new arrivals were taking their time.

Dropping the bag by her feet she turned and rested her back against the bar. She had her PA in hand. A downward glance and two finger taps on the embedded hardscreen brought what she wanted into place.

Finished, she glanced over at Dexter, hovering a few paces from her, radiating apprehension crudely masked by cool silence and languid movement.

Behind the thick black rims of his DVFrames, she saw his swollen and badly bruised eyes dart between her and the end of the short passage leading to the club's entrance.

Ruby smiled, despite her guts scrunching up around a hard pellet of tension. "I'll introduce myself, okay?"

He nodded vaguely, apparently wrapped up in his own mental dialogue.

The group that walked in were typical of the squalid criminal caste she was about to parley with. Two stubby Rottweiler types, one ginger, the other with ridiculously bad bleached hair and goatee; short sleeved sport-shirts, misshapen muscle groups and aggressive tattoos. Between them they hauled a young, skinny man with close-cropped rust coloured hair; another bleached goatee-beard; arms held behind his back. He was their prisoner. The Skinny Pup caught her interest because his shell-shocked face was too pale to be healthy, yet it had been crafted with the sort of hard edges that were suggestive of a brutal life; this was not a man whole broke easily, she guessed. He had red-rimmed eyes: recent pain and emotional trauma. Then she saw a rapid, snarling grimace of anger twist his features as his gaze fell on Dexter. No love for Dexter, it seemed.

The final, fourth figure strode up front. No doubt this was the freelancer Tough Guy said Jerry White had hired in. A solid block of aggression cast with East Euro-Fed features. Loose all points for the bad haircut. It was a short-lived amused thought as his dark gaze settled on her like she was something to be kicked away with disgust. Her face went taught under his hostile scrutiny. She spotted the bulky handgun clenched in one fist.

"This the same black cunt at Richy's last night?" The question was thrown at Dexter, guttural East Euro-Fed accent. Sounded like Russian, but wasn't.

"This is Ruby." Dex said slowly. "Ruby, this is Kofi."

Ruby nodded once.

"Uh-huh," Kofi acknowledged, more of a sneer, and strode up to the bar. Slapping the flat of his hand across the bar he twisted his head to look meaningfully at Dexter. "A drink. Barman. *Budala.*"

Dexter rocked back on his heels and moved easily around to the other side of the bar.

The two Rottweilers stood nearby, controlling Skinny Pup who continued to spear Dexter with his eyes; wiry arms still behind his back

Kofi slung his head the other way and regarded her balefully. "My monkey here says you're just a customer. What you here for? We don't give refunds."

Ruby rolled her lips together and reviewed the approach she'd planned.

"Or maybe monkey lied," Kofi continued suggestively, malice seeping into the dead expression of his face, "Eh? Why the fuck 'you here?"

Ruby smiled, the tension in her guts melting within the heat of her dislike for the prick, and savouring the notion of what might be about to happen next. She wanted to enjoy his anger.

Kofi rolled a shrug at her silent smile. He saw Dexter had poured vodka into a short tumbler, grabbed the glass and took a surprisingly small sip.

Ruby flicked her eyes at Dexter who met her glance then looked away deadpan. He was waiting for her to make a move.

The atmosphere in the small space of the club was becoming increasingly taught.

Kofi lifted his face from the glass and stared directly ahead, into the bottles behind the bar. "Maybe I should throw a contest. Turn dance floor into fight ring. Put Micky over there with you and see if his father is right about white blood." An ironic chuckle and subtle shake of his head. "Everybody is fucking lying. And I don't leave until you're telling truth."

With a deft movement of her fingers, avoiding the need to look down at what she was doing, she unlocked the PA and pressed her thumb against the large button rendered on the hardscreen.

Kofi shifted his posture as the message reached his PA with a dull notification note, probably a vibration too.

"That's from me," she told him levelly. His reaction was immediate, surprise and suspicion clouding his darkened expression. "It's a phone-tag of an associate of mine. He knows Jerry White and he wants to talk to you about an arrangement."

Kofi sighed through the prolonged glare he gave her.

She gave him her brightest smile, then let it drop as she span round and faced the bar. Catching Dexter's eyes she nodded at the empty glass she'd been using.

Dexter poured her another shot as Kofi moved away, extracting his PA and examining what she'd sent him. Dexter braved a smirk, but Ruby didn't acknowledge it. This wasn't a game.

"*Govno,*" Kofi literally spat the word as he walked across the empty gloomy dance floor to get some privacy as he made the call.

A blink of silence. Then a caustic voice from behind her.

"You're a fucking dead man walking, Dex."

It was the Skinny Pup with so much hate in his eyes.

Ruby saw Dex bristle but contain his reaction to a few chilly words, "Yeah? Why's that then?"

"You know why."

Ruby supped the whisky and let the rant and response zip overhead. She considered what she'd told Tough Guy to say to Jerry White's freelancer. Veiled threats tied together with the bonds and alliances of the network they all shared. It boiled down to this: help Ruby Torres or you'll never work for Jerry White or any other part of the organisation again.

The lack of words from Dexter was stirring Skinny Pup into an emotional frenzy. A torrent of broken sentences and statements poured out cut with rage and grief. Accusations about a girl called Nicky. Who was now dead, it transpired. Killed by Kofi.

Male bravado bullshit. And men said women were the weaker sex because of their emotions. Jesus Christ, listen to this guy.

Dexter impressed her with his reserve, and a skilful way of taunting Skinny Pup without losing control. But there was something else behind Dexter's reactions. Dexter was scared about what else Skinny Pup might say.

Ruby took a long sip of whisky without really drinking much. The acrid smell burned the soft tissue of her nostrils and rolled over her tongue to rake the back of her throat, but that's what she wanted and allowed it to linger before taking the glass away. So long as Dexter and Skinny Pup didn't threaten her plan, she wouldn't need to tell Kofi to use that big gun on them.

29

The mixed-race girl reminded him of a transsexual Spad had shagged in Barcelona. Like the tranny, she was womanly enough, had all the clothes and the make-up just right, but there was a masculine vibe from the broad shoulders and easy strength in the way she moved. Maybe it came from bloody ballet lessons and pilates, but McVee had spent his life fighting and he sensed this random bitch knew how to put down tough bastards twice her size. In any case, the bruises on her face suggested she'd recently taken a hammering.

Whoever she was, she was *connected* and was using his dad's name like large denomination currency.

Col and Jed were either side of him, shifting about on their feet like they both needed the fucking bog for a slash or something. They were restless, probably not used to this kind of hierarchical interruption happening when Jerry White was around.

His hands were fucking numb. His shoulders were on fire from the strain of having his arms pinned back for so long.

At least Kofi wasn't stuffing his head down a toilet and pouring bleach into his face.

Not yet, leastways.

Dex was looking a cool as a fucking cucumber. Smug wanker.

McVee still couldn't tell if Dex had been shagging Nicky or not. Or if it was just a mind fuck being played on him by Kofi. He guessed it would come out in the wash, eventually. The Muscle Mullet would probably try and use stuff like that to drive a wedge between them, get him and Dex sparking off each other, spilling stuff that needed to stay quiet.

Nicky lurched into his mind.

Fucking hell.

It was weird how he felt all cut up about her getting killed and at the same time didn't really give a shit. Better her than him, right?

Spad was there, waving at him from the edge of his memories with that stupid ape-man grin on his sunburned face. It was good he hadn't seen what actually happened to Spad. That would have really drilled a hole in his fucking heart. The sight of Spad's bloodied body was already losing focus as his brain scrambled to protect him.

Just good memories left, mate. McVee managed a smile, despite himself. *I won't fucking forget you.*

The atmosphere of the gloomy club became supercharged with tension as Kofi came striding back across the dance-floor, the hand cannon still clenched like he'd prefer to smack you over the head with it rather than shoot it.

The PA was gone from his hand.

"You work with some powerful people." Kofi told the girl; he went to the bar and gestured for Dex to pour him another vodka.

The girl raised an eyebrow, smiling like the Devil and turned to face him, resting on hip against the edge of the bar. Cool as ice she said, "I work *with* some powerful people. Kofi."

Muscle Mullet chuckled with a sound like he was gargling phlegm and grabbed the glass even before Dex had finished pouring. Raising the glass to the girl – a mock toast - he knocked the small amount of liquid back, then bared his teeth.

Kofi regarded her with an expression as blank as death for a moment, dark eyes reminding McVee of a shark. Then he nodded with the merest trace of a smile. "Come. We go somewhere and talk about what you want to do. You want this gang dead. So do I. So we work together."

McVee sensed Kofi was speaking for the benefit of the others.

The girl picked up her coat and bag and moved away from the bar with Kofi. As they went, Kofi glanced at Col and Jed, then waved the gun at McVee. "Cut him loose but keep your eye on him."

Kofi twisted at the waist and pointed the gun at Dex. "And him. If he shows you disrespect you have permission to break his teeth."

McVee observed Dex standing behind the bar, watching the girl and Kofi head towards a boothed area on the far side of the dance floor, looking like he'd been left out of the party.

Not so fucking smug are you now, eh?

Click of a switch-blade. Col pushed McVee in front of him and cut through the plastic strip-binders. Jed shuffled away, heading to the toilets, muttering something under his breath. Neither seemed too happy about the turn of events. McVee held his tongue whilst Col still had the blade between his wrists.

His hands fell free from behind him and he nearly fell to the floor with the sudden shift in balance; his arms felt like bars of cast iron. Heat and pain flooded into his hands. McVee staggered a couple paces forwards and turned to face Col, twisting his hands and fingers to work the cramp out of them.

"Cunt spoiled your fun, eh?" McVee taunted with a sneer.

"Fook off ya little twat."

Col shook his head and walked to the bar, close enough to McVee to give him a not-so-friendly shove with his shoulder as he grazed past. McVee let it go. His hands were beyond useless right now.

He watched Col go over and speak with Dex. Dex poured two pints of lager.

McVee waited. Massaged his fingers together as the life began to return to them, grimacing with the fucking mad pain. He glanced at his wrists. They were cut to shit and bleeding but nothing to worry about.

Col was trying to get a rise out of Dex. Dex just nodded or looked blankly at the lager flowing into the glasses.

Jed came out from the toilets, wiping wet hands on his sports-shirt. Spatter marks around his thighs.

Col saw him, picked up the pints and walked over to a table and chairs arrangement near the entrance. Jed joined him. Both took a seat and sat back like they were on sun-loungers on the Costa Del Sol.

McVee turned his head and looked over at Dex. Dex was watching him.

Feeling a little twitchy, Dex, eh? You fucking should be you cunt.

Smiling ambiguously, McVee wandered over to the bar.

"Pour me a pint then."

Dex said nothing, just reached down for an empty glass and began to pour the same cheap shit he'd poured for Col and Jed

McVee cleared his throat.

"You better be thinking about how to get me out of here."

Dex nodded. "Glasgow, right?"

McVee's mouth compressed into a thin line.

"Aye, Glasgow," he said evenly, "The second that fuck with the mullet tries to do me in, I'm gonna spill my guts about you and the twister. I'm as good as dead. I'll take you with me if I have to. Got that?"

Dex finished pouring and placed the pint on the bar in front of him.

"Guess that makes me and you friends then."

McVee sneered. "You're no friend of mine."

With an abrupt flick of his hand, Dex knocked over the pint. The glass smashed. The liquid splashed over the bar and caught McVee on the legs of his trousers as he leapt back.

"What the fuck?" McVee snarled.

Dex looked at him with grim calm, "Sorry. Beer's off."

Sound of Col and Jed laughing from behind.

McVee glared at him, physically trembling with anger. He could feel his face flushing red and burning.

"I'll try and get you out of here, Micky." Dex told him softly. It was strange hearing his real name. "I've got nothing against you. You had a rough deal with your dad. I appreciate that. But don't think you've got a hold on me. And you ever threaten me like that. I'll bury you."

"You got fucking balls, mate." A mirthless grin. "But you're full of shit. You bury me? Not a fucking chance."

Dex tilted his head, as if to say, maybe, maybe not.

McVee stepped up close, nailed Dex with a far-reaching stare. "You get me out of this, mate. Fucking hear me? Get...me...out of this."

30

The Skinny Pup was called Micky White, estranged son of Jerry who wanted the 'bastard snitch' dead. That's what Kofi had told her, along with other things. Ruby observed Micky, aka Henry McVee posturing and hissing words at Dexter across the bar.

The boy was bad news all round. Angry and carrying a cloud of pain over his head wherever he went.

The Serb was deeply impressed by Ruby and her connections. They spoke briefly about Sebastian Bonifacio Stacoli and her time running infiltration and extortion in Marseilles. Kofi had killed for Stacoli on several occasions. It was a strange moment of connection and greatly eased the mood between them.

He told her his mother was related to the illegitimate daughter of Arkan. She vaguely knew the name was an infamous part of Serbia's less glamorous nationalistic past, and made faces like she actually gave a shit.

"Zeljko 'Arkan' Raznatovic." Kofi stated the name with proud, swelling out his already expansive chest and patting it with his hand. "Bank robber, gangster, politician, paramilitary leader and national fucking hero, despite fact Hague wanted him as war criminal."

Kofi mentioned Arkan's thousand-strong army of football hooligans, under direct control of Serbia's interior ministry: shock troops in the war of ethnic cleansing.

The vodka and their abrupt camaraderie had him talking, it seemed; he went on to dismiss some woman called Ceca as nothing but a hood ornament in Milosevic's machine of National transformation.

Ruby played interested.

"She should have stuck to singing her sentimental farmer music in *kafana's*," Kofi stated grumpily. Ruby detected deep issues with his past, probably passed down through the family line. "Every twenty years they bring back fucking Turbo-Folk revivals like she was something to be proud of. What kind of music is that?"

Their meeting extended. Kofi talked. Ruby mentioned nothing about her true identity, as a Carthew, or anything about what Cray was up to. She kept Kofi focussed on the plan ahead, and distracted him every time he tried to recap on what brought her to Bristol and her 'issues' with the London gang. She didn't correct him when Kofi mistakenly theorised about Cray being part of a possible attempt to choke off supply of Pentathene IV in the city, driving up prices before unloading a supply from London dealing hubs.

She told Kofi that she'd gained intelligence that Cray and the London gang were occupying disused tunnels beneath an old monument, two miles from the centre of Bristol.

The plan was as blunt as it was simple. Kofi had a small armoury in the boot of his jeep. Kofi, Col, Jed and she would go in quickly, quietly and kill as many of them as they could.

"Drive them out," Kofi stated, chuckling thickly and clenching a fist towards her. "Like rats, like an *infestation*. We drive them out and they don't come back."

Ruby slid her tongue around the inside of her cheek. It caught her by surprise, but she had a craving for Pentathene. Too many weeks living with Kerry Lloyd.

"Listen dude," she leaned in close to him. "I think Dexter will be useful in what's coming next. He's military. Knows how to use a gun. Do you have a problem with that?"

Kofi squeezed out his lower lip and made an indifferent shrug. "I was hoping to break his balls. You know? I thought maybe these problems were because of him. Being feral. Fucking Croat. It's in his blood to lie and cheat. No loyalty. No honour."

"We all have stuff in our blood that history won't let us forget," she said obliquely.

Another indifferent shrug. He agreed to Dexter being part of the assault.

She said she wasn't comfortable about Micky White - McVee – coming along.

"No way leaving the fucking rat here. Too valuable and Jerry will smash my balls with hammer if he gets away. No, he comes with us but we can leave him in jeep."

Ruby didn't feel she had any ground to argue.

The discussion wrapped up quickly from that point. She told him they'd need torches to navigate the tunnels. Apparently there were several torches in the jeep.

In silence, they walked back across the gloomy dance floor towards the others.

Kofi started grunting orders and insults.

"We're heading out. You two, bring Micky to the jeep. Dex, grab a coat. You can keep your gun. You'll need it where we're going. Maybe prove you're less of a Croat then I think you are."

The Skinny Pup snapped a strange look at Dexter. Ruby read it as fear mixed with a warning. Another reason not to like him, and a red light of caution about Dexter. Those two were up to something. So long as it didn't risk crippling the attack on Cray, she didn't care.

THE JEEP WAS just big enough for the six of them. Col, the Rottweiler with the bad goatee beard, was driving. Kofi was beside him, sat at an angle so he could rest an arm behind Col's seat and talk with Ruby. She was in the middle row, next to Dexter. Skinny Pup was in the very back, squeezed in next to the ginger Rottweiler, Jed, who was loading handgun magazines from a box of bullets.

Ruby directed Col out of the city centre onto the A4, heading towards Bath and Wells.

Kofi tapped his fingers on Col's headrest with an endless beat, something playing inside his head. Ruby wondered briefly if it was something he was humming to himself or if the Serbian freelancer was carrying implants. In a way she hoped he was, it would make him more effective in the coming fight.

*If Cray's there...*she felt the first flicker of doubt.

He had to be there. She could 'feel' it, if that was the right term to use to describe the sensation.

Backtrack. Her thought about Kofi carrying cybernetic implants. A memory from Richy's flat, the policemen with their torches failing and stuttering to a dim bulb burn. The way electronic devices seemed to be affected by Cray's aura. Was it something Cray could control? Maybe it was better if Kofi was one-hundred percent organic?

"Kofi," she asked sweetly, "You wouldn't be a target for FABIAN would you?"

An ugly sneer from Kofi, the tapping of his massive fingers stopped, "You think I'm a machine, huh?"

"Merely a question, dude. Curious is all I am." She kept her tone light. The trick worked. Kofi's sullenness eased a little; fingers started tapping again.

"I don't like surgery."

It was a good enough answer for her. She shifted the angle of her head and stared off into the passing blur of rain-soaked streets. The weather had eased up a little but was still spitting. The clouds were low, oppressively dense and a uniform grey, filtering the daylight down to a nocturnal gloom. Traffic was heavy and slow moving. Her eye snagged on an advert recruiting colonists: high-def animation of New Tokyo going through a sunset she knew was more fantasy that fiction, holographic overlays showed the now familiar toroid shape of the space elevator rising up into the flecks of rain above the ad-shell. Sponsored by Soyar Corporation. The growing orbital colonies weren't going to be governed by national identity or government states; they were already evolving into corporate enclaves. She wondered how people like Kofi would fit into such political environments. A wry smile tugged her broad lips: Kofi would probably become the first space-pirate.

The jeep surged forward on a spurt of acceleration then braked sharply. Blare of vehicle horns. Ruby snapped her attention forward and saw a taxi had cut in front of them and was now blocking two lanes of traffic.

"What's with the manual drive," Dexter muttered, complaining.

"Put a fookin' brick in it," Col retorted angrily, finding Dexter's eyes in the rear mirror.

Kofi chuckled, oblivious to or maybe enjoying the growing tension, then twisted round and patted Dexter's leg.

"*Ko se s nama druzi, postaje mu duzi!*"

Dexter folded his legs the other way, delivered a dry retort, "*Popusis mi kurac.*"

Kofi's features lit up with caustic humour, "*Navucem te na kurac!*" A laugh more like a growl. "What, you some *Derpe*? Do you want some of my *djoka*? Eh? You want to fuck me like *zguza*?"

Dex smeared a shit eating grin across his face.

Kofi swung his eyes to Ruby, winked and twisted back round in his seat.

The jeep surged forward again, steady acceleration that brought them to a decent speed.

"It's not far now," Ruby said to nobody in particular.

Jed tapped her on the shoulder and started passing loaded magazines to her. She began handing them over to Kofi.

"Keep sum for y'self," Jed told her. "Got a nice one for ya in the back, like."

A crude laugh erupted from Col and he hunched forward over the steering wheel.

Ruby didn't feel like smiling. She let her gaze drift beyond the windows as she mechanically passed the remaining magazines to Kofi, who had now started loading a second handgun and was stuffing the mags into his jacket, both guns still in his hands.

Skinny Pup's whiney voice squirted out from the backseat, "You two were always a crap fucking comedy act."

"Shut ya trap y'little cunt," Jed muttered. "Y'wanna get through this, y'behave. Got that?"

If Skinny Pup responded Ruby didn't hear it. She noticed Dexter fidgeting with his fingers. She gave him a sidelong look as the jeep came to a stop at a red light. His eyes were lost behind the thick rims of his DVFrames and the red glare of taillights flooding through the front windshield, but the rigid set of his jaw and slack facial features described a man caught in an internal dilemma.

Better not let me down, dude.

As if he'd heard her thoughts his face snapped round to look at her. His eyes were cold and staring.

"Got enough ammo?" she enquired, her voice not as casual as she'd have liked.

He nodded, patted the side pockets of the jacket he'd gone upstairs to his apartment to fetch. "Grabbed everything."

The jeep sped forwards. She dropped her head a little to catch her bearings through the windshield and a chilly spike of apprehension slid through her guts. Abruptly she felt as if her bowels were going to empty into her knickers.

Fear, dude, just sweet sweet fear.

Up ahead, through the light rain, the blue strobing flash of stationary police lights lit up a length of the road.

"Hey-hey-hey," Kofi complained, pushing his body more upright against the seat whilst lowering his guns as far down as they'd go without letting them out of his hands. "What the fuck is *this*?"

"Relax," she called out with a commanding voice. "It's a minor problem with where we're going. I'd forgotten about it. I'm sorry. There's another way in."

Ruby leaned forward and began giving Col directions to keep driving, and then bear left. There was an old industrial estate, large plots separated by wide lanes.

"We can park up pretty much out of sight," she explained, "There's an access point to the tunnels from there. I should have thought about it earlier."

The jeep cruised past the police cordon. A couple of media vans bristling with antennae and a small crowd of protestors who were gathered under make-shift tarpaulins. It was the ongoing demonstration about the planned rebuilding of the Carthew Tower.

She found an ironic smile trembling the corners of her mouth. They had no idea what they were actually trying to stop.

Yes, dude, and neither do you.

31

McVee was surprised when he saw the pigs and demonstrators, and then he realised the girl was talking about taking them to tunnels below the ruined Carthew Tower. It didn't make any sense. Why would this rival gang from London, who he'd never heard a whiff of, be hiding out there? Unless they were cocky bastards who liked the idea of being camped out beneath the bacon snouts?

He shoved himself deep into the cramped rear seat, hoping Jed was getting a sore neck squashed in like that. The blunt point of Jed's elbow dug into him a little, a silent boundary squabble over the limited space; McVee ignored the physical dig and settled his eyes on the route.

The jeep cruised past the crowd camped outside Arnos Vale and swept through the lights at the Moon-Burger franchise on the corner of Brislington junction, taking a left, heading towards the east of the city. He listened to the black girl giving directions and realised he didn't know the area she was taking them; but Bristol was full of confusing urban cavities that could ambush the casual wanderer.

He was going to miss the place, he realised. Whatever happened next, he wouldn't be able to stay in Bristol. Not just because of his dad and the thugs he'd keep sending after him. But because of Nicky and Spad and their bloody guts spattered over the walls of his memory. Maybe he was getting soft as shit in his 'old' age but things like that, like regret, were starting to grate against his normal *fuck-the-world-and-who-you-hurt* attitude.

Or maybe he was just thinking like a fucking retard right now 'cos he was scared. Really scared.

He had Kofi pegged as the kind of psychopath who made causing pain a personal pastime. It was written in the dead stare of his dark, stony eyes. Mundane life held no passion for somebody like him. Kofi probably got his kicks through the niche perks of his trade.

Mental flash and flicker of savage and sadistic scenarios, drawn from the gang beatings he'd been party to in Manchester and from violent films and sim-stims he'd grown up with.

Kofi wasn't going to flinch when he started screaming.

This whole business, sitting in the jeep, hands free and carefree, like he was along for the ride, it was a sick prelude to the moment the violence started.

McVee's guts shifted, his chest tightened, his breathing changed.

Fuck this. I'm not going to die like that. If I'm going down, I'm going down punching with my last breath.

His gaze shifted focus from the blurry view of the road ahead to the back of Dex's head; dark, short and messy hair rubbed with styling wax, but greasy, flat in places and in much need of a touch up. Had Nicky run her fingers through that hair? The fear that had been straining through his features melted away in the heat of resurgent rage. A hot flush of blood rushed to his cheeks and a sickly sweat pumped out through his palms and around the collar of his army-surplus T-shirt.

Dex had a gun. Dex was on the other side of the fucking fence with a free-pass.

Cunt. No way I'm letting you get out of this without me.

A jarring impact as the jeep bounced over a pothole knocked his attention back to the outside world, and brought several muttered complaints from Kofi, Jed and then Col. The mood had become abruptly sombre, perhaps in response to the way the girl was hunched forward in her seat, peering intensely through all of the windows in turn, quietly giving directions.

They were rolling through a half-derelict industrial estate. Large metal-sided structures locked away behind old brick walls propped up between sections of pre-fab wood panelling, topped with rusted razor wire; big steel ventilation stacks and a jungle of weeds and creeping vines. Everything dripping wet with water. Big fuck-off puddles in the road.

The sky was weird. Low clouds appeared to be churning slowly, like in a spiral, faint traces of sunlight from high above glittering on a few edges. A haze of moisture held up by thermals, stained the colour of weak piss by the feeble light and threatening to fall as rain.

In fact, the atmosphere was distinctly odd. And it wasn't just him. He could see it in the way each person inside the jeep was rigidly holding on now, not breathing, eyes scraping every line and angle of sight.

They'd taken several turns along disused roads within the sprawling estate, so it struck him that Bristol, as a thriving city, was now remote and far away. Again, he tried to get his bearings. He guessed they were heading back towards Temple Meads.

"There, on the right," the girl pointed, "The chain-link fence. There's a gate."

The jeep slowed further, swung to the other side of the road and came to a stop in front of a narrow section of wire-mesh that had stuff like ivy growing through it.

An eye blink pause. Everyone looked.

"Locks have been cut," Kofi stated. A glance at Col. "Probably nose us through it."

Col nodded, peering left and right whilst leaning over the wheel, a little uncertain, then eased the jeep forward. Sure enough, the gate cranked open with a muffled rattle of mesh against the bodywork.

"Keep your eyes open," the girl suggested. "They're definitely here."

Col settled back into the driver seat and kept the jeep moving.

Beyond the gate, the road pushed between the brick walls of two aged industrial units; all the windows were sealed with rusting metal shutters; the signage illegible beneath moss and from decades of weathering.

The road dropped down to the right, sharply, following a natural ridge in the landscape that brought the jeep sweeping down and round onto a small flat area of wasteland next to the sluggish brown waters of a canal.

The jeep stopped. There was nowhere else to go but back up the way they'd come. Framing the wasteland where it wasn't hemmed in by the bank of the canal, was a blunt and ruddy-coloured cliff face, some thirty metres high. One of the industrial units was sitting flush to the cliff's edge above.

"There's a door over there." The girl began getting her things ready to leave.

190

The unlikely doorway was a dark aperture, set into the bottom of the cliff with a stone lintel that looked like it belonged to some Victorian factory.

"We're like fookin' sittin' ducks here." Col protested.

"No," the girl responded easily. "They'll not be expecting us to come in this way. And the tower is a good mile away through the tunnels."

"I don't like the way you make assumptions," Kofi said tersely without looking back at her, instead his head was bobbing this way and that as he methodically scanned sight-lines. "Jed, you stay here with our rat."

"Aye, will do." Jed confirmed and tossed McVee a smug look. McVee didn't look back at the ginger cunt. Instead he lowered his head to peer out through the misted window next to him and get a better view of what lay beyond the canal. A pellet of anticipation dropped into his guts and fizzed. He recognised where he was: they were amazingly close to Temple Meads train station. Bizarre if you thought how valuable land so close a major transit point must be worth. The canal was like a boundary between a modern, over-developed terrain, and this bleak, forgotten, abandoned throwback to a dead industrial era. He was able to orient his position from the tall, modern office buildings that crowded the skyline across the water.

"Everyone else. Out." Kofi rumbled, then popped open the passenger-side door and eased himself out, a gun in each hand. A quick look back inside. "Col, open up the boot and give the lady a gun."

The girl shoved her door open, reached over and scooped up a lumpy dark-coloured satchel. She gave him a look that was hostile and telegraphed immediate dislike. He realised then that she wasn't on his side.

The girl climbed out, slammed the door shut and strode around to the rear; joined by Col who bailed out of the driver side with quick, military punctuality.

The smell of rain mixed with an odour like burnt diesel swirled into the back of the jeep, followed by a cold blast of air as the rear hatch was opened.

Muttered conversations between Col and the girl. She knew stuff about guns. McVee picked out the fact all the weapons shared the same ammunition and magazine type.

Dex hadn't moved from where he was sat. His head was bowed slightly and McVee knew he was holding a gun on his lap. The pellet in his guts fizzed a little harder.

Jed had picked up on Dex's hesitation but possibly misread the vibe.

"Ya farkin' cannit get owt a'this one, eh?"

Dex rocked his head back and forth a couple times, like he was weighing up a decision, then abruptly pushed open his door, jumped down and slammed it shut.

"Soft as farkin' shite." Jed sneered, his attention rooted on some indeterminate point ahead.

Don't forget to come back for me now.

Then McVee heard Kofi's accent through the open hatch. "You want a better piece?"

"No." Dex responded flatly, quietly. "I'm good. Let's do this, yeah?"

A moment later the rear hatch banged down. McVee slid his gaze sideways to look past Jed who was now leant forwards, gawking out the side window as the others crossed the wet, hard-packed earth towards the cliff. His gaze percolated down to Jed's hands. Clutching a loaded magazine but no gun. McVee suspected the ideal moment would be to wait until the others were out of sight, until he was sure they wouldn't come back because one of them had forgotten something. But this moment was also good...

The blood in his veins turned to ice water. His mouth became instantly dry.

McVee brought his elbow up and out in a slashing arc, striking Jed on the temple. Jed gasped in shock then roared with rage, twisting in the seat, one hand plunging into McVee's chest to grab his T-shirt, the other hand jabbing at him repeatedly, the loaded magazine turned into a blunt striking weapon.

But Jed was reeling from the surprise blow. His focus was out. His eyes bulging and glassy.

McVee rose up using Jed's iron grip and rigid arm like a support, pressing himself up and back against the close confines of the jeep's interior; wedging himself in place McVee pummelled at the soft tissue of Jed's eyes and the spongy cartilage of his nose with bony knuckles hardened from years of bloodthirsty scrapping. McVee knew he couldn't risk getting into a grapple with Jed. The man's larger size and strength in the cramped space of the jeep would quickly overwhelm him. McVee rained blow after blow into Jed's face. Jed was screaming, lashing wildly; his fist struck the roof, the magazine clattered from his grip.

McVee was relentless. He knew how to exploit any advantage in the disparity between size, bulk and muscle against his lean frame.

Jed's eyes were now screwed tightly shut. Blood was flowing freely from the crushing damage to his nose.

McVee punched him again and again. He felt the strength of Jed's grip on his T-shirt weaken. McVee got into a better position, brought more force behind each blow.

Jed was yelling at him, incomprehensible swearing, a high pitch tone of panic seeping into the voice.

McVee was grinning like he was dancing.

Jed slumped forward, hands scrabbling to protect his head. For a few more frenzied seconds McVee continued to drive punches into any opening. Then Jed's hands fell away and he collapsed against the door, mouth slack, eyes closed. He wasn't pretending. And he wasn't dead. He'd gone into shock but was still breathing.

McVee reeled back, sucking in air loudly through his nose, mouth twisted in a manic curl of victory. Sweat was trickling down his skin which felt hot and tight.

A quick glance outside. No sign of the others. They'd vanished. Probably through the doorway in the cliff.

McVee wiped the back of his hand across his mouth and grimaced as he tasted blood. He wasn't sure if it was Jed's or his from the raw wounds to his wrists.

Jed moaned.

Finish it, mate.

He grabbed the seatbelt hanging down beside Jed's vulnerable figure. Looped it around Jed's neck, clambered up, so he was more or less crouching on the seat with his knees pressing down on Jed's arm, shoulder and chest, then started to strain on the belt.

Jed's legs began to kick, his body rocked and bucked, but the man was fucked from the injuries to his head. The fight was out of him. McVee pulled tight until Jed's struggles faded into a sickly trembling, and then his whole body went limp. Jed stopped breathing.

"Stupid cunt." McVee derided. He pushed himself backwards, away from the body. Mind racing, he was already following a rudimentary plan.

Behind the rear seats was a narrow parcel shelf. He worked out how to remove it and pulled it aside; frequent glances through the windows, which were steaming up, towards the cliff.

Inside the boot was like a treasure trove. A heavy-duty carbo-plastic carrying case, left open, filled with grey foam and cut outs where several weapons and a stack of magazines had been removed. Half a dozen other guns were still there, along with a deep recess packed with boxes of bullets.

Taped to the inside of the lid was a hydrogel pocket, typically used by tourists for carrying important documents and the like.

He leaned over the rear-seats to reach down and rummage inside. Came out with a handful of cashcards. A frown carved his forehead whilst a manic smile began to curve his lips. He selected one of the thin rectangular slices and thumbed the command button. The carshcard lit up between his fingers, one part of the display showing the amount current stored.

"Holy fucking Jesus Christ, I am a bad man."

And he laughed.

He checked some of the other cards. All were loaded with cash. Anonymous, non-traceable cash. Kofi's slush fund for dirty tricks? Payments gathered from dealers by Jed and Col? Who gave a shit.

McVee began stuffing the cashcards into the pockets of his baggy nylon cargo pants.

"Fuck, yeah..."

Chuckling like a chimpanzee, giddy with delight, he kissed several of the cashcards.

"Portugal. Load up the red wine. Here I come."

32

Dex hung back a few paces as Ruby, Kofi and Col trudged ahead of him towards the uninviting aperture set into the cliff. The Vortek was clenched purposefully in his fist.

Ruby had barely said a word to him since Kofi had walked into the club. Her aloofness had him feeling a little unsettled; certainly not confident of his position within the current dynamic.

He didn't trust Kofi, and the simple reason was this: when he'd offered Dex another gun from the jeep, it was a Subusu Rapid, a 9mm with a range of magazine types, including extended ones, which suited the weapon's three-round-burst to full-auto setting.

Kofi was carrying one alongside the massive Boris flechette pistol. So was Ruby and Col. Dex knew the weapon from countless operations when they'd been used for hitting targets fast and hard. The one Kofi had offered him was different. The red safety dot was on the wrong side of the lever, which suggested it was a Subusu imitation, maybe even a basic replica. The question was, why offer it to him?

Twisting at the waist he stole a look behind him and saw the ginger arsehole, Jed, grinning at him like a bloody retard from the partially misted rear of the jeep. McVee was a vague shadow beyond.

Part of his brain yelled at him to stop walking but his legs didn't obey and kept him moving woodenly forwards.

What was he going to do about McVee?

The easiest thing would be to dart back now and just shoot the guy dead. But Jed might try and stop him, and he was sure Kofi had plans for McVee that the Serb wouldn't appreciate being spoiled.

The alternative was to try and spring McVee but that was like killing a lion to save a snake. McVee had issues and if allowed to live, he was going to be a problem one way or another.

Dex peered up at the sky as if an answer might be waiting for him there. Cold specks of rain bounced off his cheeks. At least all the bandaging and tape on his forehead was keeping him warm. And he was wearing the warm cotton jacket Tarjuan had acquired for the London gig. Dex thought it was ironically appropriate that he should be wearing it now.

Killing Cray - *Attempt number two.*

The sealed pockets also held two stutter-flash grenades and a handful of tracking beads. They might come in useful for something.

The weather was strange. He'd never seen cloud formations like this before. It was if some presence was causing them to coagulate together in a swirling pattern like clotted clumps of dirty grey stuff, tinged with weak rays of sunlight.

A portent of what was to come?

It just reinforced the bad vibe he had about being here. Not that he had much choice with Kofi and Ruby working together like they were. Ruby hadn't threatened him out loud, but in some intangible way, he felt as though she had him over a barrel. He couldn't just walk away as he wanted. And Kofi was just a crude machine running a basic programme. No parameters for negotiation.

It just like being in the military. There was a ton of places he didn't' want to go and stuff he didn't want to do, but you just gritted your teeth, grazed up alongside your training and conditioning and got on with it.

But this was different. The idea of confronting Cray again injected a heart-swelling pulse of primal terror into his veins and made him feel sick with fear, so he just didn't think about it. Focus on the *getting there* rather than freaking out about what they were going to find at the other end; that was the trick he was using.

Hopefully it would be quick. Find Cray and his cohorts. Shoot the bastards until they stopped moving.

Get out. Go home. Drink a whisky or five. Plan what he was going to do next.

Kofi wasn't finished with him, that was for sure. Dex didn't have the money to pay what he owed Jerry.

So...

Tough times ahead, either way it went.

I wonder if Tonga's got good weather this time of year.

He reached the doorway set into the cliff a few moments after the others. They'd taken two torches from the boot of the jeep. Ruby had one, Col had the other. Switching them on, powerful beams criss-crossed as they probed the dank darkness of the rock-walled chamber beyond.

The entrance was normally barred by a metal gate formed of heavy-metal rods, almost orange now with rust. The lock had been smashed out. As she moved in, Ruby was staring at the damage as if to say: they're definitely here.

Weapon up, he followed them inside.

The air was depressingly cold and damp, loaded with smells that brought to mind images of unhealthy fungus, hidden in dark niches, glistening wet and reflecting the torch light.

Beyond the doorway was a small chamber; it had probably been enlarged by hand tools from a natural passageway in some forgotten era of history. The chamber led seamlessly into a tall but narrow fissure of rock that formed a tunnel burrowing deep through the base of the cliff.

He knew Bristol was riddled with tunnels and caves, but he'd never seen anything like this.

Kofi had paused by the opening and gestured with one of his guns for Dex to carry on ahead. Dex gave him a look that said – yeah, *thanks* – but thought better of causing an argument about it. Ruby got the good news next.

He glanced at her as she stepped beside him into the cramped channel of rock, her eyes were wide and fixed dead ahead. It was as if she was barely aware of his presence. Cloaked in shadow her features were rigid with tension. He didn't say anything. It wasn't appropriate.

The beam of her torch was pointing at a downward angle to reduce the signature of their approach. Anybody on stag was going to see them coming, for sure, but there was no low-light imaging technology and no other options other than groping blindly in the dark.

He made a silent prayer that Cray hadn't brought along firearms; it wouldn't be hard for anybody with a ranged-weapon and even the crappiest aim to start picking them off inside here.

Fish in a barrel.

They moved further in as Kofi and Col stepped in behind them. Col's torch light was equally subdued, and Dex suspected he'd be reversing his angle every few steps to keep their rear covered. Going at a steady but cautious pace they walked deeper into the fissure.

Did this really go on for a mile? He didn't consider himself claustrophobic but this was bloody intense. He was more scared than he thought he'd be.

At least he was with people who knew how to handle themselves.

Yeah pal and Cray didn't do so bad kicking the crap out of a squad of police in assault gear.

Dex shoved the fact to a far corner of his thoughts.

He caught sight of his breath pluming around his mouth.

Bloody hell.

They pressed on, deeper and deeper into the inky darkness, nothing but a bubble of light revealing the irregular walls looming close on either side.

He tried to judge the direction they were heading and their position in relation to the world above. He had a vague notion they were running parallel to the A4, which made sense in the context of where they were ultimately heading.

The Carthew Tower.

Or beneath it.

Words from MacAleavey's journal flared into existence within his mental vision. Strange phrases and hard-to-comprehend accusations. Apparently somewhere down here, beneath the tower, there was a stone chamber with a circular shaft placed in the centre of the floor; like a well, the capstones lining the rim marked in strange symbols. He recalled Ruby expressing her belief they were part of an occult language. What the hell did Mary Carthew find down here? What did MacAleavey eventually come to suspect that was so terrifying he fled Bristol and eventually the country?

Dumb questions.

Right, so keep your eyes and ears peeled, pal, and stick to the programme.

Yes, Sirrrr.

With the Vortek held out ahead of him, his free hand brushed the wall alongside him. It was wet and bitterly cold to the touch.

Keep moving.

Just keep moving.

THE TUNNEL, MAN-CRAFTED, penetrated into a web of natural caverns and connecting fissures. A cold, dark labyrinth, empty of sound and life. Ruby forged ahead, as if guided by some unseen force, which for Dex, was a notion more disturbing than reassuring. Kofi and Col apparently assumed she simply knew the way.

As they moved, the sounds of their anxious breathing echoed alongside the padding footfalls, and the shuffle and scrape of their bodies and clothing.

High-ceilinged in places, there were many other points where they were all forced to stoop as they moved through beneath vast sagging bulges of rock. Reflected torch light bounced off the curved and jagged walls and apertures, exposing areas of rock that looked freakishly organic; many of these seemed to flicker like demoniacal faces, leering at their foolish plunge through the shadows, only to morph into a mass of random shapes if Dex snapped a glance at them.

The darkness.

It conveyed a sense of movement, somehow. Dex knew it was his mind playing tricks; his fear cranked up beyond normal limits because of what he'd experienced in London; but it was as if the shadows were sliding above and around them to congeal into a solid darkness in their wake.

Break free from this lot and you get the upper hand, pal.

Yeah, got to shake free of Kofi first... man is sticking to my back like glue.

The sound started to touch their ears after about ten minutes of steady walking. Distorted by the acoustics of the tunnel, it was hard to describe and impossible to verify its source. The closest Dex came to picturing it was of a low, sonic vibration.

When Ruby heard it she paused long enough to look back at him and pin him with a haunted expression.

Together they knew what Kofi and Jed didn't, an awareness of the true risks lying ahead.

Dex tightened his grip on the Vortex and gritted his teeth against a shudder that ran through his whole body.

They pressed on, flashlights pointed down, the beams truncated to bright circles of light held close to their feet or the lower edges of the narrow, winding burrows.

Dex pictured what must be above their heads. The creative-industrial complex of Paintworks. The houses of

199

lower Totterdown.   The sluggish and clogged stream of traffic oozing out of the city along the A4 towards Brislington.

Eventually they would be beneath graves and an area of rank desolation older than the tower itself.   Arnos Vale cemetery.   He'd been there several times on a whim of ghoulish fancy.   A horseshoe-shaped depression surrounded by high hills cluttered with trees and seriously old headstones, bordered by a dense tangle of residential streets.

Focus, mate. You need to focus.

His attention had drifted.

The sound came back at him more distinct now.   Male voices in a baritone chorus of murmuring, droning, and muttering.

The articulation of those voices caused the hair on his arms and head to stand on end. His nerves tingled.

Was it his imagination or were the torches loosing their brightness?

He stabbed a glance at Ruby but she was suddenly ahead of him now, stooping at a point where the cramped channel emerged into a larger space.   As she went through she swept the beam of her torch up and round, giving him a glimpse of what lay beyond: a cluster of red and white hazard cones, plus some heavy machinery with yellow-painted hulls.   Abruptly, she stepped through, gun following the turn of her head.   The area beyond lit-up with a soft and hazy light in response to her entrance: it was an automated response.   No sounds of panic from Ruby.

The droning of bass voices continued without pause or interruption.

"What's al' the fookin' mumbo jumbo?" Col breathed.

If Kofi replied, Dex didn't hear him.

Dex reached the point where the narrow channel came to an end; he crouched down and stepped through the low aperture, emerging into a long, low-ceilinged cavern which was filled with recent evidence of excavation and restoration work.

Each of the hazard cones had a strip of sodalum wrapped around its midriff, rigged with a motion trigger; the cones demarked an oval area and trailed off through one of the three other tunnels exiting the cavern, the sodalum on these latter cones remaining unlit.

This exit tunnel probably led right to the surface by Arnos Vale, and would be how the workforce were getting in and out.

Quick getaway, Dex noted.

Lots of blue, white and yellow signs stated safety regulations. The machinery was a generator, currently disabled, and a bunch of exoskel-digger gloves lying on the ground and attached to the generator by coils of thick cabling; the dirt-encrusted metal gloves looked liked severed claws from some giant monster. There was a cluster of small quarry droids, parked together and inactive, some of them carrying partial loads of extracted rubble in the rectangular buckets welded to the back of their insect-like bodies.

Kofi and Jed stepped through from the narrow channel in a surly manner, their arrival triggering a few more sodalum-wrapped cones to flare into life.

Dex whispered, by way of an explanation, "I think this is part of the restoration work everyone's protesting about."

Kofi gave him a sour look.

Ruby was silent and motionless, pointing her torch at a part of the chamber wall where it appeared there had once been another tunnel, long-since collapsed. This seemed to be the focus of the heavy work.

Dex studied the area in the glare of Ruby's torch beam: the current project was probably working towards excavating the collapsed material and re-opening the adit.

The droning voices seemed to be multiplying, like echoes overlapping. Dex felt a giddy rush, as if the floor was shifting subtly beneath him, which he knew was impossible; then he moved his head and the edges of his vision swam and swirled.

Something's not right...

Dex saw several bloated flies swirling lazily within the now dimming beam of her torch where it probed the shadow-choked horizontal shaft.

"*Koji ti je kurac?*" Kofi muttered with growing irritation, noticing the fearful wide-eyed expression seeping across Ruby's face.

"The chamber. He's opened it." Was all Ruby said to nobody in particular.

"Where the fuck are they, then? Through there? Come on, let's go." Kofi growled, dismissive of her odd behaviour.

Ruby stepped back, shaking her head.

The sodalum strips, once so bright with luminescence were rapidly fading into a tarnished golden glow. The torches were now dimming significantly. It was as if some immense, invisible force was emerging into the cavern, oozing forth, smothering all light.

"Fookin' crap batteries. Ay only put new ones in last week." Col hissed angrily, staring down into the feeble brown radiance of the torch in his hand.

Kofi nudged past Ruby and marched up to the partially excavated mouth of the collapsed tunnel; he crouched down and tried to peer in, flapped one of the guns in his hand to waft away several of the larges flies that had started to settle on him.

Dex was stationary, his feet rooted to the spot as a nauseating feeling of déjà vu swept through him. His muscles were frozen, his mind shrinking down against an onslaught of recollected visuals and emotional sensations. It was like Richy's place all over again, but infinitely worse.

Eyes. Yellow eyes staring at him from the dark. But not anywhere he could see.

Oh Jesus Christ. He's here.

"Just got fookin' cald in 'ere, d'ya feel that?" Col stated without emotion.

"I can't see anything down there. What is happening to the lights?" Kofi rumbled, pissed-off and frustrated.

Dex saw Ruby's gaze had become glassy with terror; her head was darting around as if catching site of terrors squirming in the swelling shadows.

And then, in a moment of mortifying revelation...

The flies weren't coming from the collapsed tunnel.

They were coming from the overstuffed bag slung over Ruby's back.

A violent shudder of shock went through him then; it was as if he'd been plunged into ice water. His scalp contracted, his chest locked up; he couldn't move, he couldn't breathe.

"-need to get out of here," Dex croaked, but his throat was as dry as sandpaper and nobody seemed to hear him.

Kofi was squinting, his blocky face screwed up in a revolted grimace. "What the fuck is in there-"

Ruby screamed.

A shrill sound of alarm and panic.

She span away, thrashing as if multiple things were attacking her. At the same moment the torches and sodalum strips faded to dull stains of illumination within the overwhelming blackness of the cavern.

Dex began babbling. Words spilling from his lips that barely made sense, even to him. His instincts were shrieking at him to move, to get away, but fear and an overwhelming morbid curiosity held him fixed in place.

In the negligible light, with figures cast more like silhouettes, he saw Kofi lurch to his feet, yelling psychotically, both guns swinging round at the end of extended arms; whilst Ruby continued to twirl and flail her limbs. She was reaching over her shoulder, yanking at the straps, hauling off the bag as if it was scalding her.

Dex realised there was no sound. Just the maddening and incessant booming drone of male voices coming from – *where?*

The world slid sideways. Hot and acidic bile punched up through his gullet and flooded his throat. A buzzing, frenzied needle-stabbing sensation crawled across his flesh.

Kofi's mouth was a black shadow set in planes of brown-painted skin and muscle.

Kofi's eyes were wide and alive.

A sulphurous stench erupted into the cavern.

As if submerged in treacle, Dex turned his head to glance at the shadow-wrapped figure of Col, who was turning round in a tight circle of terror, gun held out, finger welded to the trigger.

Then, slowly swinging his gaze back at Ruby - his pulse surged to a stop.

In the shallow light, he saw her rigidly upright, not moving, staring right back at him with her lips moving soundlessly.

And then he saw the shape, black and formless, rise up beside her. And it kept rising.

His heart swelled to bursting point.

From above, glistening in the faint, smouldering light, an oily black tendril of some incomprehensible matter began to extend downwards towards him.

Another slow pan of his head, and he tracked a mass of oily darkness nightmarishly pouring across the walls, surging across the floor in a boiling wave of madness.

A tendril squirted forward and struck Col like a jet of tar, and kept moving, through an explosive a spray of gore as thing shredded through tissue, muscle and bone. Col had vanished in the blink of an eye. The stink of pulverised intestines washed over him. Dex nearly collapsed as his legs buckled, vomit sprayed from his mouth.

Laughter.

Loud. Insane. Ecstatic. A furious orgy of baying, guttural, sounds.

Cray!

Ruby had said Cray was in the chamber. Was he there with his cohorts? The chanting echoing up through these tunnels? The circular shaft described in MacAleavey's journal. Was Cray making this happen?

Kofi vanished from sight as a block of impenetrable darkness rolled across his lower half, and he tumbled back, eyes-wide in shock, mouth yawning open with a lung-emptying scream.

In some cosmic glimpse of utter delirium, Dex saw the error of Ruby's decision to bring the idol with her. It wasn't Cray making this happen. It was Ruby. She'd played into the hands of her enemy. She'd delivered what Cray wanted and to the very place it was needed.

The Key.

The Gate.

She had activated it.

It wasn't buried here all this time. It was *in* the idol. It was the bloody idol. The idol that Walter Carthew's father had taken from whatever shrine had been built in the base of the tower, before blowing it up.

There was now almost no light whatsoever.

He could just see the white's of Ruby's eyes, her gaze drilling into his with an expression that was lost within the near total darkness.

Darkness surging towards him.

It wouldn't be long now.

To engulf him.

Dex plunged his free hand into one of the pockets of the padded jacket and his vomit-smeared fingers locked around the egg-shaped, heavy weight of the stutter-flash grenade.

He pulled it out. Fingers already sliding over the studs at the top, pressing them down. Still holding the Vortek he brought his hands together. Twisted the bottom of the grenade. Saw a flicker of dull illumination within the rotating seam.

He let it tumble from his hand. Imagined he heard it crack against the hard rock, and then roll.

Screwing shut his eyes he turned his head.

And yelled.

A primal urge.

Light.

Bright.

White.

Painful.

Searing.

Staggered pulses of it, burning through his eyelids.

A feeling of unleashed tension ripping through the muscles of his arms and legs.

Freedom of movement.

He opened his eyes and looked, as several sounds assailed his ears.

Blood-chilling screams from Kofi.

Back of the throat snarling rage from a not-so-distant Cray and his animalistic cohorts.

Then the sodalum panels and the two dropped torches surged dramatically back to full intensity - the oppressive force dispelled by the light? - revealing a horror scene painted in blood, gristle and excrement.

No monstrous shape. Just pools of black ichor spattered across the rock floor, instantly bubbling and steaming as if boiling away. It couldn't stand the light. The light harmed it. Especially the intense burning fury of the grenade.

Most of black stuff was concentrated around the torn remains of Ruby's rubberised bag. There were shreds of the towel he'd used to wrap the idol within. Flakes of old paper lay like confetti; MacAleavey's journal and the hardcopy notes reduced to countless fragments.

Ruby was sprawled across the floor, a tumble of limbs, twitching from the disruptive effects of the grenade. Otherwise unharmed, so it seemed.

Kofi had been unaffected by the grenade. Either an optical-nerve defect or the Serb was carrying military grade blast-shielding bioware.

His eyes clawed onto Dex, wide and pleading, manic with pain and fear. Dex stared back, the impulse to flee stunted by the grisly sight.

Kofi lay on his back in the entrance to the partially-excavated tunnel, the rock walls behind him speckled in a dripping aftermath of a jettison of blood. A shiny slick of blood was steadily expanding across the filthy ground from the ruptured remains of his legs and lower torso, a mangled mess of torn meat and splintered bone. The Serb was straining his big arms and slithering in it. Pieces of skin were sticking to his fingers like some red-stained mince mix he'd plunged his hands into. Kofi had managed to get his head upright, pressed up against the rock surface behind him at a strange angle; his mouth was a trembling chasm – Dex could see the whitish yellow tongue – and the shrieking came in helpless waves.

Dex lurched away, controlling his guts, looking around, grabbing command of his senses.

There was nothing left of Col.

Ruby's eyes were partially open but vacant. Drool was sliding from her lips. She was a mess.

It was going to be a while before she started to properly come around. He knew what it would feel like. Getting her out of here was going to be tough. He moved towards her, crouching down.

The torch light and sodalum began to diminish.

"What the-"

Dex began to take cautious backward steps, his eyes swivelling between the remains of the rubberised bag and the partially-excavated opening.

Kofi's shrieks became hysterical with fright. Dex realised the Serb's sanity was as shattered as his body.

Instinctively, he pulled out the final stutter-flash grenade from the other pocket. Trembling uncontrollably, his fingers found the two studs at the top and pressed down. He kept the Vortek held out and pointing towards the opening.

Then he saw what had set Kofi off.

From the inside torn flaps of the bag numerous threads of what looked like glossy black hair were wriggling across the stone floor. With sickening dismay Dex saw the threads proceed to rapidly multiply, thicken and elongate further. An abrasive slithering sound accompanied their movement, suggestive of ground glass against stone.

The lights were now fading fast.

Grab the bag, run the hell away here with it and stop all this...

Like hell, pal. Go! Get out of here now whilst you can.

Run!

Now!

Dex stepped forward, towards Ruby, desperately trying to decide how to lift her up whilst holding onto the Vortek and the grenade.

"I SEE YOU."

Cray's distorted voice barked out from the partially-excavated tunnel.

Dex snapped a glance towards the entrance but saw nothing other than Kofi slumped there.

The floor around the bag was now infested with black tendrils, which continued to disgorge from inside, thrashing, wriggling, whipping back and forwards. He saw how they ripped the rubberised material as their oily-tar surface brushed past. He saw how a growing number of them were groping towards him, now rising up from the floor and coming together as one murderous tentacle.

The cavern was nearly in total darkness now.

Cray roared with laughter.

Dex pulled the trigger several times. The Vortek kicked in his hand. Muzzle flash. He fired the bullets into the mouth of the collapsed tunnel: hoping to hit Cray or at least keep him suppressed. Then he rapidly backed away from the seething, shuddering, amorphous mass of bubbling tar looming up towards the ceiling, towering over him, clotting together into pulsating knots that began to elongate downwards. It made a composite sound like stretching leather and a horrible plastic popping.

Blind terror gripped him then.

Twisting the base of the grenade, he tossed it towards the excavated opening then turned and ran.

Ran for his life.

He barrelled into the exit tunnel used by the workers. The enraged snarls of Cray and God knew what else leaping after him.

An expanding line of sodalum strips began to fizzle into weak luminescence as he hurtled past, showing him the way.

Time seemed to freeze.

He was sprinting, lungs working, leg muscles pumping, arms slicing the air by his side, Vortek gripped more like a baton than a weapon.

And yet it was as if he wasn't moving.

He was racing through an infinite void whilst Death boiled up behind him.

Then the lightening flash of the grenade spattering the walls of the tunnel in the distance.

And an absolute silence descended. Broken only by the scuff of his shoes on rock and his desperate breathing.

The sodalum wrapped around the hazard cones flared up to full brightness, filling the void with their pale misty light.

After less than a minute he reached the end of the tunnel at the foot of a maintenance ladder.

With limbs trembling like jelly, shoes slipping on the rungs and peddling the air, he clambered up and emerged through a stone-flagged floor, gasping and gibbering, sucking in cool unpolluted air, into the cold embrace of a crypt.

Oh, no-no-no...

For a moment he panicked, thinking his exit was blocked, doomed to return down the ladder and into the nightmare tunnels.

But the crypt door had been only pushed too, a metal wedge keeping it from closing entirely. No doubt by the workers for safety or convenience.

He pressed his shoulder against the door and slow-barged it open.

Stepped out into an amber glow. The sky was a surreal conglomeration of churning dark clouds and golden afternoon sunlight. Drifting down in shifting layers was a fine rain. Sparkling in the visible light.

A gravel path led from the crypt, past a stack of unused hazard cones and heavy-duty crates, and met an asphalted thoroughfare; this swept down the slope through dense forest towards the main gates.

Not good. Police and protesters down there.

Dex loped away from the crypt and headed up the hill. There was a wall at the top that backed onto residential gardens. That would be his way out.

Jed and McVee were a mile away, at least, and Dex doubted he'd be able to find where the jeep was parked with any ease.

Besides, why did it matter?

A strained sob escaped from his throat. His lungs heaved but he got it under control. He used his hand to smear away snot and tears as he half-trudged, half-ran up the hill. Complex emotions bubbled through his chest. Foremost was the sense of overwhelming relief.

He was free now.

He was out.

33

Dex Raškovic strode as fast as he could without looking like he had something to hide. Bristol was bristling with rush-hour traffic and crowds of people strolling briskly through the light rain. On their way home for a Monday night in, or heading off to meet friends or loved ones after work. He didn't care. It was a state of normality that was alien and stupefying mundane when considered in the context of what he'd just experienced.

He was just glad for the anonymity the crowds afforded him as he concluded his brain-dazed, sometimes stumbling, walk from Arnos Vale, past Temple Meads towards the city centre and the Strontium club.

The Vortek was stuffed into the belt at the back of his black, mud-stained jeans, covered by the warm tails of his jacket.

It would be another three hours, at least, before any staff started to arrive to open the club.

He had time to clean up, get his things in order and prepare to eject.

Dex slowed and turned off the main street into a wide lane, picked up the pace again.

Squirming in the pit of his stomach was an inescapable feeling of despair and morbid guilt towards the fate of Ruby Torres.

What would Cray do with her? Back at Richy's place Cray had said she was his blood. What did that mean? Was Cray the descendant of William Cannel? Cannel, the man who used to be Walter Carthew before fleeing to London...

Cray had survived below ground. Feeding from cadavers that his cohorts probably dragged out of graves, tunnelling beneath them, selling the jewellery - and undoubtedly partly responsible for the dozens of people that went missing in the capital every year.

What would happen to Ruby?

He closed down the line of thought and told himself, feebly, that he didn't care.

He focussed on the logical order of objectives ahead of him. Get back to the club. Wash the filth and stench from his skin. Change his clothes. Pack and leave.

Yet again he had an uncertain future, but there was the three kilos of twister locked in his safe. That was a ticket to somewhere. Duke, in Tonga? Maybe.

The wide lane brought Dex back onto another main road. He strode on like a pellet of oil fired through the rainwater. He kept his hands within the pockets of the jacket, hugging the warm material to his body as if it was armour protection, not just something to keep the shitty weather out. The spirit of Ricardo Tarjuan lived in the jacket. That's how he saw it. The jacket was his saving piece of Grace.

He stepped off the road through a metal archway into St Nicholas Market. The labyrinth of small carbo-plastic stalls, contained within the historical stone walled building, had a trickle of people moving through it, avoiding the rain. All the stalls were closed.

Reaching the doorway of the Strontium club he was confronted by mixed emotions.

He paused, suddenly uncertain if he should go back in. It was part of another life that now no longer seemed to be his. Perhaps he should just vanish. Ring Duke. Call in a favour.

A grimace carved his face. Duke was a pal but he wasn't loaded enough to get Dex over there and settled. Not in the way Dex needed.

The gene-twister will....

He saw the shadow slide behind him a moment before he felt the cold, hard jab of a gun-barrel press into the back of his neck, just below the skull.

"Hello Dex, mate."

It was McVee. Micky White. He was almost slumped over Dex's back, using an arm placed across his shoulders to hide the gun being held there.

Dex began to turn but McVee drove the end of the barrel further into the rigid muscles of his neck and made a – *uh-uh* – sound.

"Just you make it out, eh?" McVee asked rapidly, his voice a jangle of nerves. Dex got the impression he was anxious about being seen with the gun. "Eh? What's up? Cat got your tongue? Come on mate, open the fucking door. We've got some catching up to do."

It dawned on Dex, then, that McVee had no idea of what had taken place within the tunnels below Arnos Vale.

"Where's Jed?" Dex asked, calmly.

"Fucker's dead, right. Too slow and too stupid. Now open the door."

"You kill him?"

"Yeah. And I'll be popping a bullet through your fucking brain if you don't open the door now."

Dex tensed his body. "That's not going to happen, Micky."

"Don't think I won't do it, cunt."

"I'm not letting you in. And if you kill me here you'll never get your hands on the twister."

That brought a sick little chuckle out of McVee's mouth. Dex felt the man's breath on the side of his cheek. Smelled garlic and coffee.

"Fuck your twister mate. I scored massive. That Serbian cunt had a cash stash in the jeep. Fucking hundred grand at least. Mate, it was there for the taking. Could not fucking believe it."

McVee was gloating. Dex got the subtext: McVee was sorted, *he* was screwed.

Dex tuned into his immediate environment and the lane. The sound of rain splashing down from a blocked gutter a few paces away. But the absence of conversations or of footsteps. They were alone for the moment. "You took a risk, coming back here."

"Nah mate. I know how to watch this place without being seen. Open the fucking door, right *fucking* now."

Dex released the coiled tension with a rear-slicing jab of his elbow, at the same time twisting his shoulders and dropping into a crouch.

His elbow connected with McVee somewhere firm, and he heard the satisfying grunt and gasp.

But McVee was fast, and seemed to be capable of absorbing blunt damage and pain.

As Dex rotated, the side of McVee's fist slammed into his already bruised face, bringing starbursts into his vision, and leaving him stunned.

Dex plunged forward to grab him.

A stream of hateful swearing accompanied a rapid flurry of blows from McVee that drove Dex backwards against the entrance to the club, barely standing, legs arched and straining to keep him off the floor.

The barrage ceased, and Dex's vision cleared as he blinked, head reeling on the end of his neck. His hands were behind him where he'd instinctively reached to break his backwards tumble.

McVee was standing upright, legs splayed, one arm outstretched ending in a fist curled around the grip of a Subusu Rapid Shot. He was dressed in the same baggy cargo pants and the olive drab army T-shirt, now soaked through and darkened by the rain, exaggerating the paleness of his skin. The lack of jacket made him look incongruously out of place, and skinny. His bloodless, narrow face was creased with a mocking sneer.

Dex's forehead throbbed where the bandaged areas had taken a battering. He stared into the eyes of McVee and saw the intent crystallise in the same moment McVee's finger tightened around the trigger.

"Bye cunt."

- *Click* -

Nothing happened.

A microscopic tilt of the head, Dex locked his eyes onto the erroneous position of the red dot on the safety lever.

Furious frown on McVee's face. His hands flapping around the gun as his finger yanked repeatedly on the powerless trigger.

Dex reached beneath his jacket. Hauled out the Vortek. Pushed himself upright with his legs as he brought the gun round and up.

One shot did it.

The gun went off like a hammer striking hollow wood.

McVee jerked with the shock and collapsed onto his knees, blood blossoming from the wound to his centre-mass. The Subusu fell from his fingers and clattered to the cobblestoned ground. Hands clutching for the edge of the doorway, McVee tried to steady himself but could only slump, backwards and then sideways, leaving a streak of blood on the whitewashed walls. His gaze glued itself onto Dex as the life faded out of them.

Not waiting for a rush of witnesses, Dex shoved the gun into one of the jacket's deep pockets, pushed himself away from the doorway and went to grab the back of McVee's collar.

His intention was to drag the body inside, then dump it down in the cellar somewhere, hopefully out of sight until he was long gone from Bristol. He'd need to erase the CCTV footage of the doorway...

A polite cough and clearing of throat caused him to freeze mid-stride, with a fistful of rain-soaked T-shirt clenched in his fist.

Dex snapped a glance behind him and saw the old hatchet-faced bloke he'd seen meeting Ruby Torres outside the police station earlier that morning. Dressed in the same incredibly snug and warm looking, dark lambs wool coat. Beside him, in an equally impressive coat, yet portraying a far more serious and corporate image was a younger, shorter man with neat dark hair and Mediterranean features.

Oddly, hovering a dozen paces further back were two burly men in suits. Professional crowd control. Not bouncers. Dex recognised the build and the body stance and arrogant confidence born of local laws broken with indifference and immunity.

Corporate mercs.

Dex released his grip on McVee and straightened, slowly. Letting everyone see his hands were empty. A casual glance in the opposite direction revealed several more suited mercs stepping into the narrow lane.

Keeping things discreet. Nobody was going to see what had happened here unless Hatchet-Face and his friend wanted it to be so.

"Hello Dexter." This from Hatchet-Face. Almost friendly. A quick nod at the body by Dex's feet. "Cleaning up loose ends I see."

"It was self defence." Dex replied deadpan.

A crafty smirk stretched old lips. "Yeah. That fake piece was really a threat worth killing him for."

Dex eased out a shrug; took a moment to eyeball the Mediterranean who was observing with the detached calm of somebody used to making life and death decisions. Dex intuitively sensed the next few moments, and how this man perceived them, were going to be important for his future.

"Look, I'll keep this simple." Hatchet-Face told him. "Where's Ruby?"

Dex felt his heart-sink.

He must have telegraphed the bad news because Hatchet-Face went through a flux of emotions, which were then quickly and brutally suppressed. A blunt nod towards the club's entrance. "Come on then. Let's do this inside."

PHYSICALLY AND MENTALY exhausted, Dex wasn't in any state to bullshit them so told it straight. Ruby, it transpired after a few muttered words from Hatchet Face, had been under surveillance; but she had given her guardians the slip before coming to meet Dex at the club.

The only thing Dex edited from the account of what had happened in the tunnels was the existence of the...creature.

Dex used suitably vague descriptions of a foul smelling gas, of a feeling of acute unease and a sense that some terrible was lurking down there. But he didn't reveal what he actually saw.

Whilst he talked he went about his business, unhindered by the three stocky and broad shouldered mercs in their tight, expensive suits.

It was already getting dark and his instincts were tweaking with a growing urge to get away from the club, and the city of Bristol as soon as humanly possible.

Whatever he'd left below the tower wasn't going to remain down there for long after the sun went down.

He patted down McVee's corpse – the mercs had dragged it inside - and extracted a stack of cashcards, loaded with large sums of money. He went up to his apartment, dutifully followed by Hatchet Face, his silent Mediterranean companion and one of the mercs. In the apartment he freshened up, slipped on clean clothes, took the gene-twister from the safe.

They asked questions. He did his best to give them answers that stuck to the truth.

They didn't challenge his version of events.

They didn't try to restrict his movements.

Dex got the picture. They were interested in information, not exacting some kind of vengeance.

Finally, clutching a satchel crammed with the few items he considered to be of value, it was time to wrap up.

Hatchet-Face indicated he agreed it was the right moment for them to part company.

"We'll take care of the body and clear up loose ends."

Dex stared at him. "You can do that?"

"My associate here," Hatchet Face indicated the silent Mediterranean, "Is responsible for security of the Carthew family. He can make a lot of things happen, to keep things quiet. You understand my meaning here?"

Yeah, keep your mouth shut about Ruby or you'll find somebody shutting it for you, permanently.

Dex nodded, a sober expression settling on his face. "What happened today stays with me. You don't need to threaten me."

Hatchet-Face raised his hands, palms open, fingers splayed; a peaceful gesture. "That wasn't my intention. Just saying it how it is, son."

Dex conceded the subtle apology with a simple nod. Then he turned and faced the silent Mediterranean. "Look. Whatever the family thought about Richard Carthew's obsession with the secrets of the past. Forget their prejudices and ignorant lies. They don't know what Ruby...knew. There is something down there. Below the tower. Something the Carthew family needs to... deal with, I guess."

"What would you suggest, Dexter?" They were the first words Dex had heard the guy speak. The question was framed in a polite facial expression. His voice was rich like some fancy polished wood, deep, cultured, and very French.

Dex shook his head. "Well, you can't blow up the tower. The Carthew's did that already. Stop them rebuilding it. Call it an issue of family security."

The Frenchman stepped forward with an easy smile, and extended a firm but manicured hand. "Thank you. I will see what I can do."

Dex shook it and let go, hefted the satchel over his shoulder. He gave the place one final glance over. "Well, good luck."

"Where will you go?" The Frenchman asked with seemingly genuine interest.

In his minds-eye, Dex was already speed-dialling his former-army buddy Duke, and arranging a flight to Tonga. He'd be giving the Royal Protection squad a miss; no need: rather there was the idea of a new bar opening up to play with. He wanted to grin broadly but held it in check. Externally, Dex smiled sadly, "I don't know. Cities give me the spooks now. Just away from here."

- THE END -

ALSO AVAILABLE BY DAVID J RODGER:

God Seed

For acclaimed documentary film-maker, Adam Kyle, this was going to be another feather in his cap. Embedded within a team of highly-trained corporate mercenaries, he was covering the start of an operation in England. But when the operation goes terribly wrong, Kyle finds himself battling for his life, his sanity, and maybe even his very soul as a new and dramatic story unfolds, dragging him across the globe...and beyond. It isn't just his documentary that is at stake, but the fate of every living thing in the Universe.

David J Rodger delivers a gut-wrenching and epic journey in a novel that plunges deep into the crawling chaos and takes you to the edge of the membrane of human existence

Iron Man Project

Former special-forces operative, Vincent Brent, is tough, ruthless and highly trained. Now he's using his skills for whoever will pay him without cashing in the bounty on his head. In this world of the near future, the UN has failed. Wars are fought in boardrooms through attorneys and politics, and on our streets with private armies of military and criminal assets. In Sicily, Jean-Luc Korda, Chief of Security for a powerful corporate alliance wields one such army - a potent mercenary force - in the fight against kidnap, extortion, blackmail and sabotage. But unseen enemies plot to use his position against him. In England a young woman must die. Her life, or death, will decide the fate of both men. In the cross-hairs of powerful adversaries, Korda and Brent must both make decisions in a choice between command and conscience.

David J Rodger delivers a palm-sweating ride in a compelling novel that will keep you turning pages until the brutal end.

Dante's Fool

Detective Sergeant Louis Cloud is a tough London cop hungry for power and promotion, and he'll do anything to get it. When two investigations cross each other around a mysterious deep space mining corporation he quickly learns there are other forces out there - and things from other planes of reality - that will also stop at nothing to get what they want. With his life thrown into turmoil, Cloud struggles to keep his career and his sanity intact as he plunges towards a terrifying confrontation with one of the sub-princes of Hell. Hurled into this violent mix of corruption and demonism is Natalya Dorganskya; previously the adorable daughter of a deceased global movie-star, she now uses her skills as a world-class pilot in bold criminal raids. A path that quickly brings her head to head with DS Cloud and the non-human things that have come stalking through time and space to take back what she has stolen.

David J Rodger delivers a dark and edgy vision of the near-future in a novel that reveals the boundaries between the Satanism and the Cthulhu Mythos.

Dog Eat Dog

Ten years after the Earth has been devastated by a viral pathogen seventy per cent of the population is dead and only a handful of cities survive intact. The majority of urban spaces have been abandoned to the Infected. Whilst above, the orbital colonies spin within their artificial gravity wells, helpless observers to the shocking events below. Mikhail Drobná and Carlos Revira. Two survivors, both hungry for money and power, and fuelled by a desire to carve their names onto this new world. One provides services of violence and protection for powerful corporate criminals in the Living City of New York; the other is a renegade intelligence agent forever running from the demons of his past. Strangers, until events bring them face to face in a bloody confrontation. Complex politics, private armies, corruption and murder on a shocking scale. Both men seek to sieze their opportunity at whatever cost. But a cosmic Evil has infiltrated the remote corners of these brutalised lands and it has its own plans for this world. Will these men work as one to defeat it or will their bitter rivalry bring about their destruction? In the end, who will devour who?

David J Rodger delivers a novel of epic vision, character depth and nerve-popping tension.

EDGE

Ethan Carmichael is a global superstar in the world of tech. His revolutionary developments push the boundaries of electronics and science. But close to total burn out he presses eject on the stress to take time out. A luxury snowboarding resort in New Zealand seems like the perfect place. But the volcanic mountain is a gateway to something not of this world, or even this Universe. For centuries it has been absent. The Maori spoke of it only in nightmares. Now it is returning, slowly yet inexorably, with monstrous consequences for those in the resort as madness takes hold, and then the murders start to happen. On the other side of the world, Halo Santana, an unscrupulous concept scout scrambles onto the trail of a new technology that has vanished from a corporate R&D lab. Quickly out of his depth, he enters a frantic race to track down the missing components before his buyers have him killed. Both men find their fates tangled in a deadly web of lies, treachery and alien horror.

David J Rodger delivers relentless narrative pace in a tense action-packed novel.

The Black Lake

The Earth has been ravaged by an event known as Yellow Dawn. Ten years later, survivors are putting lives back together and probing the frontiers of a new Wilderness; whilst overhead the orbital colonies glide across the sky, removed and unaffected. Five men leave the fortress island of Malta on an expedition to the sub-Arctic waters above Scotland. They intend to undertake scientific observations of an alien meteorological phenomenon that has followed the apocalyptic event. What they find is a cosmic horror that seethes amongst the shadows of a shattered Earth. It is a story of escape and wonder, of madness and terror.

David J Rodger delivers a novel that tears open a rent in the boundary of reality, providing a nerve-jarring glimpse of the Outer Chaos and the horrors that hungrily cluster just beyond the threshold of our fragile, human existence.

For the latest information on David J Rodger, excerpts from his books and other projects, visit his website.

www.davidjrodger.com

Printed in Great Britain
by Amazon